Smokeshow

NEW YORK TIMES BESTSELLING AUTHOR

ABBI GLINES

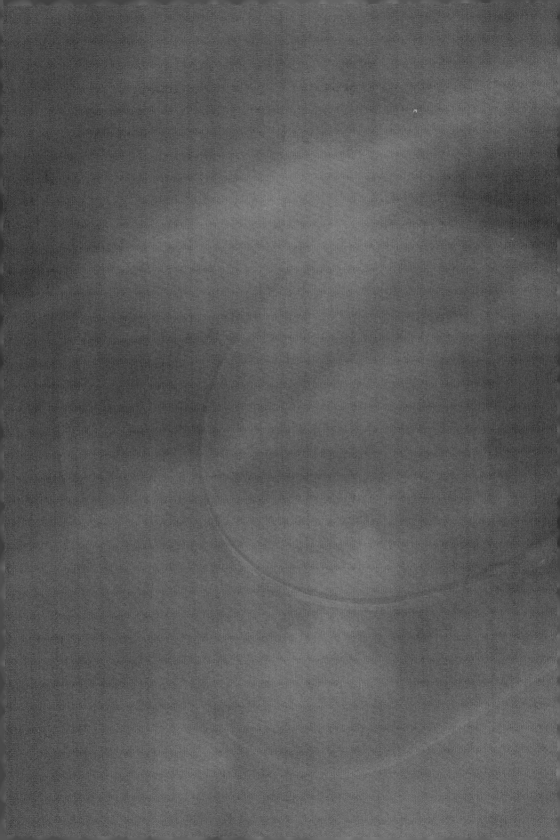

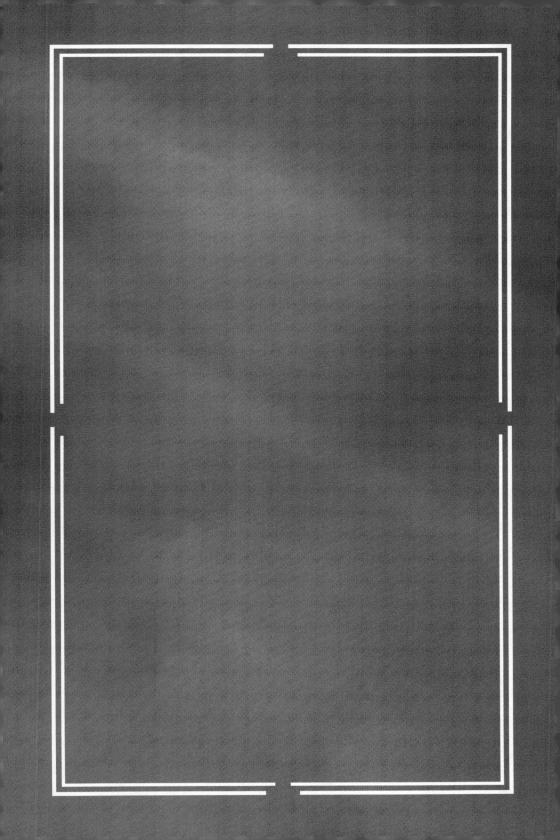

• THE FAMILY •

started by Jediah Hughes. It began with horse racing, moonshine, and illegal arms in the early 1900s

Jediah Hughes

Eustis

Elmer
(died from
Typhoid at
ten years old)

Feldman

Tipper

Garrett

Gregory
(died at three
years old in a
house fire)

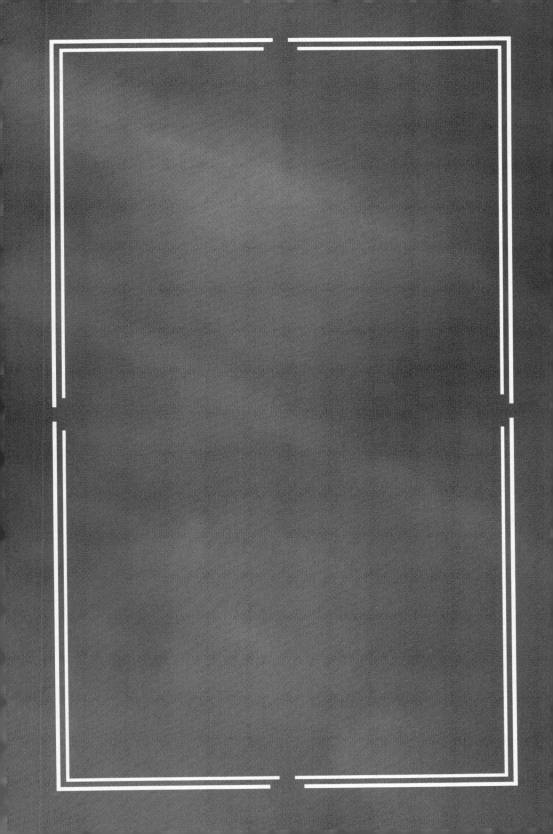

• THE HUGHES •
Hughes Farm

Garrett Hughes (BOSS in books 1-9)
Wife: **Fawn Parker Hughes** → *SCORCH*

Blaise Hughes (Current BOSS/oldest son)
Wife: **Madeline Walsh Hughes**
(parents Etta Marks/dead and Liam
Walsh/President of Judgment MC)

Trev Hughes
Fiancée: **Gypsi
Parker** (also
stepsister) →
FIRECRACKER

Cree Elias Hughes →
SMOKESHOW and
FIREBALL

• THE SHEPHARDS •
Oldest family inside the southern mafia other than the Hughes

Charles Livingston Shephard
Best friend of Jediah Hughes

Gerald

Joseph
(became a priest)

Jeffrey
(died from Spanish
influenza at
fifteen years old)

Charles II

Darwin
(died from gunshot
at twenty-four)

Charles III
(drowned in
childhood)

Joshua
(became a
missionary)

Lincoln

Lincoln II (Linc)   **Stellan**

Mississippi Branch

Linc Shephard
(left Florida to run Mississippi Branch when **Levi** was twenty-two)

|

Florida Branch

Levi Shephard
Wife: **Aspen Chance Shephard**→ *WHISKEY SMOKE*

Georgia Branch
Shephard Ranch

Stellan Shephard
Wife: **Mandilyn Shephard**

Thatcher
→ *DEMONS*

Sebastian
Book Coming
September 2024

• THE KINGSTONS •
Mars Kingston joined the family in 1921

Mars Kingston
Childhood friend of Jediah Hughes

Hollis

Son
(died in childhood)

Atticus

Son
(died in childhood)

Rollin

Raul

Creed

Barrett

Florida Branch

Creed Kingston (dead)
Wife: **Abigail Kingston** (dead)

Huck
Wife: **Trinity Bennett Kingston**
→ *SMOKE BOMB*

Hayes (dead)
engaged to **Trinity**
at his death

Georgia Branch

Barrett Kingston
Wife: **Annette Kingston**

Storm
→ *SIZZLING*
and *STORM*

Lela
*Book coming in
2025*

Nailyah
*Book coming in
2025*

· THE HOUSTONS ·
Joined the family through horse racing in 1938

Kenneth Houston Wife: **Melanie Houston**
Moses Mile Ranch

|

Saxon Houston
Wife: **Haisley Slate Houston** →
SMOKIN' HOT

|

Winter Noel Houston

• THE LEVINES •
Joined the family in 1977

Alister Levine

|

Mississippi Branch

Luther Levine
Ex-Wife: **Chloe Wall**
(Moved from Florida when **Kye** was nineteen)

|

Florida Branch

Kye Levine
Wife: **Genesis Stoll Levine** → *BURN*

|

Jagger Henley Levine

• THE PRESLEYS •
Joined the family after graduation

Gage Presley
Best friend of Blaise Hughes in high school
Wife: **Shiloh Carmichael Presley** → *STRAIGHT FIRE*

• THE SALAZARS •

Joined the family through horse racing in 1958

Georgia Branch only

Efrain Salazar

Gabriel Salazar (dead)
Wife: **Maeme Salazar**

Ronan Salazar
Wife: **Jupiter Salazar**

King Salazar
→ *SLAY* and
SLAY KING

Birdie
w/Ex Wife: **Estela Salazar**

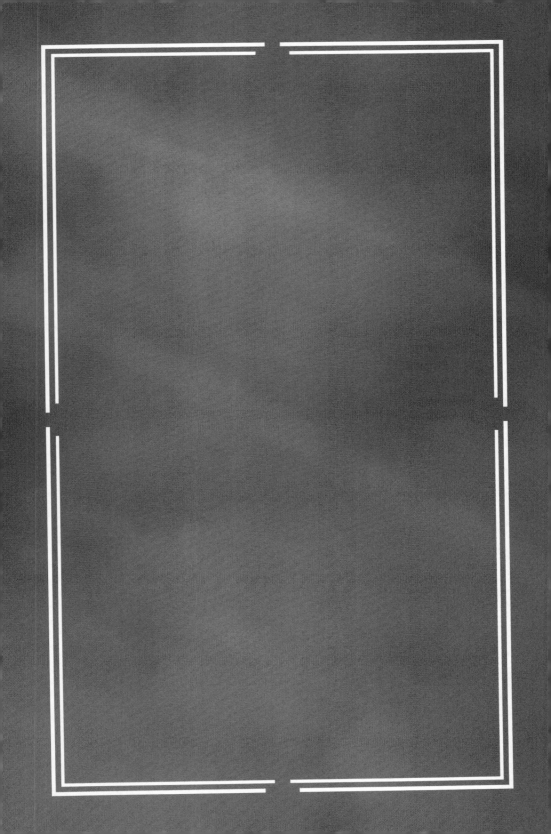

• THE JONES •
Joined the family through joined real-estate in 1966

Georgia Branch only

Hoyt Jones

Monte
Fiancée: **Bay Mintley**

Roland
Wife: **Luella Jones**

Wilder Jones
Wife: **Oakley Watson
Jones** →*ASHES*

Wells Jones
*Book date
coming soon*

Teller Jones
*Book coming
in 2025*

Sarah Jones

PLAYLIST

Carry On Wayward Son
Kansas

The Cowboy in Me
Tim McGraw

Better Than Me
Hinder

Weak
Seether

Don't Cry
Guns N' Roses

Stay
Thirty Seconds to Mars

Savin' Me
Nickelback

Love Me Harder
Ariana Grande & The Weeknd

Beautiful Lies
Jana Kramer

Love You Goodbye
One Direction

Ain't No Sunshine
Bill Withers

To Miriah Baker, the only friend I have who is my exact kind of crazy. You make me feel normal when I know I'm not. I'm so thankful I have you in my life.

I

*How often the line fades
that stands between love and hate.*

Chapter
ONE

MADELINE

This wasn't my home. It never would be. Home wasn't a place. Home was a person. If you were lucky, it was more than one person. Because of that, I'd never be able to go home again. My home had been my dad and my brother, Cole. Now, they were dead, and I was alive. I was homeless. Even though I had a roof over my head.

"Madeline, honey, breakfast is ready. No hurry though. I don't have an appointment until nine thirty," Melanie Houston called from the other side of the closed door.

I stood there, staring at my reflection in the mirror, wearing clothes that weren't mine. Melanie had bought them for me. I would have never chosen these items for myself or any of the other items she had filled the massive walk-in closet with before my arrival yesterday. My mother's best friend was someone I had never met until she walked into my former neighbor, Mrs. Miller's, living room with tears in her eyes to take me "home."

Melanie was nice. She had come to save me when I had nowhere else to go. Mrs. Miller barely made it on her monthly check from the government. Staying with her had been temporary. I had been planning on getting a third job in hopes I could afford a place to live. I was a legal adult. I wouldn't stay with the Houstons that long. Just until I could save enough money to live on my own.

"I'll be right there," I replied and bit my tongue to keep from reminding her yet again that my name was Maddy.

My mother had named me Madeline, but I didn't remember much about my mother. She had died from breast cancer before I turned three years old. My dad had always called me his "Maddy girl." I'd never been called Madeline by anyone, except on the first day of school every year. I would correct my teachers when they called roll that first time. *Had my mother called me Madeline?* There was so much I didn't know about her.

With one last look at the stranger in the mirror, I walked to the door and opened it, then headed down the hallway toward the wide, curving staircase. The chandelier that hung over the foyer appeared to sparkle as the sunlight came through the windows, hitting it directly. Everything was so clean and smelled fresh. That was the first thing I'd noticed when I walked in the large double doors yesterday afternoon.

There was no lingering hint of weed or stale beer in the air. The moldy smell that I'd grown accustomed to in our apartment was also absent. *Would I ever get used to this? Did I want to?* I didn't miss that smell, and it made me feel guilty. I had hated the stench and complained about it often to my dad and brother. If I could have them back, I would never mention it again.

"There you are, and don't you look beautiful."

I turned to see Melanie beaming brightly up at me as I descended the stairs.

"I knew blue would be your color. It was your mother's color too. Those eyes of yours are like looking at Etta. You do have her eyes."

My dad had once told me I had my mother's blue eyes. He said they were bluer than the sky and deeper than the sea. I had always wanted the hazel eyes my dad and Cole shared, simply because they looked so much alike. There wasn't anything about me that looked like either of them.

"Mrs. Jolene made homemade waffles with her special strawberry glaze. You'll love it. It's Saxon's favorite breakfast," she told me and patted my arm. "Let's go get you fed."

I followed her toward the kitchen as she continued to talk about the different milk options and the juice selection. Breakfast wasn't something I was used to unless it was cold Pop-Tarts and a glass of water before I hurried to catch the bus.

"Oh good," she said as we entered the spacious white kitchen. "Saxon, you're eating in the house this morning."

Melanie moved to the side of the island, and when she did, the guy standing there studied me. I, in return, did the same to him. He was tall—at least six foot, if not more—with broad shoulders and dark brown hair that held the slightest bit of curl. His brown eyes were set off by his thick, dark lashes. They would almost seem feminine, if not for his chiseled jawline and the small scar on his left cheek. When the corner of his mouth lifted just barely enough to form a smile, I noticed the hint of dimples.

"Madeline, this is my son, Saxon," she said before looking at him. "Saxon, dear, this is Madeline." She turned back to me. "He gets up early to go out to the stables. Racehorses are what the Houston men eat, sleep, and breathe. You'll find that it takes over every part of our lives here."

Saxon kept his gaze locked on me as he finished the glass of milk in front of him. I had been too tired yesterday after our flight from Dallas, Texas, to Ocala, Florida, to stay up and meet the family for dinner. Instead, I'd taken a shower and gone to sleep.

Although Melanie had told me all about Saxon during our flight. He was her only child, my age. He had been the all-star high school quarterback his senior year and worked with his

father, raising and training racehorses here on their five-hun-
dred-acre ranch, even though he had been offered several football
scholarships. Kenneth, Melanie's husband, had been born into a
racing family, and Moses Mile Farm had been in his family for
over eighty years.

"You left out a few details," he said to his mother, raising one
eyebrow at her, then smirking. When his gaze swung back to me,
he asked me, "You ever ride a horse?"

I shook my head.

"But you're from Texas," he stated the obvious while looking
confused. As if being from Texas meant we all had our own horses
and rode them around for transportation.

"And yet I'm not a cowgirl. Go figure," I replied.

He laughed, and both dimples were out in full force. "I've got to
get back out there before Dad realizes I snuck inside for a second
breakfast. Jo didn't make this out at the barn kitchen." He nodded
his head toward the back door. "The waffles are delicious, trust me,"
he added. "When you're done, you can head out to the stables. I'll
show you around."

I wasn't sure how I felt about horses or going out to the stables,
but what else was I supposed to do with my day? I simply nodded,
and he turned and exited out the door in the far-right corner of
the kitchen.

"He grew up on horses. He forgets that there is a life outside
racehorses," she said as she walked over to the kitchen cabinet and
began getting me a plate. "We aren't formal around here for breakfast. Mrs. Jolene, who Saxon has been calling Jo since he could talk,
cooks breakfast for the ranch hands early every morning and then
comes in to make sure we have a hot breakfast before returning
to clean up the workers' breakfast. Kenneth always eats with the
hands. Saxon eats in here the days he has classes, but he's not taking
any classes this summer semester. Which reminds me, we need to
talk about college. If you want to attend locally, we need to get you
registered for the fall term. Anyway, Mrs. Jolene will always have

food to eat in the house. You just come in and make yourself at home." She paused. "I want you to feel at home here. I truly do."

"Thank you," I replied, although I didn't see that ever happening, but Melanie was trying her best to make it so.

"After breakfast, go on out to the stables and find Saxon. He can give you a tour and then show you some things you can do every day to help out. We all have some chores, and I think that'll help you feel like a part of the family."

I nodded. "Yes, ma'am."

"Working out at the stables would be better than anything you could do inside the house. Besides, I am willing to bet you're gonna fall in love with horses. Your mama sure loved them. I imagine it's in your blood."

My mother had loved horses? How had I never known this?

Melanie had told me how she had grown up with my mother. They'd been best friends all their lives. Dad had never told me we had lived in Ocala, Florida. He never mentioned Melanie or where my mother was from. Whenever I asked him about grandparents, he would tell me they were all dead. I had assumed there was no other family or friends.

"I didn't know my mother loved horses."

Melanie's smile faded, and she looked away. "Well, I can imagine your father wouldn't have wanted to talk about that much," she replied, then began talking about the fresh juice options, as if she hadn't mentioned my mom or dad at all.

When Melanie had arrived to pick me up, she'd been dressed as if she had walked out of a magazine and into the wrong reality. Mrs. Miller frowned at her, as if she'd spoken another language, and asked if she was confused. I had thought the same thing. I couldn't envision someone in my family knowing anyone who looked like Melanie. My dad hadn't even been able to show me a picture of my mother, so all I had were the small things he would mention on occasion. I learned not to ask him about her though. Dad wasn't mean to me, but he had a temper. Talking about my mother always sent him into a drinking spell. I had done everything I could to keep him happy.

"Maddy girl, where is the fucking milk? I told you to get milk when you went to the grocery," Dad yelled from the kitchen.

I glanced over at Cole nervously, hoping he would speak up and say something. It was his fault we didn't have milk. I'd barely had enough money left after he took most of it from me before school this morning. Cole shrugged as he stayed silent, watching a basketball game on the television.

"Did you use it all?" I whispered.

Cole glanced over at me. "I had to, Maddy. I owed Rev," he replied, as if it were my fault he'd gotten hooked up with a dealer.

"What am I supposed to tell Dad?" I asked.

Cole shrugged again. "Just tell him you didn't have enough. I don't care what you say."

"He asked me—" I stopped talking the moment Dad's large form filled the doorway.

His angry scowl went from me to Cole. If he knew about Cole selling party favors for Rev at school, he'd beat him.

"You want to say that a little louder, Maddy girl?" he asked me, not taking his eyes off Cole.

"I was telling Cole I had forgotten to get the milk and asked if he had money I could borrow," I lied.

Dad didn't seem convinced as he took a long drink from a can of Natural Light. Dad always had money for that. "What'd you spend all that money on then? There's barely shit in that fridge."

He had left me a hundred dollars. That was all he left me every two weeks, and I was supposed to buy the groceries with that. Most of the time, I would babysit the Johnson kids three doors down at night to help buy us more food. But lately, Cole had been finding my hiding spots and stealing my money. Instead of selling cocaine, I knew he'd

6

started snorting it. He said he wasn't, but I could tell when he was high. It was becoming more and more frequent.

"Eggs have gone up in price, and so has fruit," I explained, which wasn't a lie.

"Don't need the fucking fruit. We ain't damn uppity folks. Use that money for some damn milk and them chips I like. Stop trying to make us healthy," he said with a growl, then went over to flop down in his faded green recliner.

"Yes, sir," I replied.

Apples were the only thing I ever bought for me. They might not care about eating healthy, but I did.

"Make us some grilled cheeses tonight, why don'tcha, Maddy girl?" Dad told me.

"Okay," I agreed, thankful he hadn't lost his temper over the milk.

"Why can't you be more like your sister? Huh, boy?" Dad asked Cole.

I hated it when he did that. It only upset Cole, and that led to him getting high.

Chapter
TWO

MADELINE

Melanie continued to talk while we sat and ate breakfast. She barely touched her food, but she had three cups of coffee. When I was finished, she told me she had a tennis match at the club and then a luncheon with friends. Before she left, she sent me down to the stables and told me where I would most likely find Saxon.

I passed several large, circular fenced-in areas with horses inside them. Some were alone while others had someone riding them. I froze when one massive horse raised his front legs and tried to toss the rider off his back. However, another man jumped over the fence and stood in front of the horse with his hands up in the air, talking to it. The horse came back down on all fours, swinging his head side to side. I was amazed the rider hadn't fallen off.

Melanie had talked about me working here and going to college. My plans were to get a job, save some money, then get a small studio apartment somewhere. I wasn't her child, and I doubted very much that her husband wanted to pay for my education. I also didn't think I was going to love horses the way my mother had.

"Just when I thought this day was going to be shit, you walk right out of my dreams," a voice said close to my ear.

Startled, I spun around. Piercing gray eyes met mine, and I stepped back because he was standing too close. His black hair was long enough to be tucked behind his ears, and he had a square jaw with lips that were entirely too lush to be fair—the combination was startling.

"Ignore him. He's an asshole," Saxon said, and I tore my eyes off the stranger to see Saxon walking up behind him.

"He's just jealous. Always has been," the guy replied, then winked at me.

Saxon chuckled and rolled his eyes. "Yeah, that's it."

"Shiiit," he drawled and smirked at me. "The package doesn't get better than this."

Saxon ignored him and looked at me. "Madeline, meet Trev. I'd apologize, but he comes around a lot. He's one of those things you get used to."

"I might come around more often now," he said with those eyes of his still locked on me.

"I doubt that's possible," Saxon replied. "What's up? You don't normally show up this early. It's not even noon yet, and you're awake."

He finally moved his gaze to meet Saxon's, but he did it so slowly, as if taking his eyes off me was difficult. I knew guys like him. I'd been exposed to them enough to know how to handle them. The flirting was not something to take seriously. It was in his nature. He enjoyed female attention and knew he was charming. I doubted he'd ever been rejected.

"My dad woke me up at seven. Who the fuck gets up that early? Well, other than you," he replied.

Saxon found this amusing. "What did he want?"

Trev frowned. "He wanted me to work."

Saxon raised his eyebrows. "Where?"

9

Trev shrugged, as if this was a good question. "Got me. What do I know about working with horses? I ride them, I watch them race, I enjoy the alcohol at the track, but that's the extent of my knowledge."

Saxon looked back at me, grinning, as if he wanted to laugh. "Trev is a Hughes," he said, as if that explained this conversation. When I had no response to that, he continued, "Hughes Farm is the biggest racehorse establishment in the South."

"With the most wins, the best horses, an Olympic-sized pool, and a hot tub big enough for twenty-five people," Trev added.

I didn't need to look at him to see the cocky smile on his face. I could feel it. He was too much like my ex. Except my ex, Hank, hadn't been wealthy. Not even close. He'd just been blessed with looks that got him what he wanted. I decided I would be careful around Trev for that reason alone.

"Khan's gonna have some competition," Saxon said as he looked out over the fences toward a horse that seemed much calmer than the one I had been watching. "Firefoot is going to give him his first dose of a real match."

Trev didn't seem to care. He shrugged. "Great. Hope he does," he replied. "I'm not here to talk horses or racing. Not my thing. I thought you might want to come over later for a swim. I've invited over some people." He was looking at me, so I met his gaze. "It would be a good chance for Madeline to meet everyone."

"Maddy," I corrected him.

Saxon's gaze was on me then, and I gave him a small smile.

"I go by Maddy," I explained.

"Mom knows this?" he asked.

I nodded, and he rolled his eyes.

"She's got this thing about not shortening names," he told me, then looked back at Trev. "What time?"

"Around four," Trev replied.

"We'll be tired and hot by then. You up for a pool party?" Saxon asked me.

I wanted to say no and go find a place to be alone and read. However, Saxon's eyes looked hopeful, like he really wanted me to go. Hiding in my room wasn't going to make this any easier.

I managed to nod. "Sure."

Saxon's smile got bigger, and his dimples flashed. "Okay then, we'll be there at four thirty."

"Excellent," Trev replied, sounding pleased. "I'll see you both later."

When he finally walked away, I felt relieved. I must have sighed that relief because I heard Saxon chuckle.

"Don't worry about him. He's a flirt. It's how he is wired."

I gazed out over the ranch and shrugged. "Other than the fact that he's rich, I've dealt with guys like him before. It's fine."

"Yeah, I guess that's something you deal with a lot."

I turned my attention back to Saxon. "Why would you think that?" I asked, hearing the defensive tone in my voice. I hadn't meant to sound like he had insulted me.

He almost looked embarrassed, and I found that interesting.

"Well, the way you look ... guys notice you."

I felt certain that was a compliment and only that. There was no flirty gleam in his eyes.

"Oh, um, thanks." My response sounded awkward, and my cheeks warmed.

Saxon nodded his head toward the stables behind him. "Come on. Let me show you around."

I fell into step beside him as he started walking. "Your mom mentioned that I needed to pick up some chores. I think you're the one who's supposed to give me some. She said I was needed out here more than inside or that I'd like it better. I'm not sure."

"How do you feel about working around the horses?" he asked me.

I shrugged. "I don't know. I'm certain I don't want to ride one or get too close."

"Why's that?" he asked.

11

"Before Trev arrived, I was watching one of these four-legged monsters rear up like he was trying to throw the rider off. It was terrifying."

Saxon chuckled. "Iron War. He might be great one day. He has some emotional damage, but our best trainers are working with him now. Hopefully, they can turn him around. Don't judge all horses because of him though."

I didn't feel convinced, and apparently, I didn't look it either because Saxon led us into the stables and directly over to some stalls with horses in them. I stayed a few feet back as he walked up to a horse and began rubbing him and talking to him, as if the horse understood him.

"This is Rig," he told me. "He's brilliant, and he comes from a winning line of thoroughbreds. No first places for him yet, but he's only two. He's got a couple of third places and a second place."

Saxon took a carrot out of his pocket and fed Rig from his hand. "That's a good boy," he said, then patted his forehead. "Come on," he urged me, waving me closer.

Fine. I'd move a little closer.

"She's scared of you, Rig. Be a gentleman," he told the horse.

Rig made a sound, as if he were attempting to respond.

I moved another step closer.

Saxon reached out and took my hand, then pulled me close enough so that Rig could nudge me with his nose. I jumped, and Saxon laughed.

"He's trying to ease your mind."

"Oh. Well, it looked like he might eat me, like he did that carrot," I replied.

"You're not orange and crunchy," Saxon said. "Here." He took my hand and placed it on the horse. "See, it's easy."

When Saxon took his hand off mine, I began to slowly rub him the way I had seen Saxon do. Rig moved closer to me, and I felt a smile tug on my lips. He wasn't scary at all.

"He's like a big puppy," I said in awe.

Saxon laughed. "Now, that's the first time I've ever heard a thoroughbred being compared to a puppy."

A phone started ringing, and Saxon pulled it out of his back pocket. I saw him glance at the screen before putting it to his ear.

"Hey," he said into the phone, then moved away from me, leaving the horse and me alone.

I watched him walk to the other side of the stable. Surprisingly, I wasn't nervous. I glanced up at Rig. He was beautiful.

My thoughts went to my mother. A woman I barely remembered. Dad had never told me about Mom loving horses or riding them. Just like he'd never mentioned Melanie or Florida. I wanted to know more about her, and maybe being around horses would do that for me. For now, I would stay and find out all I could about my mom and her past.

Why had my parents left here? Why hadn't Melanie come to see me sooner?

There was so much I wanted to know.

Chapter
THREE

MADELINE

After spending my day at Moses Mile, learning to muck stalls, helping Mrs. Jolene prepare and put lunch on the table for the workers, and spreading fresh hay, I felt a little more like I understood the ranch. It was the first distraction I'd had since the accident. I found myself looking forward to tomorrow, and that wasn't something I'd expected.

Going to Trev's pool party wasn't what I wanted to do, but I showered and put on one of the six bathing suits Melanie had bought for me. I'd hoped Melanie had forgotten to buy me a bathing suit so I wouldn't have to go to the party. There hadn't been one in my closet. However, Saxon texted his mom earlier today to buy me one without my knowledge, and she went shopping. All six of the ones she had brought home were bikinis, so I chose the one I thought covered me the most, then put a sundress on over it.

Getting out of the house without Melanie asking to see how it looked on me was pure luck. She wasn't downstairs when I met

Saxon at the front doors, and we went out to his truck to head to Hughes Farm.

"You caught on quick today," Saxon said to me as we left Moses Mile.

"Thanks."

"Dad was impressed with the stalls when he got back from the auction. When I told him you did it, he said he looked forward to meeting you."

I started to ask what the auction was when I saw a massive arch up ahead with elaborate horses made out of iron standing on either side. Over the top of the arch, the words *Hughes Farm* appeared, gold-plated. Oak trees lined the entrance, and the pavement turned to red brick as we pulled to a stop in front of the closed gate.

Saxon rolled down his window and reached over to punch in a code on an electronic screen. The gate then slowly swung open.

"And this is the Hughes fortress. It's a bit ..." He paused.

"Over the top?" I suggested. "I mean, it's a horse farm, right?"

Saxon grinned at me, then drove down the red brick road, lined with the old oak trees that shaded the path. "Hughes Farm has been breeding and racing thoroughbreds for a hundred years. They have put out more champions than any other ranch in the Southeast. It's less of a family-run operation, like Moses Mile. This is more of a corporation. The Hughes have power."

I frowned, thinking about my interaction with Trev today. He hadn't seemed like someone from a powerful family. He was more self-absorbed than anything.

"Garrett Hughes, Trev's dad, is someone you keep on your good side. You don't want to make an enemy of him. My dad respects that, and we've always gotten along with them just fine."

As the shade from the trees broke, I was sure I gasped at the view of the house—no, that wasn't a house. It was a mansion. "Whoa," I whispered.

"Insane, isn't it?" Saxon said beside me.

15

I managed to nod. The place had more square footage than the low-income apartment complex I had lived in the past ten years. *Why would any family need so much space? How many kids were there?*

"Please tell me Trev has nineteen other brothers and sisters, and that is the reason they need this house."

Saxon let out a bark of laughter. "Uh, no. Trev has one older brother. Different mother though. Garrett is currently in search of wife number four. Trev's stepmom left him a year ago."

"What happened to his mom?"

Saxon shrugged. "Not sure. I remember her from when Trev and I were younger, but not much. She was rarely around, and the nanny took care of him. One day, she was just gone. We were about four, I guess. Trev didn't seem to care, but he barely knew her."

My life hadn't been easy, and Dad wasn't always the ideal parent, but he was there for me and Cole. Even on nights he hadn't made it home or he had drunk too much and I had to go get him out of the bar, he had always been sorry. He would make it up to us.

I felt sad for Trev, and I hadn't expected to ever feel any sympathy for him.

Saxon parked his truck in front of the house, where a circular drive was filled with other vehicles. Most of them expensive and flashy. There were only two other trucks that looked a lot like Saxon's. I stepped down out of the truck and walked around the front of it to meet Saxon.

He gave me a crooked grin. "Ready for this?" he asked me.

I stared up at the house, then back at him. "No."

"Too late."

I sighed, and he started for the stairs leading to the front doors "You'll be fine. Besides, you need to meet some people."

I disagreed, but said nothing. He rang the doorbell just as I reached the top step. The left door opened almost immediately, and a short, round woman appeared on the other side. The smile that lit her face made her dark eyes twinkle. There was a kindness in her expression as she stepped back so we could enter.

"Hello, Saxon," she greeted. "You've come to join the gathering out back, I suppose."

I followed Saxon inside, and her gaze finally met mine.

"Oh, aren't you a pretty thing," she said to me.

"Ms. Jimmie, this is Maddy. She's a friend of the family who will be living with us," Saxon told her. "Maddy, this is Ms. Jimmie. The best biscuit maker in the county, but don't tell Jo I said that. She'll never cook for me again."

I held out my hand toward her. "It's nice to meet you," I told her.

She looked down at my hand, then up at Saxon, grinning before reaching out and taking my hand in hers. "It's a pleasure to meet you too. Don't let that circus out there scare you off."

"I'll make sure she survives," Saxon assured her.

She let go of my hand and waved us on our way. "Go on then. You know how to find it. Follow the sound of bad music and high-pitched squeals," she told us.

Saxon laughed and looked at me. "This way."

I started to follow him through the grand entryway, my eyes taking in everything all at once. This house was unreal. They could hold a ball in the foyer alone.

"GARRETT!" a deep male voice boomed, and I jumped. "WHERE THE FUCK IS MY HORSE?" the voice demanded, and then the body it belonged to appeared as he stalked toward us.

He was tall with shoulders and a chest so wide that his black T-shirt stretched tight, leaving no question to the number of muscles beneath, paired with faded jeans that hugged his thighs. His skin was so deeply tanned that he had to live outdoors, and his dark blond hair was tucked behind his ears and covered with a worn cowboy hat. Stubble ran along his firm jawline, and his eyes were the color of the greenest grass. If the expression on his face wasn't terrifying, he would be beautiful. The boots he was wearing clicked against the marble floor as he stalked past us as if we weren't there.

"Where the hell is he, Jimmie?" the man asked, his tone slightly softer when he spoke to her.

17

"Well, now, Blaise, the last time I saw him was this morning. With the party going on out back, I don't think he has plans to return today. Have you called his phone?" she asked.

"Yes," he growled out and took off his hat to run a hand through his messy blond locks. "He won't answer the damn thing."

Saxon reached for my hand and tugged me, drawing my attention away from the scene in front of us. I started to follow him.

"Sax!" the guy called out.

Saxon froze, then looked back at him. "Yeah?" he asked.

"Moses Mile know anything about Empire?" he asked him.

Saxon shook his head. "Not a thing. Why? He missing?"

The guy scowled, and even then, he was breathtaking. "Yeah. Fucking Garrett," he snarled.

"Language, Blaise. There are ladies present," Ms. Jimmie scolded him, not appearing intimidated by the furious Greek god at all.

His eyes swung toward me for the first time, as if he just realized someone else was here. That stung a bit, considering I had been ogling him since he stalked by us. His gaze scanned my body, then came back to my face. There was a flash of disgust in his eyes, as if what he had just seen turned his stomach.

"Come on," Saxon said to me.

Still holding on to my hand, he led me through a hallway and into a large, open room full of expensive furniture and paintings. I had no time to focus on any of it though. Saxon was walking quickly, as if he was trying to escape the force that Ms. Jimmie had called Blaise. Two more turns, and we were exiting the house. Saxon let go of my hand while we were walking out onto a back patio. Loud music, too many people, and a pool that looked as if it belonged at an exclusive resort greeted us.

I wanted to ask Saxon about this Blaise, but Trev was already walking in our direction. Teal-blue swim trunks hung on his hips, and his dark hair was wet and slicked back while his chest glistened with drops of water. If I hadn't just seen a remake of Adonis inside his house, his chest might have been impressive.

18

"You made it," he said, his eyes locked on me.

"Have you talked to Blaise?" Saxon asked him.

Trev frowned. "No. It's been a lucky day. Why?"

"He's looking for Empire."

Trev shrugged. "That's horse business. Not my thing. He can call Dad."

"He said he wasn't answering," Saxon told him.

Trev flashed him a bright smile and held up the drink in his hand that I was sure wasn't just soda. "I don't care. His issue, not mine. I got a party to host."

"You're late," a brunette with the body of a runway model said as she reached us. She pressed her chest right up against Saxon's and placed her hand against his cheek before leaning in to cover his mouth with hers.

"Maddy, meet Declan," Trev said, then held out his hand to me. "Now, let's leave these two alone to grope and go find you a drink."

I didn't feel like I had much of a choice. I knew two people here, and standing beside the one who was currently making out seemed awkward. However, I wasn't going to hold Trev's hand either. Instead, I moved to stand beside him, and he smirked at me, as if my not touching him was something I would get over soon.

"I've got it all. What's your poison?" he asked me, and I walked with him toward a bar with an actual bartender.

"Club soda?" I asked him.

He rolled his eyes. "Come on, Maddy. You can do better than that. What about some vodka in that club soda?" he asked.

I shook my head. "I don't drink." Because my dad had been an alcoholic, and because of his addiction, he and my brother were both dead. I didn't say the last part though.

"Club soda," he told the bartender, then leaned on the bar and studied me. "You want to give me the sundress? I'll make sure it's kept dry."

I looked around at everyone else and realized I was the only one in clothing. My bikini was modest compared to most of what I was seeing. I gasped when a girl with long blonde hair turned around and her bare breasts were on display. I scanned the others in the pool and found two other topless girls.

I shook my head. "I'm okay."

He groaned but kept his smile in place. "You're going to tease me with that sundress?"

I shrugged. That wasn't why I was keeping it on, but if that was what he wanted to think, then fine. My bikini would be more coverage than what the other females here were wearing, but I preferred to stay covered.

My gaze moved back over to Saxon, who was now talking to the girl Trev had called Declan. She had her arm wrapped around his and was tilting her head back to look up at him. Her hair hung in thick, luxurious waves down her back, barely brushing her waist. She was beautiful, and it was clear Saxon thought so too. She had his complete attention. She was also still wearing her bikini top.

"She's going to hate you," Trev said, drawing my attention back to him. He handed me a glass with ice and club soda.

"Who?" I asked, taking it from him.

"Declan Delamore," he replied, grinning as he took a drink of the dark liquid in his glass.

I recognized the smell of whiskey. When my father had had a good week, he'd splurge on a bottle of cheap whiskey.

"Why is she going to hate me?" I asked him.

"Because you're gorgeous and living in Saxon's house. Right down the hallway." He shrugged. "Granted, Saxon has never once cheated on her in the year they've officially been together. But she'll still see you as competition."

I took a drink of my soda. "Has she looked in the mirror?" I asked, thinking that her being jealous of me was ridiculous.

"Have you?" Trev asked me.

I rolled my eyes. He was flirting, and he would continue to until some other girl came along who welcomed his advances. I knew the drill. Soon, I would be sipping this drink in a corner, hiding from the action.

"I've not been introduced." A guy slightly shorter than Trev with a slimmer build and sandy-blond curls and friendly brown eyes stood in front of us.

"Oliver, this is Maddy, my new friend," Trev replied, then leaned down to whisper loudly, "Maddy, this is Oliver. He's brilliant, he goes to Harvard, and he's terribly boring."

Oliver looked amused. "I'd say that, one day, you will be working for me, but we'd both know it was a joke."

Trev laughed.

"Trev won't be working for anyone. When you're royalty, you don't need a job," a redhead with nothing but tiny black bikini bottoms on and perfectly smooth, pale skin said as she sauntered up to us, then wrapped her arms around Trev's body. Her bare chest was pressed against him, and I felt uncomfortable, as if I were watching something that I wasn't supposed to see. "Swim with me," she said, batting her long, thick, dark lashes up at him.

Trev gave her a crooked grin. "Ah, I would—and I will—but at the moment, I have a new friend I can't abandon."

She cut her cat-green eyes at me and quickly took in my face and body. "She looks more like Oliver's type. You know, boring."

"Tsk-tsk, kitty," Trev said, affectionately tucking some of her hair behind her ear. "Be nice."

"I'll keep Maddy company while you go swim. It will give us a chance to bore each other," Oliver offered, his voice amused instead of insulted.

Trev frowned in Oliver's direction, as if he had said something distasteful.

"That's sweet of you, Ollie," the girl said and ran a long red nail over his jawline. "You're always so nice to everyone." She drew out the last word and shot a triumphant smile back at me.

If she thought she was winning something by taking Trev away from me, she was way off course. Oliver seemed like an easier person to talk to anyway. I'd never met anyone who went to an Ivy League school. I was curious about it.

"I think I'll stay here with Maddy for now," Trev replied.

"Chanel!" another topless girl in the water, who was perched on a guy's shoulders, called out, and the redhead turned to look toward her. "Come play!"

The redhead, who I assumed was Chanel, gave Trev one last pouty glance. "Come find me once you have her all … settled in." She walked away as if every eye at the party was on her. If they were male, there was a good chance she was right.

"Always so pleasant," Oliver said in such a sarcastic tone that I had to smile.

I would have enjoyed Oliver's company just fine.

"You think that's funny?" Trev asked, and I looked up at him to see he was grinning at me.

I lifted a shoulder. "A little."

"Ollie is a regular ol' comedian," he agreed, then winked.

"Trev!" another female voice called out, and he sighed, then reached for my arm.

"Sorry, Ollie, my man, but we got somewhere to be," he said, then pulled me behind him as he walked past the bar and toward another house. A regular-sized house that was hidden just around the corner.

"Who lives here?" I asked, surprised that there was a house so close to theirs. It seemed odd.

Trev glanced back at me. "Where?" he asked.

I pointed at the house we were walking toward.

"The pool house? No one lives there. It's a pool house."

I stopped walking and looked at the house closer. "This?" I asked him.

"Positive," he replied with a soft chuckle.

"Trev," I said, putting a hand on my hip as I continued staring at the house, "why would anyone need a pool house this big? If no one lives in it, what is the point?"

"Hell, I don't know. What do you mean? It's a pool house."

I realized no matter how I phrased this, Trev would not understand what I was asking. I turned my gaze back to his. "Why are we going to the pool house?" I asked him.

His eyes dropped to my sundress. "To get rid of that dress so we can swim. Or better yet, get in the hot tub."

"I'm not doing this … with you," I said. "This flirting you're doing? You're wasting your time. I know your game. It's not for me. Also, I don't intend to bare my boobs, if that is a requirement at this party."

His smile faded, and he ran a hand over his still-damp hair. "You think I'm playing a game? We just met. You barely know me. I could be the most genuine guy you've ever met," he replied.

Even though he looked sincere as he said it, there was a twinkle in his eye that told me he was teasing me.

"I know your game, millionaire. I'm not interested in playing it."

"Ouch," he replied, placing a hand over his heart, as if I had hurt him.

"But we can be friends. If you want to be my friend, that is."

He said nothing at first, then finally nodded. "All right then. Friends it is," he said. "But only if you go topless."

I shot him an annoyed glare, and he threw his head back and laughed. Shaking mine, I started walking toward the pool house that a family of five or six could live in comfortably.

"Hey, Maddy," he called.

"Yeah?" I asked, looking back at him.

"I'm not a millionaire," he said.

I frowned and held out my hands toward the pool house. "Oh, is that so?" I asked sarcastically.

He nodded his head. "Yeah, it's so," he replied, then reached past me to open the door. "I'm a billionaire," he replied, then winked.

Chapter
FOUR

MADELINE

I didn't even have the luxury of Section 8 housing, my dad was an alcoholic who struggled to keep a job, and now, I'm a penniless orphan," I whispered to myself as I looked in the mirror.

What was I doing in this house with these people, wearing a hot-pink bikini that, on second glance, really didn't cover my boobs that well? Turning so I could see my butt, I winced at the lack of fabric. Did Melanie not realize I wasn't built like her? I wasn't overweight, but I also wasn't as thin as she was.

Sighing, I thought about letting my hair back down so it could fall over my shoulders and cover my cleavage some, but then it would get wet and do very little for coverage.

A knock on the door startled me.

"You ready yet? My glass is empty," Trev called out.

I gave myself one more look and grimaced. I should have just stayed at the Houstons' house and read a book. This was not what I had expected when we were invited to a pool party. But then this was the first pool party I'd ever been to.

"I'm coming," I replied and headed for the door.

When I opened it, Trev was near the pool table and picking up a ball.

"Do you pl—" He stopped talking when he turned to look at me. "Pool. Play pool … " He trailed off and then held up his glass. "Yep, gonna need another drink, buddy."

He went to the door and opened it up. "After you," he told me.

"I don't have a towel," I told him.

"We have them out by the bar in a warming closet. You can grab one when you need it."

"Of course you have a warming closet for towels," I replied, smirking as I walked past him.

When the door closed behind us, he let out a breath he had been holding. "Jesus," he muttered, and I glanced back at him to see he was staring at my butt.

"Trev," I said, and he jerked his attention back up to my face reluctantly.

"Yeah, uh, right, a drink," he muttered.

I waited until he was beside me before walking. I was not going to walk in front of him if he was going to look at my backside. I might not want to date Trev, but he was a guy, and I didn't relish the idea of him studying me close enough to see my flaws.

I didn't make eye contact with anyone. I focused on getting to the bar so Trev could get his drink and I could get a towel to wrap around me.

"Uh, you, uh, going for a swim?" Saxon asked, and I turned my head toward his voice. He was alone, sitting on a lounge chair with a drink in his hand.

"I was going to get her into the hot tub," Trev replied.

He moved to stand up. "I'll join you."

"Great," Trev drawled.

Saxon narrowed his eyes as he looked at his friend. "You don't sound like you want my company."

"Where is Declan?" Trev asked him.

25

Saxon shrugged. "I don't know."

"Don't you need to find her?" Trev asked.

"No," Saxon replied.

Trev set his glass down on the bar, and the bartender gave him another without needing an order.

"You want a fresh club soda?" he asked me.

"No thanks. I'm good for now."

It was ninety-two degrees outside, so the hot tub was empty as it sat perched up on a large rock that overlooked the pool. Beside it was a waterfall that came from yet another large rock.

"Trev," the deep voice I instantly recognized from earlier called out.

Trev groaned and turned around slowly to face Blaise. "What?" he asked, annoyed instead of terrified.

"Inside. Now," he demanded. "Bring your phone."

"I'm in the middle of a party," Trev replied. "See the people?"

Blaise's expression didn't change. "Get the fuck inside with your goddamn phone before I end this party."

Trev slammed his glass down on the bar. "Fuckin' asshole," he muttered.

Blaise stood there, waiting for Trev to move, when Trev's hand touched my arm.

"I won't be long."

Blaise's angry gaze shifted to me for a brief second, then back to Trev. "You move fast."

"So?" Trev replied and stormed past Blaise toward the house.

When they disappeared inside, Saxon leaned closer to me. "Want to swim? That hot tub isn't going to be very refreshing in this heat."

He was right, of course, but there was one problem. I couldn't swim. This was the first swimsuit I had worn since I had been nine years old. Even then, I didn't swim. I played in the sprinklers at the different apartments we lived in. Dad didn't take us to lakes or pools. There had never been vacations or summer activities in our house.

"I can't swim, and besides, I think I'm overdressed for that pool."

I'd decided to just be honest. He would find out eventually. I was living in his house, and it was the summer in Florida.

His brows drew together. "Really? You can't swim?" he asked.

"No, Saxon. I like to lie about things that are embarrassing," I replied sarcastically.

"Yeah, good point. Sorry." He looked thoughtful as he stared out at the water. "We have a pool. I mean, you've seen it, I'm sure. It's not this impressive. How about you let me teach you how to swim?" he said as his gaze shifted back to me.

I wasn't so sure how I felt about that. What if I couldn't swim and drowned while he was trying to teach me? I was about to ask him to let me think about it when Declan appeared by his side, wrapping her body around his arm—or at least, it looked like she was trying.

"You didn't come back in the water." She pouted up at him. "Jeremey had to become my base during war."

Saxon gave her what looked like a forced smile. "Sorry."

She glared over at me with clear hatred. Of course, it was my fault Saxon had left her. I wanted to roll my eyes.

"I was just going to get another drink," I said, needing a reason to leave this situation.

Not waiting on Saxon's response, I stepped away from them and went to get another club soda. As I stood behind a few other people in line, loud voices carried out over the pool area, and I turned to see three guys who were clearly older than college students. The crowd parted for them as if they were royalty, or perhaps they moved out of their way because they were scared. Two of the guys had on cowboy hats while the third one had a buzz cut. Their jeans and boots made it clear they weren't here for the pool party.

"Shit," the guy in front of me muttered under his breath as he looked their way.

"You're just jealous," the girl beside him said to him.

"Whatever," he replied, then walked off, leaving her standing there.

She laughed at him, then went back to watching the three older guys.

"Looks like we might be interrupting something," the one in the black cowboy hat said with a smirk.

I thought no one was going to say anything when Saxon stepped out of the crowd. The guy with the buzzed hair looked at Saxon.

"Shit, Sax, haven't you realized you're better than this crowd yet?" he drawled.

"Gage," he replied with a smile. "Didn't know you were back from your leave."

He ran a hand over his almost-shaved head. "Just got home yesterday."

Then, Sax held out his hand toward him. "It's good to have you back."

The guy he'd called Gage slapped his hand in Sax's, and they shook.

"You grew up. 'Bout damn time," the guy replied with a grin.

"Hell yeah, he grew up," the guy wearing a brown cowboy hat said, then slapped Sax on the back. "You should see him breaking in the mustang over at Moses Mile. Regular fucking badass."

"You can stay," the one wearing a black cowboy hat said loud enough for everyone to hear. "The rest of you can go," he then said, glaring out over the crowd. "Except that one." He pointed to the topless redhead. "Bring those double Ds right on over here and sit in daddy's lap."

I cringed. Had he really just said that? The redhead beamed at him and walked out of the pool, not looking away from him.

"She legal?" the guy asked Saxon.

"Yeah, she's eighteen," Saxon told him.

I stood there, watching as people began to gather their bags. People talked in groups among each other, and gazes would cut toward the three older guys, then quickly look away. Two other topless girls made their way over to the guy Saxon had called Gage. He seemed pleased by their attention. When the first one reached him, he cupped both her breasts in his hands and said something in a low voice that caused her to giggle.

I was no longer in a line for a drink since the people in front of me had moved to get their things and leave. I looked at the bartender, who was watching me. Unsure if I should order a club soda or not, I glanced back at Saxon. Declan was now with him, and they were discussing something. She didn't look happy about whatever it was.

"You staying?" the bartender asked me.

I shifted my gaze back to him. "I have no idea," I replied honestly.

"You might want to go," he offered.

I nodded. Maybe I did. Instead of ordering another drink, I glanced back toward the pool house and decided to go get my things. This entire scene was weird and confusing.

"Maddy!" Trev's voice called out my name, and I turned to see him walking my way. I waited for him to reach me. "Where are you going?" he asked.

"To get my things," I said, then looked around him at the three guys. "Not sure who the rodeo squad is, but they told everyone to leave, and since the crowd is obeying, I assumed I should too."

The corner of Trev's mouth curved up. "Did you call them the rodeo squad?" he asked.

I nodded.

Then, he laughed. "Fucking brilliant." He reached for my hand. "Come on."

I hesitated, then put my hand in his. At the moment, he was the safer option. Especially if a scene from Pornhub was about to break out.

Saxon was still talking to an annoyed Declan. She had her hands on her hips, talking rapidly. Something had set her off. I felt bad for him, but then he was the one staying in the situation. He could just walk away from it.

"Uh, you want to go inside?" Trev asked me, looking back over my shoulder at something.

Out of curiosity, I glanced back to see what had him looking so serious. I wished I hadn't. The redhead was straddling the guy she'd sauntered over to. He had her left nipple in his mouth, sucking, while she rocked back and forth on him. Both of his hands were cupping her almost-bare butt.

I quickly snapped my head back around and felt my face heat up.

"It's going to get much worse than that," Trev said to me. "Knowing Skylar, she'll end up taking two of them on at the same time."

"Are you serious?" I asked him in a whisper.

Trev smirked. "Deadly."

"Oh," I replied because I honestly had no words.

Chapter
FIVE

BLAISE

The fucker had moved my horse without talking to me. It was another one of his power plays to remind me who was in control. For now. He had already moved me into a position I was aware would one day be mine. Horse racing was also in my blood, and he knew it. He used it against me. The son of a bitch was vindictive, and I should have considered he'd do something like this to get me to take the next step.

I was the son he had prepared to step into his shoes. I was the one he'd trained to be ruthless. If it was just about the horses, this would have been easy, but my father wasn't just a horse breeder. My legacy wasn't to just take over Hughes Farm. It was darker than that. A darkness my little brother could never handle. Trev knew, of course. We all knew. It had been our life from the moment we had been born. Trev was just too much like his mother. Soft, fragile, unable to become what our father wanted.

Using more force than was necessary, I shoved open the door leading out to the pool, feeling a brief moment of relief when the crowd was gone. I reckoned I owed the boys for that one. It had been ten years since we had graduated high school, but the legacy never seemed to fade. Even this new generation held on to the stories. Hell, it had been at least six years since one of us had been arrested. We had been hotheaded and stupid back then. Age had taught us that to be successful in our world, you had to be smart. Not stupid. Keeping cops as friends was the first thing I'd learned. Of course, I knew it wasn't our past that struck fear in them. There were also the whispers, things they would never say in public, truths they all hoped were lies.

"You find him?" Levi called out from a lounge chair with a topless red head draped over his chest.

"Yeah," I replied, heading straight for the bar.

The bartender was already pouring up my choice of bourbon when I stopped in front of him. He'd been working parties out here since I had been in school. I nodded my thanks, then took the glass and turned back to scan the place and see who hadn't fled.

"Fuck this shit. It's too damn hot," Huck said, tossing his brown cowboy hat toward an empty lounge chair and then jerking his shirt off. "Stand up, baby, and let me get these jeans off. Then, you can ride my cock like a good girl."

The blonde stood up and began taking off her bikini bottoms. Leave it to them to clear the place out but keep some barely legal pussy around to fuck.

"We have bedrooms, you know." My younger brother sounded annoyed, and I glanced back at him and smirked.

He was pissed his party had been cut short. I started to say something when I shifted my gaze from him to the blonde he'd been with earlier. The one who had arrived with Sax.

Madeline.

Her eyes met mine, and like earlier, the blue color that stared back at me was fucking insane. Especially under the sunlight. Unable to help myself, I did a quick take of her body in that hot-pink bikini. She hadn't gone topless, but I wasn't surprised.

32

I swallowed hard, then took a long drink from my glass. A body like that didn't belong on a nineteen-year-old.

Holy fuck. Sax and Trev were gonna end up beating the hell out of each other over her. It would be a complete waste of Trev's time and energy. They didn't know who she was. Not really.

I did.

A splash and a loud female squeal drew my attention to the other side of the pool. The squeal had come from the youngest Delamore girl. I'd gone to school with her sister, Heidi—or was it Hannah? I couldn't remember. Didn't matter. Sax was making a mistake with that one. Those girls had been raised to do nothing but look pretty and marry well. That one would be no different. She might be acting silly and batting her eyelashes at Gage, who had jumped in the pool naked, but her arm was firmly locked around Saxon.

Saxon's focus, however, was not on her. He was watching Madeline.

"You gonna wait around until the old man gets home?" Gage asked as he got back out of the pool, wrapped a towel around his waist and walked towards the bar.

"He made sure I didn't have a fucking choice," I replied. The annoyance clear in my tone.

"At least we cleared the place out for you," he said. "Well, except for the ones with the biggest tits and the one with Trev. Speaking of which, your brother is my hero. Have you gotten a look at the blonde he's with?"

I gave a singular nod, then took a drink. They'd know soon enough. I didn't want to discuss it, especially here. With her so close.

"She's not like the others. She's seen shit. It's in her eyes," Gage said.

"Her eyes?" I asked him, knowing what it was he saw.

Madeline's life had been a fucking shit show. Leave it to Gage to notice she was different.

"She's not some spoiled brat. There is a maturity there," he said.

I cut my eyes at him. "You've been deployed too long," I drawled, although he was closer to the truth than I was comfortable with.

She was tough. She had never had a choice to be anything else.

Gage grinned. "If you mean I need to get laid, you're right." He reached over and squeezed the right tit of the girl that had come over to hang onto his arm. "You ready to suck my dick, sugar?" he asked her.

"Probably want to find someone who can legally drink," I tell him.

"This mouth looks sweet enough," he said, rubbing a thumb over her bottom lip. "I bet you can suck real nice."

I knew he'd have her bent over a chair soon enough, fucking her from behind.

I glanced over as Trev leaned in close to Madeline. He was saying something to her, and then they turned to walk to the pool house. The backside view was as good as the front.

Gage released a low whistle, and I didn't have to look at him to know he was watching her walk away too.

"Damn," he said.

Yeah. Damn.

"I swear to God, I am living vicariously through Trev right now, and I never thought that would happen," he added.

I took another long drink to keep from saying anything more.

"Now, baby, don't be like that. Your hot little mouth is gonna make me forget every woman but you. I swear it."

I glanced over at Sax to see he was sitting up now, completely ignoring his girlfriend while watching my brother and Madeline go to the pool house.

Three … two … one …

And he was standing up. Yep, this shit was not going to end well for the girlfriend. He was following them now, and the Delamore girl called out his name, but he ignored it.

"My money's on Sax," Huck called out.

34

Shaking my head, I took another drink. Although, where Madeline was concerned, I agreed. She would see right through my brother.

As far as fighting went, Trev was a pretty boy who was fucking spoiled, but he was a Houston. Sax knew that, and he knew what it meant. There wouldn't be a fight between them. The guys knew that as much as I did.

The Delamore girl stood up and glared after Saxon before flipping her hair over her shoulder and going for the entrance to the house.

"Ah, leaving so soon?" Huck asked her.

She paused and looked at him like she might move on to him. But she didn't. I respected that.

The red head now riding Levi was moaning as he grabbed her waist and lifted her up and down on his cock.

"Oh God!" she cried out loudly.

Her tits bounced, and I enjoyed the view while I took another drink.

"Suck it, baby," Gage groaned from behind me. "That's it. Just like that. I'll shoot my load in that little mouth, then fuck you until you can't walk."

His breathing got heavier, and I could hear her gag. The sound made my dick harden.

The pool house door opened back up, and Madeline came walking out with the sundress she'd arrived in and both boys beside her. She'd let her hair down, and it hung over her right shoulder. Although she couldn't be more than five-six, she had fucking legs for days.

I watched her face when she saw the several sex acts going on around me. When her eyes met mine, I tipped my hat at her and smirked. The shock on her face as her eyes swung to the girl screaming out Levi's name made my dick throb.

Chapter
SIX

MADELINE

They were legends in this town—or at least, that was the way Trev had explained it to me. Not because they had won anything or been some sort of sports stars, but because they had broken laws.

Gage had gone into the Marines because his father had forced him to, not by choice. Levi had been in prison for two years for grand theft auto. Huck had left home at seventeen and now owned a repair shop for motorcycles. And Blaise was their leader. He'd been arrested and let go several times for different things. His father had always gotten him out of trouble.

Trev told me all that, then warned me to stay clear of them. They might have gotten older, but that only meant that they'd gotten better at covering things up.

When I had asked what things, he had frowned, then shaken his head and told me, "Just stuff."

As I took in the scene around me, I wondered if underage porn had been involved in those crimes. I decided that I didn't want to know any more. The way he'd said "just things" sounded dark. As if he wished didn't know. From the looks of it, they didn't seem to follow any kind of rules.

With Saxon and Trev on either side of me, I felt as if there were some barrier between me and the scene taking place. I was ready to get away from this here. Watching people have sex and listening to what the guys were saying while doing it made me feel strange. I knew my face was red, and I tried to keep my gaze on the ground so no one would notice my glowing cheeks.

"Let's go home," Saxon said to me.

I nodded with a quick glance up at him. He looked relieved to be leaving too. Hopefully this was more than he cared to witness.

"Leaving so soon?" Blaise asked.

I didn't want to look at him. He made me nervous. It was just hard not to look at him. There was a powerful energy around him that drew you in. That, and his eyes. Even if there was nothing friendly in their depths.

"Since you crashed my party and turned the place into a free sex show, yeah, they are," Trev replied.

Blaise didn't even acknowledge his brother's response.

"Sax," he called out instead, and Saxon turned to look at him.

"Yeah?" he replied.

"If you hear anything about Empire, let me know," he told him. It sounded like a demand more than a request.

Saxon nodded. "Will do."

"Dad's just making a point," Trev whispered—so that Blaise couldn't hear him, was my guess. "Reminding him that he does have some power over him."

Saxon glanced at Trev as we reached the door to the house.

"I don't want to get in the middle of any war between Garrett Hughes and Blaise. If I hear anything, I'm telling you, and leave me out of it," Saxon said to Trev.

Trev just nodded once, like he understood. His expression more serious than the carefree grin he seemed to always flash.

37

Maybe Blaise and their father had some bad blood between them.

Neither of them said anything as we walked back through the house to the front doors.

"I'll see you later," Sax told Trev, then opened the door and looked at me. "Let's go."

"Later, Maddy," Trev said to me, and when I met his eyes, he grinned. The serious expression had faded.

"Thanks for including me today," I told him, feeling like I should say something.

He chuckled. "Yeah, glad you got to experience all this." Then, he leaned closer to me. "You are welcome here. Anytime. It's not always like this."

"Good to know," I replied and hurried after Saxon, my face feeling warm. I didn't want to think about all I had seen outside.

When I reached the truck, Saxon was looking down at his phone. He lifted his gaze to mine and then walked over to the passenger door and opened it for me.

"Thanks," I told him awkwardly, then climbed inside.

No one had ever opened my car door for me before. Not even Saxon when we had gotten in the truck to come over here. Was he doing it for Trev's sake?

Saxon walked around the front of the truck and climbed inside. When he closed his door, he turned to look at me and sighed. "And that's the Hughes family," he said. "Wealthy, powerful, arrogant, and sometimes terrifying."

I frowned. "Isn't Trev your best friend?"

"Yep," he replied, then started the truck. His gaze shifted to the house in front of us and Trev walking up the stairs. "He has been since preschool. First time Dad took me to the track, we sat in the Hugheses' box. Garrett had bought a racehorse, but he was green and needed a lot of work, so Garrett asked Dad to work with him.

Dad is a horse whisperer. He can turn any horse around. Anyway, we were there in their box to see the horse Dad had turned into a potential champion. That's my first memory of Trev. The following year, we started preschool together. We've been tight since then."

I found myself wanting to hear more of their story. I couldn't imagine having a friend for that many years.

"Did the horse win?" I asked him.

The corner of his mouth curled up. "Won the triple crown twice before it retired. The day I met Trev was his first victory. Goliath proved true to his name."

"Where is he now?"

"He's living the posh life as an old man in the Hugheses' stables," Saxon replied.

I smiled, happy to hear he was still alive. I might not be sure about my feelings toward horses just yet, but I was warming up to them. The one I'd met today was lovable. Perhaps I had a little of my mother in me. A part of her I hadn't known existed.

"Sorry if today was a bit much," he said to me, changing the subject. "That crowd is a lot. Then, add Blaise and his crew ..." Saxon shook his head. "I hadn't expected them to show up. Blaise doesn't come around much. He keeps Empire there, and he does own a percentage of Hughes Farm. Just not a controlling percentage. Anyway, I wouldn't have taken you or gone myself if I'd known all that was going to happen."

He had tried to help me fit in and make friends. There was no reason for him to apologize for something that he'd had nothing to do with. I found it sweet that he had though.

"I appreciate you taking me. You didn't have to," I replied.

He smirked then. "You say that, but you don't know Trev. If I hadn't taken you, he'd have come and gotten you himself."

I didn't ask him why. I didn't need to. Guys like Trev loved girls, and they especially loved a challenge.

Chapter
SEVEN

MADELINE

Dinner wasn't the event I'd feared. Melanie called as soon as we returned to the house to tell us that Kenneth would be staying in Lexington overnight and that she would be having dinner at the club with friends. I knew a family dinner would come for me eventually, but after today, I was relieved it wasn't tonight.

My family hadn't done dinner together. Dad would eat in front of the television, and so would Cole. I typically made a meal for them from what food we had and then cleaned up the kitchen while they ate. That had been my normal. Not living in a house with someone who cooked for the family and served them in a fancy dining room.

After standing in my closet for over ten minutes, staring at the clothes and wishing my cutoff sweatpants and faded Texas A&M T-shirt were in there, I finally chose a pair of white shorts and a black tank top. It seemed like the most casual pieces of clothing I had been given. My other clothes had gone missing. I didn't have to ask to know Melanie hadn't approved of them. They had been secondhand clothes, but they were mine.

A knock on my bedroom door brought me out of my thoughts on clothing, and I walked over to see what Saxon wanted. It had to be him. We were the only ones home.

He smiled when I opened the door. I liked his smile, but then again, he also had dimples. That was hard not to like.

"Hungry?" he asked.

I was indeed hungry, but I didn't want to leave this house again today. I paused for a moment before replying, "Yes," almost cautiously.

"Good. I ordered pizza. I wasn't sure what kind you liked, so I ordered a cheese, pepperoni, barbecue chicken, and veggie. Jo was going to fix us something before she left, but I told her we wanted pizza."

All of those pizzas sounded good.

"I like them all," I told him.

He beamed at me, as if I'd said something brilliant. "Perfect."

A chime went through the house, startling me before I realized it was the doorbell.

"It's here," he said. "Let's eat."

He started down the hallway toward the staircase, and I followed behind him. My stomach growled, and I was suddenly ravenous.

I couldn't remember the last time I'd had pizza. Well, this kind of pizza. I used to make bread pizzas at home. Expired white bread was cheap, as were dented cans of tomato sauce. When we'd had enough grocery money to splurge on cheese, I would make us pizzas on slices of bread. Cole loved them. If we could afford pepperoni, then Cole was thrilled. That was rare though. Every dollar had counted in our house.

"Declan, I didn't know you were coming over," I heard Saxon say, and I paused.

I wasn't sure if I should keep going down the stairs or turn around and go back to my room. Seeing Declan again did not sound appealing. But the thought of pizza made my stomach rumble, and I decided I was hungry enough to deal with it.

When I reached the bottom step, Declan glanced over at me, then back to Saxon, as if I weren't even standing there.

"I thought we could watch a movie. Today was a bust, but tonight doesn't have to be," she told him, stepping inside and pressing closer to Saxon.

"Uh, well, I guess," he replied, then looked back at me. "Want to watch a movie, Maddy?" he asked me.

I knew that Declan hadn't meant me when she suggested "we" watch a movie.

Not wanting to make an enemy since it was obvious I would be seeing a lot of Declan, I shook my head. "Oh, no, that should just be the two of you. I can get my pizza and go to my room and read." Which was exactly what I wanted to do.

A pleased smile spread across Declan's full lips, and I was glad I'd made her happy. I didn't see us being friends, but as long as she knew I wasn't after her boyfriend, I figured we could exist peacefully.

"Did y'all order pizza?" she asked, looking back up at Saxon.

He nodded, but he was frowning at me. "You don't have to stay up in your room, alone."

I started to protest, but Declan stepped around Saxon and farther into the house as she leveled her gaze on me. "He's right. That sounds terribly boring. Stay down here with us. You can help me decide on a movie. If we let Saxon pick, it'll give me nightmares or put me to sleep," she said with a friendly smile that concerned me.

There was no way she was suddenly open to me being here.

"My movies aren't that bad," Saxon said defensively.

Declan rolled her eyes and shot him a look over her shoulder. "Yes, they are." Then, she turned back to me. "The last movie he picked out, I was asleep within the first twenty minutes."

Saxon closed the door and smirked at me from behind her back. I wanted to laugh, but I kept from doing so.

"I don't watch much television. I'm more of a reader," I explained.

Declan grimaced. "I can fix that," she replied with a wave of her manicured hand, as if I were broken because I read books. "When is the pizza going to be here?" she asked, turning to Saxon as she placed a hand on his arm.

"Uh, well, I thought you were the pizza, so any minute," he replied.

"Did you get a vegan on gluten-free crust?" she asked him.

He shook his head. "No."

Declan sighed, and her shoulders dropped, like he had disappointed her. I hadn't known they made vegan or gluten-free pizzas.

"I'll go ask Jo to make me a salad then," she told him.

"Jo left for the day," Saxon informed her.

Another long sigh. "Then, I will go make myself a salad." She flashed a smile at me. "Come with? You can help me get the plates and flatware," she told me, then began walking toward the kitchen.

I looked from her retreating form to Saxon. I didn't want to be alone with her since I was ninety-nine percent sure this was an act for Saxon. Once we were by ourselves, I feared her claws would come back out. However, I didn't see a way to escape this, and Saxon said nothing. He just shrugged.

I wanted to sigh this time, but I forced a smile and turned to follow Declan to the kitchen. I had dealt with my share of Declans in high school. I knew what to expect. I'd thought once I graduated, I was done with this kind of thing. Apparently, it was something that not everyone grew out of.

The kitchen smelled clean and was spotless when we entered. I didn't like the idea of messing it up. Didn't seem fair to Mrs. Jolene. She'd left it pristine before leaving for the day.

Declan opened up both of the doors to the massive fridge and stood in front of it with her hands on her hips. "I've never actually made my own salad. I don't cook," she said, then flashed a bright smile at me. "We have a chef for that."

I wasn't surprised. I didn't say anything because I had no polite response.

Declan went back to studying the fridge while letting the cool escape, but reached for nothing. I knew that the Houstons could afford the electricity bill, but the longer she stood there, the more stressed I got. Why wasn't she getting things out and closing the doors? There was no reason to leave them open like that. When she finally moved, it was to look at me again.

"I don't know where to start," she said. "Do you know how to make a salad?"

I didn't want to make Declan anything, but if it would get her to stop standing there with the fridge doors open, then I would do it. I nodded and walked over to look inside the fridge. Quickly, I grabbed a head of lettuce, some vegetables, and a bottle of dressing.

"Does that dressing have dairy? I'm vegan," she said, causing me to pause.

It was ranch dressing, so I nodded.

She shook her head. "Can't have it then."

I put it back. "There are a few other dressings," I told her and moved back so she could look at them.

She did a quick glance. "Are any vegan?" she asked me, as if I knew.

"I'm not vegan. I don't know what you're looking for," I explained, feeling more annoyed by the second.

She frowned and reached in to pull out an oil and vinegar bottle. "Just use this," she told me.

Relieved, I took it and finally closed the doors.

"Are you going to, like, wash and chop that stuff?" she asked me.

Since it all needed to be washed and chopped, I nodded.

She beamed then. "Great. I'll be in the movie room with Saxon." Then, she spun around and strutted out of the room without a *thank you* or a *do you need help*.

I would have been annoyed by that if I wasn't being left alone. If getting rid of her was the outcome, then I would happily take my time making a salad for the princess. At least I was alone again. This would also give me the chance to clean things up. When Mrs. Jolene returned in the morning, the kitchen would be exactly like she had left it.

It took me several minutes to find a colander, cutting board, salad bowl, vegetable peeler, and knife, but once I had all my supplies, I went to work on the salad, making extra for Saxon and myself. Lost in the process, I didn't hear Saxon walk into the kitchen and jumped, startled, when he placed the pizzas on the counter.

"Wow, you can really make a salad," he said to me. "Declan said you insisted on making it, and now, I can see why. Hers wouldn't have looked anything like that."

I'd insisted, huh?

"I made enough for all of us," I told him. "We could use some veggies with our pizza."

He held up a box. "This is veggie pizza."

I grinned. "That's been cooked with cheese, and it's full of grease, taking all its nutritional value out of the picture."

He smiled. "I don't normally eat salads, but since you made it and pointed out my lack of proper vegetables, I'll have some."

I started to reply when Declan came back into the kitchen.

"Is it ready yet? I didn't expect a simple salad to take so long. I would have stayed and helped you if I'd known you were going to struggle with it." All the while, she kept her friendly smile in place.

I imagined taking the salad bowl and tossing it in her face. The thought made me feel better.

"It's done now," I replied. "Saxon, what dressing do you like?" I asked him, taking the attention off Declan.

"He doesn't eat salad," Declan announced. "But I hope you do. That's entirely too much for me, and I'd hate to waste any of their food. You should have been careful. Jo might need some of those things tomorrow."

So, she was worried about wasting their food, but not about wasting their electricity. How did Saxon deal with her? Did she not drive him nuts?

My brother had always said, "Guys think with their dicks, Maddy. The hotter the piece, the more bullshit they will put up with."

I'd always rolled my eyes at that saying, but in this situation, that had to be the case.

"Maddy made enough for all of us. She pointed out the lack of nutritional value in the pizza, so I agreed to eat salad too," he explained to Declan, then looked back at me. "I like ranch."

I nodded and went to get the ranch from the fridge again. I liked it, too, so this would work for both of us. Closing the door, I went over to set it on the counter.

"I'll get the plates," I said since I had found them while looking for a salad bowl earlier.

"Are we eating in here? Wouldn't the dining room be better?" Declan asked.

"No need to mess up the dining room. It's just us," Saxon replied and walked over to me to take the plates.

He handed one to Declan, and she took it as if it were a foreign object. Saxon didn't seem to notice and began putting one of each of the pizzas on his plate, and then he took the tongs I'd put in the salad bowl and added a small portion of salad on the space left.

I took my plate and followed his lead while Declan watched us, frowning before moving toward the salad bowl and putting an even smaller portion than Saxon had gotten onto her plate. Realizing I had indeed made too much salad, I went back and put a much larger portion of the salad on my plate. I didn't want to waste the salad, and it was clear that Declan wasn't going to eat more than a few bites.

Once she had her food, Declan walked out of the kitchen with her plate and toward the dining room. Saxon watched her then looked at me and rolled his eyes before taking his plate to follow her. My new plan was to eat, then claim a headache and get back to the solitude of my room. There was no way I was staying down here and watching a movie with the two of them.

Chapter

EIGHT

SAXON

Declan was either trying to be friendly with Maddy or she was faking it. My bet was on the latter. I knew Declan was unhappy about Maddy living here. Once Declan had seen her today, that unhappiness had escalated. She hadn't known that my mother's orphaned best friend's daughter was also gorgeous. Neither had I.

Tonight, I had hoped to get to know Maddy better and make her feel comfortable here. Mom wanted her to feel like this was her home. Truth was, my mother had always wanted a daughter, but after I was born, the doctors had warned her that her body couldn't handle another pregnancy. She'd tried anyway a few years later and lost the baby at twenty weeks. I didn't remember it, but I knew from things Dad had said, Mom had been heartbroken. The baby had been a girl.

Maddy was exactly the kind of daughter my mother would have wanted. My mother loved beautiful things, and Maddy fit that category. When she'd gone to get Maddy in Texas, I had wondered if the girl would be what my mother wanted. Not to say Mom was shallow, but a part of me felt like if Maddy didn't meet her expectations physically, Mom might not want to offer her a home. I never voiced that concern, and when Maddy had walked into the kitchen this morning, I understood my mother's buoyant mood. She had gotten the perfect daughter.

Dinner was exhausting. I did my best to control the conversation so that Declan wouldn't say anything to make Maddy feel uncomfortable or unwanted. However, when Maddy stood up from the table with her empty plate, I could see the look on her face. She was going to bolt, and honestly, I didn't blame her. Nothing about this meal was what I had planned. Declan had made sure that Maddy didn't get a chance to say much. She'd managed to turn the topic to herself every chance she got.

"I'll clean up in the kitchen and put things away. I've got a headache that I hoped food would cure, but it's not getting better. The two of you enjoy your movie. I'm going to head up to bed. I think the travel yesterday is just getting to me."

As much as I wanted to beg her to stay and watch the movie, I knew Declan would make it awkward. The weary look in Maddy's eyes said she'd had all she could handle for one evening.

I nodded and stood up, taking my plate. "We will help you clean up. No reason for you to do the cleaning on your own when we all ate dinner."

She shook her head. "Oh, no, that's fine. I don't mind. It won't take me long."

I was torn now. It was clear she wanted to get away from us, but I hated the idea of her cleaning up. "Go to bed. You made the salad. We will clean up," I told her.

"We will?" Declan asked, and I ignored her.

Maddy looked torn. She wanted to escape, but it was obvious she didn't like leaving the cleaning to us. I picked up Declan's plate and put it on top of mine.

"I swear, I got this," I told her again.

After a brief pause, Maddy finally nodded. "Okay, if you're sure."

49

I started to tell her I was positive when the door chime began to play. Who the fuck was that? With my parents gone, the only answer was that it was someone for me, and I hadn't invited anyone.

"That's Trev!" Declan announced, springing up from her seat.

"Trev?" I asked, confused, looking at her.

"What? I invited him. I didn't want Maddy to feel like a third wheel. But now that she has a headache and is going to bed, that ruins everything," she said with a touch of a sour note in her voice.

"You didn't mention it to me," I said, unable to keep the annoyance out of my voice.

She shrugged and pushed her lips out into a pout that I'd once been affected by. Back before I got to know her and when I was getting hot sex from her in the locker room at school and blow jobs while I was driving. She was every teenage boy's fantasy. But like I'd said, that was before I got to really know her. Declan was a lot to deal with. She had daddy issues, and I knew her home life was hard. Her mother ignored her and was rarely home. I felt bad for her, and because of that, I overlooked a lot.

"I didn't know I needed permission to invite your best friend over," she said as if this conversation were ridiculous. "Besides, I thought it would be a better setting for Maddy to get to know us. Today wasn't exactly a success. Blaise ruined everything."

The door chimed again.

Declan raised her eyebrows. "One of us needs to go get it. Or are you planning on making Trev stand outside?"

I looked back over at Maddy, who remained, still watching us.

"You don't have to stay down here," I told her.

She nodded and turned to leave the room. I wished I could do the same.

"That was rude," Declan said, glaring at the door Maddy had exited.

"She has had a shitty week. Her head hurts," I said to Declan through clenched teeth.

"Whatever. I'm going to let Trev in," she said to me.

50

I didn't watch her go, but picked up the dishes and glasses on the table, then went to the kitchen to load them in the dishwasher. Declan could entertain Trev. Not that he needed entertaining. He knew this house as well as he did his own.

Maddy was washing her dish in the sink, along with the other things she'd used to make the salad. I placed the dishes down beside the sink, and she gave me a tight smile that didn't meet her eyes.

"Sorry about all this. Trust me, I didn't know this was how the night was going to go. I'll wash these up and get them put away. You can escape now."

The corner of her mouth lifted slightly. "It's fine. The pizza was delicious. Thank you for ordering it. I've got the dishes. Y'all go watch your movie. Once I'm done here, I'll go up."

"You shouldn't have to clean up after us," I argued. She'd made Declan a salad, which Declan had barely touched. Watching her clean up our dishes, too, bothered me. "We've got an excellent dishwasher," I told her. "I can just load the dishes in there."

She shook her head. "That's not fair to Mrs. Jolene. She left things spotless. The dishwasher is empty and ready for tomorrow."

I knew Jo well enough to know that she wouldn't mind. She'd be glad I had eaten a salad. However, the determined look on Maddy's face told me she wasn't going to budge.

"Then, I'll help," I replied.

She sighed and stopped washing to look up at me. "I would really rather do it alone. If you stay in here, then ..." She paused and glanced over her shoulder.

She wanted to say Declan would come back and she didn't want that. I could see it in her eyes.

"Yeah, okay. I get it," I replied.

Her shoulders sagged in relief. "Thanks," she said softly.

I didn't like her washing the dishes, but I couldn't ignore her obvious desire to be alone. Declan would come bursting in here with all her energy any moment. I wanted to say more, but I gave

51

her a nod, then walked away. If Mom knew I'd let her wash the dishes, she'd be pissed. Hopefully, she would never find out.

Trev and Declan were headed toward the kitchen when I met them in the foyer. It was a good thing I had left when I did.

"I brought the good stuff," Trev said, holding up a bottle of his favorite rye whiskey.

Unlike my father, who kept tabs on the contents of his liquor cabinet, Trev's dad had an entire cellar and didn't notice when a bottle went missing.

"I'll grab glasses from the bar and meet y'all in the theater," I told him.

He glanced over my shoulder toward the hallway leading to the kitchen. "Where's Maddy?"

"Not feeling good. She's got a headache and going to bed," I explained.

He grinned and held up the bottle. "I got the medicine she needs," he replied, then started to walk past me.

"Wait. I doubt she wants that stuff," I told him.

He shot me a cocky smirk. "She might not know she wants it, but she will."

"Seriously, man, she's had a long week. Let's give her space," I argued.

Trev looked slightly concerned, but only for a moment. "I won't bother her if she doesn't want me to. But just because she is trying to escape you two doesn't mean she won't appreciate my charming company."

"Come on," Declan said, running a hand up my chest and pressing a kiss to my neck. "Let him go check on her. She might want to see him. It'll give us some alone time."

Trev pointed at Declan. "Listen to your woman," he said, then walked off before I could say anything else.

Damn, this night had gone to shit.

Chapter
NINE

MADELINE

"Hey, gorgeous. I got your headache fix right here," a familiar male voice said.

I turned around to see Trev with a bottle of whiskey in his hand. He was flashing me that smile of his that said he knew he was attractive and he enjoyed using it to get his way. I liked Trev, and we had agreed to be friends, but not tonight. Dinner with Declan had been more than I could handle.

"I don't drink. Remember?" I replied.

He set the bottle on the bar and walked around it to come stand beside me. "Well then, let me help you wash the dishes," he said.

I didn't argue. I figured there was no point. He took the bowl I'd just washed from me and began to rinse it.

I smirked. "I would bet money this is the first time you've ever washed dishes."

He cut his eyes to me, then chuckled. "You'd win."

I laughed. It felt good to laugh. The tension in my body eased, and I was suddenly glad that Declan had invited Trev over.

"I'd be willing to bet your headache starts with a *D* and ends with a bitch," he said.

I bit my bottom lip to keep from laughing again. "You'd win," I replied.

He laughed out loud this time and reached for the plate I had finished washing. "I keep waiting for Sax to dump her, but he's too nice. I think he's hoping she'll break it off. Dude's delusional."

I handed him another plate. "Why does he think she will break it off?" I asked.

Trev rinsed the plate and began to dry it. "He never asks her out anymore, he avoids her the best he can, and he doesn't text or call her—he only responds to her texts with brief replies after waiting hours to do so. The kind of shit most girls would get the hint from, but Declan has her talons in and isn't going to let go."

That sounded miserable. For both of them.

"That seems like too much work," I replied.

"Yeah, it does. Wears me the fuck out, thinking about it," he agreed.

We continued washing dishes for a few moments in silence, and then Trev leaned down closer to me.

"Wanna skip out and go have some fun?" he asked.

I glanced over at him, realizing he was really close. "What do you mean?" I asked, turning my attention back to the almost-empty sink.

"We can go out that back door and head over to my place," he suggested.

I shook my head. "No, I don't think so." I wasn't about to walk into that circus again.

"I swear, no pool, no hot tub, no Blaise, and no live sex shows. You ever played Grand Theft Auto?" he asked.

I handed him the last bowl. "I really hope you mean the video game," I replied.

He took the bowl as he grinned. "Yeah. Unless you got a wild side I don't know about and want to try your hand at the real thing."

I laughed and pulled the plug from the sink so the water could drain out. "Definitely not. But I've never played a video game."

Trev placed a hand over his heart, like he was wounded. "What? Are you serious? That's a fucking tragedy."

I took the dish towel from his hand and popped him in the chest with it. "Dramatic much?"

He picked up the dishes. "Do you know where this shit goes? We've got to put it away and go fix this."

"Fix what?" I asked.

"You!"

"What's wrong with me?"

"Well," he said, letting his gaze scan down my body and back up, "until a couple of minutes ago, I'd have said not a damn thing. But you're lacking one big skill that I didn't know about."

"And that is … playing video games?" I asked, highly amused.

He nodded, as if this made complete sense. "Abso-fuckin'-lutely," he replied. "Now, let's get this shit put away and get out of here before they come looking for us."

Part of me still wanted to go to my room and read. Even though I did enjoy Trev's company. He was charming and made me laugh. His mischievous grin reminded me of a little boy who was up to no good. I found myself unable to tell him no.

"Okay, fine," I agreed. "If you swear the rodeo squad is gone?"

"I swear!" He lifted his fist into the air. "Hell yes! Let's do this."

I laughed at him, shaking my head, then walked over to the cabinet where the plates went and opened it for him to put them inside. Then, I took the other items and placed them all back in the spots I'd found them. Once I was done, I wiped down everything and turned off the lights.

"Ready?" Trev asked me in a whisper even though the theater was far enough away that there was no way they could hear him.

I nodded, going along with his game. He grabbed my hand, and we exited out the back door. It wasn't completely dark yet. The sun had been setting later and later, leading up to the summer solstice. However, the sunset was our only light as we walked down the path leading to Trev's parked car. We moved quietly, which was probably unnecessary, but it made the idea of escaping more exciting. I was smiling when I realized we had reached his SUV.

The shiny black vehicle looked expensive. I knew little about cars, but it was obvious this one was considered a luxury SUV.

Trev opened the passenger door. "Hop on in," he told me, no longer whispering.

I climbed into the vehicle, and the smell of leather and new car filled my senses. Looking around, I took in the screen in the dash that was the size of the television my brother and dad had watched daily at our old apartment. The leather was red and softer than any car interior I'd ever felt. When Trev opened the driver's door, he was still grinning. I wondered if he was ever unhappy or angry. I doubted he had reason to be. His world was perfect. Nothing to worry about. It was all taken care of. I couldn't imagine how that must feel.

"Like it?" he asked me.

"The car?"

He looked offended. "This isn't a car, Maddy. Calling it that probably hurt its feelings. You should apologize."

I laughed. "I am not apologizing to a vehicle," I informed him.

He reached forward and petted the dash like he would a dog. "It's okay, baby. She doesn't know any better. I've got a lot to teach her."

Amused, I watched him, and then he glanced at me before starting the engine.

"It smells new," I said.

He nodded. "It is. My dad bought it for me as a bribe. It worked," he replied.

"This looks like an expensive bribe," I said as the smooth ride felt as if we weren't in a car at all.

Trev shrugged. "Not really. Not to him."

I waited a moment, and when he said nothing more, I decided to ask another question. "What kind of vehicle is this?" I asked him since I couldn't recall ever seeing one like this before.

His grin stretched across his chiseled face. "This is a Bentayga," he said with pride. "It would appreciate it if you remembered that."

I nodded, biting back a smile. I had no clue what a Bentayga was, so I didn't reply.

He glanced at me when he came to a Stop sign. "It's a Bentley, Maddy. Surely, you've heard of those."

A Bentley I had heard of, but other than television, I hadn't seen one in person.

"They make SUVs?" I'd thought Bentleys were cars driven by rich, old men.

"Hell yeah, they do," he replied and then caressed his steering wheel.

I laughed, unable to help myself. At least he appreciated his extravagant car. His phone started ringing as we pulled through the entrance to Hughes Farm, and he smirked, looking at the screen on the dash.

"It's Sax," he told me, then pressed something on his steering wheel.

"Hey, bud. How's the movie?" he asked him, then winked at me.

"Where's Maddy?" was Saxon's response.

"Are you accusing me of abduction? And here you are, my best friend," Trev replied, sounding offended while he grinned at me.

"Cut the shit, Trev. She's not here, and neither are you," Saxon replied.

He sounded angry, and I wondered if my leaving with Trev and not telling him had been a bad idea. At the time, it had seemed fun and exciting. Now, I wasn't so sure it had been the right decision.

"Ah, yes, well, we both agreed that a movie with the lovely Declan didn't sound very appealing. Then, Maddy revealed that she had never played a video game. Can you believe that? Never. She's missing out on so much in life. So, being the good guy that I am, I decided I would introduce her to the beauty that is Grand Theft Auto. The game. Not the actual felony itself."

I was torn between laughing at Trev's explanation and worrying that I needed to go back to the Houstons'. I didn't want Saxon to be mad at me. I should have told him I was leaving. It was thoughtless of me.

"I'm sorry I didn't tell you," I said then, unable to sit quietly any longer.

Saxon didn't say anything at first, and I felt a knot form in my stomach. I'd made a mistake. Trev was a ball of energy that could wrap you up in the moment. I had acted out of character and not thought about anything more than that.

"No, that's okay. Trev should have told me. But I understand," he replied.

That should have made me feel better, but I only felt guiltier.

"I'll come back," I told him.

There was a pause, and Trev frowned at me and shook his head.

"No, stay. You wanted to go, and I get it," Saxon replied.

"I'll keep her safe, bro," Trev assured him. "Go watch your movie."

"Okay," Saxon said, and then the call ended.

Trev looked over at me. "You look like you kicked a puppy. Stop stressing. Sax is fine. Declan will make him forget in seconds. One of the reasons he started dating her was because of the way she sucks co—"

"Please do not finish that sentence," I said, holding up a hand to stop him.

He winked at me, then shut off his expensive vehicle and opened his door. "Let's go get our game on."

The Hugheses' mansion was even more impressive at night. With the setting sun almost gone, the place was lit up, making it appear like something from a fairy tale.

"Are we the only ones here?" I asked, noticing no other cars.

"The dick squad left—or is it the rodeo squad?" he asked me with a grin. "I know they are gone, but I'm not sure if my dad's back or not. There is a ten-car garage back that way, to the left. It's not visible from here," he replied as we climbed the stairs to the entrance.

I watched as Trev lifted a brass plate beside the doors, which revealed a keypad. He pressed in several numbers, then opened one of the large double doors. He waved a hand for me to enter, and I walked past him inside.

"My room is up those stairs, but first, let's go get snacks," he said with a grin and a nod of his head toward the open arched entrance to the left of us.

I followed him, quietly taking in everything around me. This place was something else. Even seeing it the second time, I was amazed. What kind of life Trev must live.

When the bright, opulent kitchen came into view, I noticed we weren't the only ones looking for food. Trev sighed audibly and groaned, then walked into the room.

He looked back at me. "I swear, I thought he was gone. He's like a fucking stray dog that won't go away," he said.

Blaise's back was to us as he stood in front of the open refrigerator. My stomach knotted up at the sight of him. He made me nervous.

"You're still here," Trev drawled in an annoyed tone.

Blaise closed the fridge doors and turned to look at us. A carton of milk was in one hand and a bowl in his other. His gaze barely touched me before his eyes locked on his brother. "When the bastard comes back and gives me my damn horse, I'll leave," he said, then put the bowl down on the counter in front of him. "Fuck knows this is the last place I want to be."

"You could always leave, and I'll let you know when he returns," Trev suggested with a hopeful tone.

Blaise ignored him and poured milk into the bowl.

"Let's get some food and head up," Trev told me.

I said nothing. I was afraid to speak. He'd barely acknowledged me, and I preferred to keep it that way. There was something in his eyes that sent out a warning. One that Trev didn't seem to notice. But then again, he was his brother.

"Letting a hot piece of ass come between you and Sax is a dumbass move," he said, shooting Trev a disgusted look.

I tensed.

"Shut up," Trev said, walking over to the fridge.

I didn't move. I wasn't getting closer to the man.

Those intense green eyes locked on me then, and it became hard for me to take a deep breath.

"You're making a mistake, sugar. But then your kind always does," he said to me.

My kind? I stared at him, knowing he had insulted me, but not sure exactly what he meant by it. *What was my kind?*

Anger began to stir in my chest, and the nervous feeling paled in comparison. He didn't know me. How arrogant it was to assume he did.

"What exactly is my kind?" I blurted before I could stop myself.

He studied me a minute while he took a bite of the cereal in his bowl. How could he still appear to be dark and dangerous while eating what looked like Frosted Flakes? I wasn't sure, but he managed it.

"Beautiful and cunning with daddy issues, looking to move up in the world from the meager life you were born into," he drawled as he tilted his head and studied me.

"Dude, shut the fuck up," Trev said, slamming the fridge door with two bottles of water and a soda in his hands.

"You got a look at this place today and realized you were reeling in the smaller fish with Sax," Blaise said, narrowing his eyes.

Blaise Hughes was a bully. I hated bullies.

"I don't measure a person's worth by their bank account, and I will never trust a man to take care of me. Judging someone by their looks is a mistake I would've thought you'd have outgrown by now," I shot back at him. My face felt hot, and my heart was racing.

Trevor cleared his throat. "Guess she cleared that up for you, bro," he said with an amused tone.

Blaise didn't appear as if he cared that I had spoken. His expression didn't change. He took another bite of his cereal. I wished Trev would hurry and get the food he wanted so we could get out of here. As if he could read my mind, Trev walked over to a door, opened it, and stepped inside, then was out in seconds with a bag of chips, a box of snack cakes, and what appeared to be a bag of candy shoved under his arms while still holding the drinks.

"Let's go," he said to me.

I followed him, relieved to be getting away from the other Hughes in the room. Besides the fact that my stomach was even more twisted up, there was a lump forming in my throat. His words had affected me when I wished more than anything that they hadn't.

Blaise was an elitist jerk. What he thought of me meant nothing. I had heard much worse from people in my life. I was tougher than this. I mentally coached myself out of letting Blaise get to me.

We walked back to the stairs, and as we climbed them, Trev glanced back at me.

"Sorry about that asshole."

I swallowed hard and nodded, not sure I trusted my voice just yet. I didn't want Trev to know how much those accusations had bothered me. I could see the concern in Trev's eyes and wanted to say something, but I couldn't yet.

Trev stopped at a door and lifted his shoulder to point to it because his hands were full. I should have offered to carry something.

"This one," he said.

I stepped forward and twisted the knob, then pushed the door open before stepping back to let him enter first.

"Sorry, I should have carried some of that," I told him.

"And make me look like less of a man?" he asked with a teasing tone.

The tension in my chest eased some. Had there ever been two brothers so completely different? Trev was the complete opposite of Blaise.

I followed Trev into his room and paused to look around. This wasn't a bedroom. It was an entertainment room. A huge screen covered most of the left wall. I assumed that was a television screen. Maybe? There was a brown leather sofa, two matching leather chairs, a pool table, arcade games, and a bearskin rug in the center of it all.

"What is this?" I asked him as he dropped the stuff on the large rectangular table between the sofa and screen.

"My bedroom," he replied.

"There is no bed … or dresser," I pointed out, still confused. "Is this where you tell me you're a vampire and you don't sleep?"

Trev looked back at me. His lips curled up. "You think I don't know that reference, but you're wrong."

I wasn't surprised. He'd probably had to watch that movie with more than one girl. I seriously doubted he'd read the book.

"But really, where do you sleep?" I asked him.

"You asking to see my bed, Maddy?"

"No. Just pointing out that your bedroom has nowhere for you to sleep."

Trev held out his arms. "This is the first section of my room. Through that door are my bed and closet." He pointed to the closed door to my right. "And that door is the bathroom." He pointed to the door to the far left.

"You have your own suites," I muttered, thinking this was something I'd read about in historical romance books but I decided not to mention it.

He shrugged. "If that's what you want to call it," he replied, dropping down to sit in the middle of the sofa. "Let's hijack some cars," he proclaimed and picked up a remote that made the screen-covered wall light up and come to life.

"Wow," I whispered, watching the screen.

Playing a video game on that was going to feel like we were in the game. I walked over to the closest chair and sat down.

Trev shot me a frown. "I can't help you from there, and the food is too far away. I don't bite. I'm not Eddie or whatever his name was. Come here," he said, patting the seat beside him.

"His name is Edward," I told him, then reluctantly moved over but kept a proper distance between us.

I didn't think Trev had me in here to make a move, but I was still cautious. I didn't want him to get the wrong idea. He appeared to sincerely want to teach me how to play this game, but I wasn't taking my chances.

Trev leaned forward and grabbed a chip, then popped it in his mouth. "Here, this is your controller," he told me as he handed it to me. "I'll play first; you watch me. Pay attention to the buttons I press and how I work the controller."

I nodded and held the new device in my hands as the game came to life in front of us.

The next two hours went by so quickly that I didn't realize the time. When Saxon walked into the room, I was surprised.

"What up?" Trev said as he continued working the remote in his hands.

"I came to get Maddy. Mom's home and was asking about her," Saxon replied as his gaze held mine.

I glanced at the time and quickly stood up. "I didn't realize it was so late," I told him.

He shrugged. "No worries. She's not upset. I was just sent to make sure you got back safely."

"I was going to bring her," Trev replied, pausing the game and looking over at Saxon.

"No need."

Trev held out his remote to Saxon. "Wanna play?" he asked.

Saxon smirked. "Not tonight. I'd hate to whip your ass in front of your student."

Trev laughed. "Whatever."

I listened to their banter as I slipped my shoes back on and started cleaning up the snacks scattered on the table. I hadn't thought I was hungry, but at some point, the sour gummy worms had looked appealing. Then, I'd moved on to the chips.

"You don't have to clean that up. We have people for that," Trev told me.

Of course he did. He had people for everything. This was not my world. Now that I was immersed in it, I needed to remember it was for a brief time. When I could afford it, I would be moving on with my life. A life where this kind of thing didn't exist. A life where I would be the help.

"You ready?" Saxon asked me.

I simply nodded, then looked back at Trevor. "Thanks. This was fun."

He beamed at me. I liked his smile, and I realized I'd enjoyed spending time with him. In the future, I'd need to be careful. I didn't need attachments.

Chapter
TEN

MADELINE

Melanie had misunderstood my being at Trev's. She thought there was more to it than just the friendship I had agreed to. However, I was finding it hard to explain that to her because she wasn't open to listening to me.

The next morning, she chose my clothing, shoes, and accessories for the day. After more than an hour of her preparing me, we left the house to go visit her salon, where my hair was trimmed and highlighted. I didn't understand that part since my hair was already blonde. The platinum streaks didn't make much of a difference in my appearance, although Melanie seemed to think it did. Next, I was given a manicure and pedicure. After that, I was subjected to waxing and something called threading, which hurt like hell.

The afternoon was almost over when we finally left the salon. Melanie talked nonstop about how perfectly everything had turned out. I felt like her doll. One she was obsessed with dressing up to suit her whim. It wasn't that I was ungrateful. It was just that I didn't see the need in all of this. The only thing that I did understand was that Melanie had it in her head that I would soon be dating a Hughes. This idea thrilled her, and she appeared almost giddy with excitement.

I had one thing to be thankful for by the time we reached the Houstons' ranch. Melanie had to meet Kenneth at a business dinner in two hours, and I would finally get a break. I plucked at the top I was wearing, wishing it were longer instead of stopping just above my waistline. The fact that I would be able to change into comfortable clothing soon was a relief.

"I'm sure Saxon will be working with the horses until late. With his father busy, he has more work to do. But don't you worry about going to help. It will mess up your nails, and they look so lovely in that shade of pink. If Trevor comes by or calls, you are allowed to go wherever he wants to take you," she said as we came to a stop in front of the house.

I wasn't expecting a call or visit from Trevor, but I nodded my head. I had given up trying to explain that we were just friends. She didn't seem to think that was possible and acted as if I weren't even speaking when I tried to tell her there was nothing more going on.

Saxon was walking from the stables toward us as we got out of the car.

"Saxon, honey, I've got to hurry and get changed to meet your father for a dinner party at the Royces'. I'll have Mrs. Jolene make sure you and Madeline have dinner," Melanie called out to him before making her way up the steps to the front doors.

I waited on Saxon since he was still headed in our direction.

He gave me a once-over and smirked. "Looks like Mom had her way with you today," he said.

I nodded.

"Looks good," he told me.

I frowned and glanced down at the clothing she'd chosen for me. I didn't want to say anything that might sound ungrateful, but I wasn't comfortable being dressed up by someone else.

He laughed then.

I lifted my eyes back up to meet his. "What?" I asked.

"Your face is so damn expressive that you don't have to speak for someone to know what you're thinking. Don't worry; this is all new for her. She'll move on to something else soon. Just roll with it until she's over having a girl in the house. She means well even if it doesn't seem like it," he said with a smile.

I had to hope he was right. I couldn't do this for long. Melanie was turning me into someone I didn't want to be. The image of Declan made me want to grimace. I wasn't like them. I never would be. I'd seen life outside of this world of wealth. That was who I was. Not a pampered debutant.

Before I could think of a proper response, a black truck pulled up the drive.

"Shit," Saxon muttered under his breath.

I turned to look back at him. "Who is it?" I asked, seeing the dread on his face.

"Not someone I want to deal with," he replied quietly.

Curious, I watched as the driver's door opened, and out stepped Blaise Hughes. I suddenly understood his reaction. Not liking Blaise was something we could agree on.

Blaise's gaze cut to me, but only for a brief second. It was clear he wasn't impressed with my makeover. He tilted the black cowboy hat on his head back with his pointer finger, and the sunlight made his green eyes stand out, even from this distance.

"I need boarding for Empire. You got room?" Blaise asked Saxon as he approached.

Saxon's eyes widened. "Yeah, uh … I mean, I need to call Dad, but we have room. You found him?"

Blaise scowled. "Yeah, I found him."

"Uh, that's good," he replied, and I could see he wanted to ask him more, but didn't.

"Took my guys all fucking night," he said with annoyance. "I'll have him brought over before noon tomorrow. If there is an issue, have Kenneth call me."

67

Saxon nodded. "Sure. No problem."

Blaise looked over at the stables. "Do you have a stall farther away from the other horses? More secluded?" he asked.

Saxon cleared his throat and shifted his feet. Was he scared of Blaise? I hadn't gotten that impression at the party. But right now, he appeared nervous.

"We can make one," he assured him. "The horses are pretty evenly spread out, but I can move things around so Empire has his privacy."

A horse that needed privacy? I rolled my eyes and looked off toward the house with a sigh. Blaise was infuriating. This was Saxon's ranch. He didn't have to bow down to Blaise simply because he was rude, arrogant, and liked to intimidate people.

"Am I bothering you, Madeline?"

Blaise using my name made my head snap back around, and I met his gaze.

His eyes still held that air of superiority, but there was a twinkle of amusement there that surprised me more than him knowing my name.

Unfortunately for me, my body liked Blaise more than I did. Blaise Hughes was beautiful—I'd give him that. However, the rest of him I could do without.

"Your arrogance is," I said aloud instead of in my head. Oh well, he needed to hear it. No one else around here was going to call him out on his attitude.

A brief tug on the left corner of his mouth hinted at a smile that didn't form. He studied me for a moment, and the intensity made me nervous. I didn't like that he could do that to me.

Frustrated at my reaction, I turned to look at Saxon. "I think I'll go inside," I told him.

Saxon's face was tense. He seemed to be more worried than nervous now. All he did was nod his head.

I didn't give Blaise another look as I walked toward the front doors of the house, but I could feel his gaze on me. It made the back of my neck warm. My knees felt slightly weak, and I didn't care for that at all. Not to a man like Blaise Hughes. He would not intimidate me. I had been around dangerous people. He was just some rich, pampered trust fund baby.

Although the term *baby* didn't exactly fit the muscular, six-foot-two, in-need-of-a-shave man with black boots, jeans, and leather bracelets on his wrists.

Chapter
ELEVEN

MADELINE

Over the next week, life began to fall into a pattern. I woke up and had breakfast with Melanie, who didn't actually eat, and then I went out to help Saxon with whatever chores he had for me.

Melanie hadn't been happy when I voiced wanting to work outside with the horses. She mentioned that my nails would break or chip. However, Saxon had managed to talk her into it.

Dinner had yet to become a family affair, like Melanie had led me to believe it would be. I wasn't upset about that and found sitting at the bar in the kitchen with Saxon, eating whatever Mrs. Jolene had prepared for us, was a nice way to end the day. There were even moments that I felt comfortable here—until I felt guilty for it. I missed my father and brother. Living this life felt like I was forgetting them and who I was.

Twice, Declan had come over after dinner, and those nights, I had gone to my room to read. I didn't mind reading in my room. I was happy to get the time to do it. I just didn't understand why Saxon kept seeing Declan. He didn't appear to like her when he spoke of her. It was weird, and although I didn't care for Declan, it made me feel sorry for her. She was clearly more into Saxon than he was into her. It seemed unfair of him to make her believe otherwise.

I heard Trev's voice before I saw him. He had also become a part of my daily routine. At least, he'd made himself one.

I gave Jinx one last carrot, then rubbed his ears and head one more time.

"We've got company," I whispered to him before stepping back and moving down three empty stalls to Firefoot, who was watching me closely.

He knew I had carrots, and he was trying not to appear anxious, although the way his ears twitched proved otherwise.

I was just about to pull out a carrot from the bag I carried with snacks when Trev and Saxon walked into the stables.

Saxon stopped and patted Jinx, who wasn't ever going to win a race—or at least, that was what Saxon had said—but he was Saxon's. He'd been there when Jinx was born, and they shared a bond. It was clear that Jinx adored him.

"You're getting attached to the horses," Trev said as he walked past Saxon, his eyes locked on mine.

I shrugged. "They aren't as scary as I thought," I replied. Then, I ran my hand down Firefoot's neck, which seemed to be his favorite spot to be rubbed.

"When are you going to let me teach you how to ride?" Trev asked me.

That was something he had brought up more than once this week. I wasn't sure I wanted to do that just yet. These were racehorses. They had been bred and trained to win races. As much as I had found myself growing fond of them, I didn't want to get on their backs. They were massive animals, and I'd watched the jockeys work with them in the arena. That was not something I wanted to experience. The speed terrified me.

"She's just started warming up to them," Saxon said as he left Jinx to come stand with us. "Stop rushing things."

I nodded. "What he said," I replied.

Trev chuckled. "Fine. I'll wait."

He might be waiting much longer than he anticipated, but I didn't say that. I went back to feeding Firefoot his snack. He seemed to be annoyed by our having company. He liked to eat his treats without an audience.

"More important news," Trev said, grinning. "My dad's out of town for the weekend. I've invited over some people tonight. A small gathering, not like the last one, and Blaise hasn't been around now that he has Empire moved over here. So, no interruptions."

Saxon moved his gaze to meet mine. He wanted to go—I could tell without him saying anything.

"Okay," I said when Saxon said nothing.

"Of course, Declan is invited, if that's who you want to bring," Trev said to Saxon, then looked back at me. "And I want you there."

Although we hadn't been alone again since the night I had snuck out of the house with him, he'd been by daily to visit. I hadn't felt the need to remind him we were just friends because he had been acting like a friend and nothing more. I wasn't sure if this was his way of saying I would be his date or not.

"You up for it?" Saxon asked me before he replied to Trev.

I nodded. "Sure."

"Excellent," Trev said, looking pleased. "I told everyone eight, but if y'all want to come on over early, that's cool." He kept his gaze on me when he said it.

I glanced toward Saxon, wanting him to make the call on when we went over.

"Okay," was all he said.

Trev nodded his head back toward Empire who was further away from the other horses.. "How's that one doing?" he asked. "Blaise been around much?"

I continued to rub Firefoot.

Blaise had been here twice, but he'd not spoken to me—or acknowledged me for that matter. Not that I cared or expected him to. It was a relief when I didn't have to be around him. He checked on Empire, spoke with Kenneth or Saxon, then left. His last drop-by had been two days ago. Not that I was keeping track or anything.

"He's good. Kip has been running him daily," Saxon told him. "Blaise has been by a couple of times."

"Better here than my place," Trev replied, then looked back at me and winked. "See you tonight."

Trev gave Saxon a nod before heading back out of the stables.

Once he was gone, Saxon turned his attention to me. "You don't have to go if you don't want to," he said, studying me, as if he thought he could read my feelings by my facial expressions.

I shrugged. "I'm good with it."

Although I was questioning that decision. I did my best to avoid Declan, but that was when she was at the house with just the three of us there. At a party, I wouldn't be forced to be around her. Besides, Trev was my friend. He wanted us there.

Saxon didn't seem convinced with my response. It was clear in the way he continued to frown. "You seem to have bonded with Firefoot," he said.

I turned my attention back to the beauty I'd been giving treats to and smiled. "He's a good boy," I said.

"Want to ride him?" Saxon asked me.

I thought about it for a moment. It wasn't the first time I had considered it, but I wasn't sure I was ready to trust the horse or myself just yet. Just because he liked my attention and the carrots I brought him didn't mean he wanted me on his back.

I shook my head. "Not just yet," I replied.

Saxon grinned then, as if he had expected that response from me. "All right. Just let me know when you change your mind."

"I will," I assured him.

I didn't watch Saxon head back out to finish whatever he had been doing before Trev arrived. Instead, I gave my full attention to Firefoot before he got annoyed. He was by far the easiest male to deal with I had ever met. All you had to do was feed him carrots and rub his neck.

After I finished with Firefoot, I glanced over at Empire. He was watching me with his head out of the stable. I wasn't supposed to give him any snacks. He had a very strict dietary plan that Saxon handled himself. However, lately, he had been watching me with Firefoot. I walked over to him, keeping my distance, unsure of his demeanor.

"I'd give you a treat, too, but I can't. You're on a special diet," I told him as he studied me. "I'm sure Saxon will be over soon with something for you."

He was bigger than Firefoot, and there was intelligence in his eyes. Something about him made me feel as if he understood everything I said. Perhaps that was what made a horse a champion—his ability to understand humans.

"I've been told you don't want to be touched. That's why I don't pet you like I do the others," I explained to him.

"He's not a dog," a deep voice said, causing me to jump.

When I looked behind me, Blaise stood there, staring at me.

"I know that," I managed to say calmly even though being around Blaise made me feel anxious.

He scowled at me. "He also does not require you to speak to him."

Although he was speaking of his horse, it felt more like he was talking about himself. I straightened my shoulders as my own annoyance grew.

"I'll remember that," I assured him stiffly, then turned to walk away from this obnoxious, infuriating man.

"While you're at it, stay away from my brother," he added, and I stopped walking.

Anger began to slowly simmer underneath my skin, and I took a deep breath in order to calm my temper. It was rare I showed that emotion at all. But Blaise seemed to stir it to life with ease. I turned back to shoot him my own glare.

"Trev is my friend," I said simply. Although I wanted to say more. Much more. Like tell him what a complete asshole he was and that I didn't care one bit what his elitist ass told me to do.

Blaise narrowed his eyes as he stared at me. "Is he aware of that?"

Through clenched teeth, I replied, "Yes."

Blaise let out a hard laugh then, which held no humor in it at all. "Somehow, I doubt that."

My hands fisted at my sides. Had I ever hated anyone as much as I was beginning to hate this man? I couldn't remember if I had. "You might have an issue with my not being from your world of wealth and privilege. However, Trev does not."

Blaise smirked, as if what I had said was stupid. I imagined how good it would feel to throw the rest of the carrots in my pockets at his face. Maybe wipe that stupid, arrogant look off of it.

"You have no idea," he said, then began to walk past me toward his horse.

I wasn't in the mood to let this go. I should leave the stables and go to the house, but my stubbornness wasn't going to let me. "What does that mean? I have no idea what Trev wants from me? Is that what you mean?" I asked him.

He paused for a moment, but he didn't turn back to me. "No," he replied, and I thought that was all he was going to say, but he glanced back at me over his shoulder. "I'm sure you know what he wants. You've not lived in his world of fairy tales. You don't entertain thoughts of love."

That was not what I had expected him to say. I stood there, speechless. What did Blaise Hughes know about me? As far as I knew, no one knew about the life I'd lived before now, except Melanie, and I doubted even she truly knew. She hadn't seen our apartment. I hadn't opened up to her about any of my past, and she hadn't asked me.

"Lucky guess," I replied.

Although I hadn't meant it as a question, he answered with, "No."

I opened my mouth to tell him he didn't know me, but Saxon entered the stables and called out to Blaise in greeting. When he turned away from me to look at Saxon, I knew this conversation was over. I hoped it would be our last.

Chapter
TWELVE

MADELINE

This party might not have many people in attendance but it was already similar to the last party I'd been to here. I was the only female not topless. A girl I remembered from the last party was currently kissing Chanel while the guys watching cheered them on.

If they wanted the males' attention, they had succeeded. Where Trev hadn't paid much attention to all the bare breasts at the last party, he was completely captivated by two females making out. It didn't bother me. I would have been surprised if he'd not wanted to watch.

"Fuck yeah!" a guy called out, encouraging the girls to keep going.

Since I wasn't into looking at boobs or females kissing, I waited until Trev walked toward the bar before heading to the door that led inside. It would be quieter in there, and maybe I wouldn't be missed. The idea of sneaking off and walking back to Moses Mile was appealing. The house would be empty, and the idea of silence sounded wonderful. I was fairly certain this would be my last Hughes pool party.

I would get through this one though. Eventually, either Saxon or Trev would notice my absence, and I didn't want to worry them or interrupt their fun. I could hide out in here for a bit, then go back out to the party after a break from it all.

Not sure which way to go to find a bathroom, I walked down a hallway in hopes that one would appear.

A soft cry that sounded like pain caused me to pause. I waited, and then I heard it again. Concerned, I hurried farther down the massive hallway, looking in doorways I passed until I found a large arched entrance leading into a brightly lit kitchen.

My eyes scanned the room until they found a girl that I didn't recognize from the party. She was standing with her back toward me, facing the sink. Long, dark hair hung down to her waist. She wasn't topless or even wearing a swimsuit. Instead, she had on a white sundress that looked like something Melanie would buy for me. Her shoulders barely moved as she cried out again.

"Hello? Are you okay?" I asked, stepping farther into the kitchen to see if I could help her.

The girl spun around then. Large, wide eyes that were more aqua than blue stared back at me. Her pale skin reminded me of a china doll, as did her perfect features. However, when my gaze dropped to her hands, I gasped. There was a knife in one, and blood slowly oozed from the other arm.

Had she cut herself? She was clearly not an employee. This wasn't an accident from preparing food.

"Oh shit," I said as I began to move again, scanning the room for anything I could find to stop the bleeding. "It's okay. You're gonna be fine," I assured her as I reached for a hand towel folded neatly on the end of the marble countertop. "Here, let me wrap it up to stop the bleeding," I said.

Not waiting on her to hand me the injured arm, I took her wrist and looked down, only to see there wasn't just one cut. There were several small cuts along the inside of her arm. They weren't deep or life-threatening. They were shallow, and the blood was seeping out.

I lifted my gaze from her arm to her face. She was trembling and looked at me as if I were about to hurt her, which was ridiculous since she was the one holding a knife. Dropping my gaze back to her arm, I noticed it then—the pale scars along her skin that were almost camouflaged completely by her fair skin color. I inhaled deeply through my nose, then exhaled through my mouth. My heart was still racing, but I understood now. I'd seen this before.

She was a cutter.

"Can I have the knife?" I asked her softly.

For starters, I didn't want her doing any more damage to herself. Then, there was the fact that I didn't know this girl, and clearly, she was troubled. I wanted to help her, but I didn't want that knife finding its way into a part of my body.

She didn't speak or move. She was frozen with those large eyes watching me, as if I were there to harm her. No one had ever been scared of me before. I didn't know what it was that had this girl so terrified. She was my age or possibly older. I wasn't dealing with a child.

"My name is Maddy. I'm a friend of Trev's. I won't hurt you." I spoke to her as softly as I could.

She blinked once but continued to tremble. I glanced at the knife still clutched tightly in her hand, her knuckles white from the grip she had on it.

"Could you put that knife down? I want to help you or get someone you know. Maybe Trev?"

Still nothing. No response. How was I going to get Trev when she wouldn't let go of that knife? I couldn't very well pull her along with me, and leaving her alone in here was not an option. I'd known cutters. This was not normal. Not that cutting was normal, but something was off with this girl or woman. I didn't know what exactly. She wasn't … okay.

"Angel," a familiar, deep voice said, startling me.

79

I feared what Blaise's appearance would do to this very fragile female. I looked from the knife to make sure she wasn't about to stab me and run, then to her face. What I saw shocked me. It was relief. Tears filled her eyes.

"Let go of her," Blaise said softly, although he still made it sound like a demand.

I did and stepped back. He moved me farther away from the girl and took my place. He reached for the hand that still held the knife, and she let him take it easily. He placed it on the sink, then glanced around, as if looking for something.

"Here," I said, holding out the hand towel to him.

He didn't look at me as he snatched it from my hand and wrapped it around her abused arm. "I told you to stay in my room," he said gently. "We've talked about this, Angel. You promised me you would stop."

The girl said nothing, but when he cupped her face in his large hands, she didn't flinch, nor did she shy away. She stared up at him with almost a worshipful expression. The trust and love in her gaze were clear.

I should go. She was okay and no longer needed my help. I felt as if I were spying on something that I hadn't been meant to see. I turned to go as quietly as I could.

"Why were you in here?" His voice was no longer soft and gentle. It was harsh, and accusation was clear in his tone.

I didn't need to see him to know that question was directed at me. Not his Angel.

I stopped and slowly turned back around. The girl was now clinging to his side as he glared at me. I had done nothing but try and help the girl. It was obvious she needed help—and not just with those cuts.

"I came inside to get a break from the party. I heard a cry and then another one. I followed the sound and found her in here, bleeding. I was trying to help her. Or at least get her to put down the knife so I could get some help." I hated that I sounded defensive. I shouldn't have to defend myself for helping someone. I hadn't been the one holding the knife. "I realize I scared her, and I'm sorry. I didn't mean to."

Blaise's jaw stayed clenched, and his body was rigid. She whimpered against him and buried her head into his side. I still didn't understand what it was about me that had upset her other than me catching her causing harm to her body. She should be glad it was me and not one of those sheltered princesses outside. I'd seen this and worse in my life. I was positive they had not.

"When you are at this house, you are Trev's guest. Stay with him. This isn't Moses Mile. You aren't welcome to walk around as if you own it," Blaise said with a coldness I had come to expect from him.

"Got it," I replied and started to leave, but my stupid temper stopped me. Instead of going back outside to what could have by now turned into an orgy, I glared at Blaise. "She needs help. That will only get worse if ignored, and it looks like that's what has been happening. You've got the money. If you care about her, then help her."

I didn't wait for a response before getting as far away from Blaise Hughes and his damaged Angel as I could.

Chapter
THIRTEEN

MADELINE

I was sure there had to be a shortcut from the Hugheses' house to Moses Mile when on foot or horseback, but I didn't know it, and it was dark. So, I took the route I did know, which was the road. I needed to burn off some steam anyway. Going back outside to that party was not an option. Pretending like I was okay and not upset after that encounter wouldn't have been possible.

Once I was off the Hugheses' property and headed down the road leading to Moses Mile, I slipped the cell phone out of my pocket and sent a quick text to Saxon and then Trev. I claimed I had a headache and that I hadn't wanted to bother them, but I was headed back to Moses Mile and going to bed. It was only a couple of miles, and if I hadn't worn sandals tonight, I could have run back quickly. A run would have felt good, but a long walk was going to have to be enough. Hopefully, neither boy would realize I was gone or see my text until much later. I didn't want them leaving a good time because of me.

The moon was almost full, so it wasn't completely dark on the road, but the sounds of animals and others I didn't recognize made me slightly nervous. Sure, I'd walked home alone on dark city streets many times, but I'd been prepared for whatever came at me then. I knew self-defense, and I had always carried a knife. I was sure neither of those would help me if I was pounced on by a wild animal.

Trying not to focus on that, I thought about other things. Like the possibility of letting Trev or Saxon teach me how to ride a horse. It was that thought I was fleshing out when headlights lit up the road, and I had to move off the pavement onto the gravel and shade my eyes to keep from going blind. I turned around just as the vehicle was slowing and decided that maybe my self-defense moves might be needed after all. I didn't have a knife hidden in my combat boots since I wasn't wearing any, but I still knew how to disarm a man.

When it came to a stop, I could make out that it was a truck, which wasn't surprising around here. However, when the door swung open and Blaise stepped out, I was not relieved. He happened to be the last person I'd wanted it to be.

"Am I not getting away from you fast enough?" I snapped. "I would have run, but unfortunately, I am wearing these sandals. You'll have to be patient."

"Get in the truck," he ordered me.

I let out a laugh. "You have got to be joking," I replied, not moving.

"I don't have time for this shit. Get in the goddamn truck." He raised his voice this time.

"Fuck you," I shouted back at him, then spun around and continued walking toward Moses Mile.

Perhaps I could take off the sandals and run. My feet were tough. I'd gone without shoes an entire summer once. What was a few miles on a country road?

"You can't walk that far in the dark! You were supposed to go back to the motherfucking party." His deep voice almost sounded like a growl.

I kept walking but looked back at him over my shoulder. "I have walked in worse places for farther distances. Trust me, I can hold my own. Now, go away."

Blaise let out a string of curses, and that made me smile.

"Stop being a child and get in the damn truck, Madeline," he roared. "I don't have time for this shit."

I stopped and turned around, placing my hands on my hips. "Then, leave! Let me walk. Why do you care?"

He began stalking toward me then, and I had a moment where I considered running. I could run fast, but these sandals had a heel on them, and I wasn't sure I could outrun him in heels. I should have taken them off. Instead, I held my head up high and waited on him to reach me. If he wanted to yell in my face, I could take it. I'd yell right back at him.

None of that happened when he got to me. He was there one minute, and the next thing I knew, I was being tossed over his shoulder, as if I weighed nothing. For a second, I was speechless as I stared down at the ground and his boots, which were making the gravel crunch as they walked back toward his truck.

My voice finally returned, and I used my fists to punch his back. "Let me down!" I screamed, now completely furious.

He ignored me and continued walking.

"I don't want a ride in your truck! I would rather be eaten alive by wolves!" I informed him with another whack to his spine.

"Don't fucking care," he replied as I heard his truck door open.

I was then tossed haphazardly into the backseat before the door slammed in my face. I opened my mouth to scream when my eyes met the same big, terrified ones from the kitchen in the rearview mirror. She sat quietly in the passenger seat, watching me.

The driver's door jerked open, and Blaise climbed inside. He didn't look at me as he shifted gears and began driving. My screaming at him and calling him all the names I could think of weren't going to happen now. Something was wrong with the girl beside him, and I didn't want to cause her any more trauma. It was clear she was suffering.

Instead, I crossed my arms over my chest and sat quietly. If these two weren't going to talk, then neither was I. Although I had several things I wanted to say. I bit my bottom lip to keep from sharing them and watched the road, thankful for every second we got closer to Moses Mile.

I lifted my gaze to see the girl in the front seat. Her eyes were locked on Blaise now. She seemed calm and relaxed.

"Why did you come looking for me?" I asked, unable to stay quiet.

"I didn't," was his only response.

"Then, what were you doing?"

"Going home," he replied.

Going home? Did the girl live with him? Where was his home? I wanted to ask all of this, but I bit down on my bottom lip harder to keep from doing it. None of this was my business.

The truck turned into the entrance of Moses Mile, and I sighed in relief. This was almost over. The silence continued until the truck came to a stop in front of the main house. I reached for the door handle. I wasn't going to thank him for this ride. I hadn't wanted it. I'd much rather still be walking than have to sit this close to him.

"Why didn't you go back to the party?" he asked me.

I shrugged. "Not my scene." Then, I jumped down from the truck.

I didn't know if he was going to say more, and I didn't care. I closed the door with more force than necessary, then headed for the front steps. The headlights didn't move until I opened the front door and stepped inside. When I closed the door, I walked over to the window and watched as he backed the truck up, turned around, and drove away.

85

I wanted to hate Blaise Hughes. I wanted to believe he was the complete asshole he had portrayed to me over and over. However, I now had some conflicting facts to deal with. One was the way he had been so gentle with the girl he called Angel. I wasn't sure if that was her name or just an endearment. Regardless, she trusted him completely. Then, there was the fact that he'd been concerned for my safety. He refused to let me walk alone in the dark. Although he'd used his brute strength and force to make me accept his offer. Lastly, he'd waited until I was safely inside before leaving.

Those three things were going to bother me.

Chapter
FOURTEEN

BLAISE

"You're gonna have to handle this shit," Gage said to me as he leaned back in the leather chair and propped his boot-clad feet up onto the desk in front of him. "Levi's ass is too hotheaded, and he'll end up behind bars again. Huck runs this shop. Without this place, we have no fucking cover."

I didn't move from where I stood, staring out the window across the room. Gage didn't have to say why he couldn't do it. We both knew the ranks. He was dead last. My father wouldn't allow it. Gage wasn't family blood. Even if he was as close as family and I trusted him with my life, it didn't matter.

Running a hand through my hair, I cursed under my breath. I had known this day would come eventually. This hadn't been a secret. Nothing about this life had ever been kept from me.

My father hadn't allowed me a childhood, like Trev had been given. There had been no pool parties and video games in my youth. Trev wasn't completely helpless. He was a Hughes, and with that had come training. Under that charming smile and carefree persona of his, he had what he needed to survive. But he didn't have the power to shut off everything else.

"How much does he owe?" I asked finally, shifting my gaze to Gage.

"Two hundred," he replied with a disgusted look. "Levi should have watched it closer."

I nodded and sighed. "I'll handle it," I said with finality.

Gage looked relieved.

"Are we sure that's all he owes?" I asked Gage as I walked over to pick up the paperwork on the desk.

"Yeah," he replied. "Levi checked it all out."

I should have caught this before now. I knew it. Gage fucking knew it. This was on me. My head had been elsewhere. They didn't know yet. I wasn't ready for them to know. It wasn't time. Too much was still undecided. If those stupid fuckers hadn't been so damn greedy, it wouldn't have had to come to an end so soon. Addicts were all the same. Why my father hadn't let me handle that shit sooner, I didn't know. His reason was weak. Deep down, he blamed himself.

The door to the office opened, and Huck walked inside.

"Made a decision yet?" he asked as he looked at me.

I'd never been given that power. The decision had been made for me years ago.

"I made the decision when I ordered the kill. This is just the next move," I said.

Huck smirked then as he put a cigarette between his lips.

"When are you going to get her?" he asked.

I didn't look up from the paperwork in my hands when I replied, "She's already here."

Chapter
FIFTEEN

MADELINE

The expensive dress, professionally styled hair, and red-soled heels didn't give me a sense of belonging. Instead, I felt more like an imposter. Whenever I passed a mirror and caught a glimpse of my reflection, it startled me. I didn't recognize the woman looking back at me.

It was as if I had been dropped in the middle of a movie and expected to blend in without knowing the plot. Finding my place in the stables had been easy. It was comfortable. But this was a different world from Moses Mile. The elite of the horse racing world mingled with the wealth and power of those in high places.

Here I stood, among them, wearing the silver dress Melanie had chosen for me, feeling like everyone who looked at me saw the girl from the wrong side of town. A glass of champagne in my right hand slightly trembled, and I had to will myself to relax.

I could make it through this evening. It was important to the Houstons, and I owed them.

"You still haven't taken a drink," Saxon said as he came to stand beside me. "Drink it, Maddy. It'll calm your nerves. Then, you can go dance with me and appease my mother."

I glanced over at him and forced a smile. "Do I look nervous?" I asked him.

"No," he replied. "You look stunning. That's all the people here will see."

I felt a blush warm my cheeks. I lifted the glass to my lips and drank slowly.

"That'll help," he said with a grin.

Seeing him in a tux, all clean-shaven and his hair smoothed and not in a messy disarray, had been shocking. He appeared older and intimidating—until he flashed his dimples at me.

"I'm not sure what I am expected to do here," I said honestly.

Saxon shrugged. "Look beautiful—which you do—dance, and enjoy yourself. Drink the champagne, eat the food—although if they offer you the shrimp on that black shit, don't take one. It's disgusting, trust me."

I smiled and felt a laugh bubble inside my chest.

Saxon raised his eyebrows. "I made that mistake once. Never again."

I gave him one nod. "Noted."

His gaze scanned the room, and I took another sip of my drink. I was fairly certain it was helping my nerves. Saxon had been right.

"See that man talking to my dad?" he asked me.

I looked over to where his father was standing with an older gentleman with a balding head and glasses. "Yes," I replied.

"That's probably going to be our next president—if the people in this room have anything to do with it, which they normally do," he said in a low whisper.

I studied the man closer, wondering if Saxon was right. Could these people truly have the power to place a man in the most important political rank in the US? I wanted to ask him how they could do that, but as I was turning my gaze back to Saxon, they found someone else.

The sight of Blaise Hughes in a tuxedo wasn't exactly fair to the female population. His hair was pulled back tightly in a ponytail. There were no loose strands of hair that had broken free tonight. I'd never seen him without his cowboy hat. His jawline wasn't freshly shaven though. It was a small defiance that didn't surprise me. I doubted he wanted to be here. From the little I knew of him, he didn't like to be near his father, and Saxon had pointed out Garrett Hughes to me earlier.

It was then that his green eyes met mine. I didn't like him. I was almost sure I hated him. However, my female parts weren't on board with those feelings. At least not completely. Neither was my stomach. It felt weird, and I wasn't sure why. Other than that he was possibly the hottest man in this room. Which was frustrating and incredibly shallow of me.

His gaze traveled down my body slowly. Then, as if he was done and not at all impressed, he shifted his attention elsewhere. I didn't allow myself to follow him as he moved through the crowd. Even if I wanted to.

"I didn't think Blaise would come to one of these events," I said aloud before I could stop myself.

Saxon lifted a glass to his lips, and a serious expression crossed his face. After he took a drink, he replied, "He's expected."

And that was it. Nothing more.

"Is Trev expected to?" I asked him.

I hadn't seen Trev in the twenty minutes we had been here.

"He's here. Somewhere. He'll eventually show up." Saxon then cut his eyes in my direction. "Want to go see the view from the balcony?"

That sounded like an escape, and I was on board for one of those. I nodded my head, and Saxon waved his hand toward the entrance we had come in. I followed him as he made his way through the crowd, only stopping to take two more glasses of

91

champagne while moving toward the glass doors that overlooked the city.

He held the door open for me, then handed me another full glass. I finished the one I was already holding, then placed it on a high table as we walked over to stand away from the doors and the two other couples talking out here.

"What exactly is this for?" I asked Saxon.

Melanie had told me we were going to a charity event, but nothing more. She had been very focused on my hair, makeup, and clothing. I'd even been given a brief etiquette lesson on speaking, eating, and carrying myself tonight. The stress of it all had me missing my home, even more than I already had.

"The gala?" he asked me, glancing back over his shoulder at the party going on inside.

"Yes," I replied.

He smirked. "This one is to raise money for scholarships— locally, of course—given by the Horse Racing Commission to those who are underprivileged but show promise. Or something of that nature. You'll realize that the events or galas are mostly a way for the powers that be to do business. Sure, they raise money, but it's more than that." He stopped talking then and took a drink. "I believe the next one is the annual masked ball, which raises money for the Red Cross. It's one of the few I enjoy."

I hadn't realized they did this often. I started to ask him how many they did when an arm wrapped around my shoulders.

"Damn, you look smoking hot," Trevor's familiar voice said close to my ear.

"And there he is," Saxon said in an amused tone.

"Were you looking for me?" Trev asked as his eyes met mine.

Like Saxon, Trevor looked older in a tuxedo. More sophisticated.

"I was curious if you, too, were made to attend these things," I replied, not wanting to give him the wrong idea.

A corner of his mouth lifted. "Unfortunately, it's a must. How are you enjoying your first elitist private party?" he asked me, then took a drink of a darker liquid in a glass. It smelled like whiskey.

I shrugged. "Surviving," I replied.

Trev let out a bark of laughter that caused the other people on the balcony to look over at us. Trev lifted his hand in a wave.

"Where did you get the whiskey?" Saxon asked him.

"The bar," he replied.

"They didn't card you?" I asked.

"Please, I'm a Hughes," he replied, then took another drink.

Saxon glanced back at the doors we had come out of. "How much longer before we can escape, do you think?"

"We'll have to survive the dinner first. Once the auction starts, we should be able to sneak out," Trev replied. "How did you get out of bringing Declan?" he asked Saxon.

Saxon shrugged. "I told her my mother expected me to escort Maddy."

I winced. I hadn't realized that. This would only make my interactions with Declan even more difficult.

"Ouch. You're gonna pay for that one," Trev told him.

Saxon didn't reply. I felt like apologizing, but then was it truly my fault? Instead, I stayed silent and took another drink. Glancing back toward the glass doors that were now standing open, I scanned the crowd until my eyes found Blaise. He was standing with a redhead. Even from here, she appeared elegant. The diamonds around her neck glittered under the lights.

"Ready to go back inside?" Trev asked me, and I jerked my gaze off Blaise and his date before Trev realized who I had been looking at.

"Should we?" I asked him.

"Probably," Saxon answered instead.

"They'll all move to the dining room soon. We'll be seated at the same table. The Hughes and Houstons always are," Trev told me.

That eased some of my nerves. I hadn't been sure where I was supposed to sit, and the thought of having to make conversation with these strangers was slightly terrifying. I knew nothing of their life or what they wanted to talk about.

"Why didn't you bring anyone?" Saxon asked Trev as we made our way back inside.

Trev shrugged. "I didn't want to be expected to entertain someone."

Melanie's eyes found me as we walked inside, and she noted Trev standing beside me. The pleased smile on her face made it clear she was happy about it. This would only further her belief that Trev was interested in me romantically. I wished she could just accept we were friends.

"You've made Mom's night," Saxon said in a whisper beside me.

I didn't have to ask him what he meant. I'd noticed it too.

"Is Melanie still Team Traddy?" Trevor asked with a smile.

"What the fuck is Team Traddy?" Saxon replied.

I understood his meaning. A smile spread across my face, and I fought the urge to laugh.

"Trevor, Maddy—Traddy. It's called shipping. Jesus, do you not watch television?" Trevor asked him.

Saxon frowned at him, as if he had just spoken a foreign language. "Apparently, we aren't watching the same things," he replied.

This time, I did laugh. Maybe it was the second glass of champagne getting to me. I'd broken my rule of not drinking tonight simply because I needed the courage. I didn't plan on making this a habit, but right now, I was glad I had done it. Laughing felt good.

Trevor took my hand and placed it inside the crook of his arm. "Let's make Melanie's night even better," he replied.

I was led through the people all slowly making their way to the next room. Several of them spoke to Trevor, and he introduced me. I could feel the women studying me, as if they were looking for my flaws. The men appeared much nicer and welcoming.

I knew I'd never remember any of their names, but I smiled politely. It wasn't until Garrett Hughes stepped in front of us that my nerves returned. Although he was smiling at his son, I could see tension and disapproval in his stance. There was no doubt Garrett knew exactly who I was, and no amount of dressing me up could trick him.

"Trevor," he said, then turned his attention to me. "Madeline." He said my name with a nod of his head. "I see my son was quick to make sure the loveliest lady here was on his arm. He is rather charismatic that way."

My tongue suddenly felt swollen, heavy, and stuck to the roof of my mouth. My nerves were not only back, but they also exploded inside me, to the point that I feared I might be trembling slightly. I wasn't going to look around, but I felt eyes on me. Watching me, as if I were under a microscope. I didn't like attention, and this was way beyond that.

Somehow, I managed to smile. He had complimented me. I should thank him or something. My mouth, however, wasn't working.

"I've got excellent taste," Trev replied, filling in the silence.

His father looked over our heads toward someone else, and I could see a slight narrowing of his eyes before he looked back at us and smiled once again.

"That you do," he agreed. "Saxon," he said then, looking over at Saxon, who had walked off to speak to someone else when Trev was introducing me to the senator and his wife. I hadn't realized he'd joined us again. "Keep this son of mine in line, would you?" he said to him.

Saxon nodded. "I'll do my best."

Garrett chuckled, but the amusement didn't meet his eyes. Those were cold and calculated. The similarities between him and his oldest son were easy to see. Whereas I saw very little between him and Trev. They shared the same color eyes, and that was where it ended.

Chapter
SIXTEEN

MADELINE

The large round tables that filled the room were covered with black tablecloths and had ice sculptures of a different Greek god or goddess in the center of each one. The massive chandelier that hung from the ceiling caused the sculptures to glisten. This elaborate decorating must have cost a fortune.

How were they raising any money when they were paying so much for the ambience?

The table that we followed Garrett Hughes, Kenneth, and Melanie to sat close to the front of the stage. I hadn't noticed the others walking with us because my complete attention was on the ice. However, when we reached the table, I realized there were assigned seats. How strange these people were. Why were they telling people where to sit? It seemed controlling, but then I wondered if that was the point.

Trev led me to the seat that had a small rectangular piece of ice on a silver stand. My name was carved into the ice in an elegant script. I looked from the ice to Trev.

He grinned at me and raised his eyebrows, as if to say, *What did you expect?*

I started to pull out my chair, but Trev's hand made it there before I did, and he pulled it out for me.

I whispered, "Thank you," and he gave me a slight bow that caused me to laugh.

Once he pushed me in, I expected him to take one of the seats beside me and Sax to perhaps take the other. It made sense that they'd put the children together, so to speak. We weren't here to do any business.

However, Trev walked around the table and took a seat beside a girl I'd never met. She wasn't one of the friends who had come to his parties. He spoke to her, and although I couldn't hear what he said, it must have been charming because she smiled at him. I felt someone beside me and turned to see Blaise taking the seat to my right. My spine instantly stiffened, and I gripped my hands tightly in my lap. Not what I'd expected. Of all the people at this table, why had I been placed beside him?

On the other side of me, I turned to see Garrett taking a seat. This was only getting worse. I wanted to sit beside Saxon, or Trev, or Melanie.

Why had I been placed here? Between these two men?

My eyes went to Saxon, who was sitting on the other side of the girl Trev was beside, and then on the other side of him was another girl I didn't know.

I looked down at my hands and managed to take several slow, calming breaths. I could get through this. I had to, for Melanie's sake. Glancing up to see where she was located, I found her sitting beside Trev, and on her other side was Kenneth. I didn't study the rest of the table. My thoughts were all over the place, and I started wondering if I could claim I'd come down with a migraine and escape this.

I felt eyes on me and lifted mine to see Melanie watching me with a strange look on her face. She seemed confused and concerned. That didn't help me calm down at all. *Why did she look like that? I* didn't understand the way these people chose seating, and I hoped this made sense to her. From the look on her face, it didn't appear to.

Kenneth leaned in and whispered something to her, and I watched as she nodded and relaxed. I wished he'd say something to me to help me relax.

"At least try and act like you belong here," Blaise said in a low, deep voice.

I turned to see his eyes on me, and the disapproval on his face was clear. Not that I cared. I hadn't wanted to be seated beside him either. In fact, I would have rather been between his father and anyone else.

"You're so fucking tense," he said.

I took a deep breath and forced myself to smile in case one of the many people at the table was watching us.

"Because I don't want to be here," I said through my teeth.

He smirked then. "You'll get used to it."

No, I wouldn't. I didn't intend to live in this world that long. I had plans. When I didn't reply, he looked to the lady on his other side and said something. At least he was done with me. I opened my hands in my lap and attempted to straighten them and lay them flat instead of fisting them so tightly that my nails were biting into my skin painfully.

"How are you liking Moses Mile?" Garrett asked me.

I lifted my gaze to his and prayed I could speak without stumbling over my words. He was just a man. He wasn't someone I had to impress or be accepted by. Just because he had a demeanor that made one feel as if they should cower before him didn't mean I had to. Garrett Hughes was nothing to me.

"I'm enjoying it. The Houstons have been wonderful," I replied honestly.

He smiled then, softening the overpowering presence he seemed to exude. "I hear you're warming up to the horses. I expected you would. Your mother loved them," he said with a touch of fondness in his tone that took me off guard.

He had known my mother? I'd not made that connection or considered that. Melanie being her friend was one thing, but I hadn't placed my mother any further into this circle of people.

"You knew my mother?" I asked then, always wanting to know more about the woman who had given me life.

Although he continued to smile, sadness flickered in his eyes. "Yes. Very well."

I wanted more than that. *How did he know my mother? Where had he met her?*

I wasn't sure where to start when servers arrived at our table and began placing a salad in front of everyone at the same time. As if it were choreographed.

From the quick glance I took of the salad, I could see it wasn't what I was used to. There were things in it that I didn't recognize. The meat might be lobster. I wasn't sure. The small amount of lettuce wasn't normal lettuce, and it sat on top of chunks of avocado. I didn't care about the food though. I wanted to hear about my mother.

"Fresh lobster," Garrett said, as if he were reading my thoughts. "Many believe Maine has the best lobster, but there are those who argue they haven't had Florida lobster."

I had never had lobster. Sure, I'd seen it on television and the cooking shows I would watch on the public broadcasting station, but I had never been able to afford something like lobster. Garrett took a forkful and held it up before putting it in his mouth, as if showing me it was safe to eat.

I decided to try it since that was where his focus was at the moment, then get the conversation back to my mother.

Melanie hadn't told me much. Her details had been sparse. I realized now just how sparse they had been. She'd never mentioned my mother knowing Garrett Hughes.

The salad was indeed delicious. I took several bites while listening to Garrett engage Kenneth in conversation about the upcoming race. I'd been hearing about the Belmont Stakes at the stables. I knew nothing about horse racing, except what I heard among the trainers and jockeys at the stables. Interrupting their discussion didn't seem like a way to get Garrett to tell me more about my mother. While I waited, I drank my water and finished the salad.

A few times, I glanced over at Trev or Saxon to see who they were speaking to. The girl between the two seemed to be more interested in Trev than Saxon, and I wondered if it was always that way. Trev had more money, and his family clearly held more power.

Blaise was speaking with the lady on his other side. I was happy to be ignored. Especially if my only option was to speak with Blaise. My eyes met Trev's as I reached for my water. He winked at me, and I smiled back at him. It would have been a much more pleasant dinner if he'd been the brother on my right.

Who had chosen where we sat anyway?

"Careful. The senator's daughter doesn't like competition," Blaise said close to my ear.

I stiffened, startled, then turned my head to see he had leaned close to me. He'd not wanted anyone to hear what he was saying.

I glared at him. "She doesn't need to worry."

Blaise raised his eyebrows, as if he didn't believe me. "Why is that?"

I set my glass down and placed my hands in my lap, fighting the urge to ball them into fists. "Like I told you before, Trev and I are just friends."

The corner of Blaise's full lips curled up slightly. "Then, act like it," he replied before leaning away from me and reaching for his drink.

I wanted to yell at him or use my fist to pound on his arm. Not that it would do much good. His arm looked as if it were made of stone. Very nicely carved stone. Even under the tux he was wearing, his broad shoulders and thick, muscular arms were hard to hide.

The servers arrived again in unison to take away the plates in front of us. It was so smoothly and efficiently done that I wondered if they had to train for this sort of job.

"Have you tested Madeline's riding skills?" Garrett asked.

My head snapped to attention, and I looked from Garrett to Kenneth and Melanie. He appeared to be speaking to them both. About me. It seemed rude, considering I was sitting right here. He could have asked me this question. It was as if I were a child who was unable to answer questions about herself.

Melanie smiled softly at me in a reassuring way.

"She's not ready to get on a horse just yet," Kenneth informed him. It seemed odd for him to be answering when he barely knew me. Yet he smiled as if he knew every detail about my days at Moses Mile.

Garrett frowned and turned to me. "You don't want to ride?" he asked me, as if this was unheard of. Something completely foreign to him.

"Until I arrived at Moses Mile, I'd never seen a horse up close. I've warmed up to them, and I do trust a few, but I'm not sure I trust myself not to panic and spook them," I explained.

He glanced over my head and looked at Blaise. "Teach her," he said.

Blaise? Teach me? Uh, no thank you.

Blaise didn't reply, but Garrett seemed pleased, so I assumed he had nodded his head. I looked back at him with my own frown this time. *Had he agreed to that? Why?* I'd rather Trev or Saxon teach me. Blaise glanced at me for a brief moment, then turned his attention back to the lady on his other side.

"Blaise is the best teacher you could have. He can outride my best jockey, and he outweighs him by forty pounds," Garrett assured me with a smile.

The soup was brought next, and I didn't even taste it as I ate. My thoughts were on Blaise and getting out of lessons with him.

Besides, Garrett wasn't my keeper. Why did I have to do anything he said?

The entrée was enjoyed by everyone, it seemed, and I managed to respond to those who spoke to me without sounding like an idiot. Melanie seemed off, however, and her gaze kept finding mine. I wondered if she, too, was thinking of a way to get me out of lessons with Blaise. I sure hoped so.

Once dessert was taken away, the band began to play again, and people were making their way to the dance floor. Saxon stood, and my eyes went to his. His mouth curved into a crooked grin, and I knew what was coming next. I watched him as he made his way around the table, then stopped behind me.

"You promised me a dance," he said.

I took the napkin from my lap and placed it on the table, then met Melanie's gaze. She was smiling, but there was something in her eyes I didn't understand. *Concern? Fear?*

"I always knew Saxon was the smart one," Garrett said, and there was a tinkering laugh from Melanie that sounded more like relief. *How odd.*

I turned to look up at Saxon and placed my hand in his, then stood. I knew he was only doing this to get us both away from the table. I'd much rather be dancing with him than feeling as if I was being watched and judged by every person at that table.

Thankfully, in my inner-city school, ballroom dancing had been offered one semester as an alternative to physical education. I was one of four students who took it, and that was the only semester that the dance instructor donated her time to the school. Her good-will had been short-lived, but it had lasted long enough that I felt confident enough to dance with Saxon.

As I fell in step with his lead, I managed to relax and enjoy myself. It had been a while since I'd danced, and never had I done so outside of the school gymnasium.

"You're good at this," he said to me.

I tilted my head back so I could look up at him and smiled. "You expected me to step all over your feet, didn't you?"

He smirked. "Maybe."

His hand was warm on my bare back, and our bodies were close enough that they brushed against each other; however, there was no spark. It was comfortable. Easy. I trusted Saxon. He wasn't complicated or full of himself.

"You handled yourself well with Garrett," he told me.

I sighed, thinking of how nervous and uncomfortable I'd been. "I'm just glad it's over," I admitted.

Saxon leaned closer to me then, his mouth hovering near my ear. "Blaise is headed this way," he whispered, then straightened back up, holding me away from him so we barely touched at all.

Before I could respond to his information, another hand was on my back—lower than Saxon's hand was—and Saxon stopped dancing. He let my hand go and stepped back with a smile, then gave me a nod before walking away from me. Confused by the sudden change, I turned to see Blaise behind me.

His teeth were clenched tightly, causing his chiseled jaw to stand out even more. He turned me toward him completely and pressed my body against his as one of his hands threaded with mine. I had never danced like this before. Never this close to someone else. The arms holding me felt like iron bars, but I didn't intend to try and break free of them. My mind was turning so quickly that I had little time to adjust to the change when we began to move.

I lifted my eyes from his chest to meet Blaise's eyes. They were hard and cold. As if touching me and dancing with me were being forced upon him at gunpoint. I stiffened, and his gaze dropped to mine. The darkness in his eyes made me feel breathless. As if I knew I should be terrified, but instead, I was intrigued.

"What are you doing?" I asked him.

We both knew he didn't want to be dancing with me, and it couldn't be for his father's sake. He didn't care what Garrett thought of him.

"Dancing, Madeline," he replied through his clenched teeth.

"I can see that, Blaise," I replied with a forced smile. "I meant, what are you doing, dancing with me?"

His hand flexed as it rested on my back, but he said nothing more.

I decided to finish the dance. Get it over with. Whatever point he was making would be made. We continued on in silence. The only thing changing between us was my traitorous body enjoying the feeling of his. I told myself any man who was built like him would feel the same way and that my body didn't take into account personalities.

I tried to focus on anything else in the room to distract me when my eyes found Trev's. He was watching us closely, and I could tell he seemed worried about me. I managed to give him a reassuring smile. The song would end soon. I would survive this.

"The dress fits you perfectly," Blaise said in a low voice, startling me. I hadn't expected him to speak again.

My eyes flew back up to meet his. He wasn't looking at me, but his jaw moved, and I knew he was aware of my gaze on his face.

"Melanie buys my clothes," I told him, feeling as if I should say something.

It appeared as if a smirk wanted to tug at his lips, but he managed to stop it. Either that or I had imagined it. Blaise inhaled deeply. I was in tune with every move he made. Even his breathing. I didn't want to be. This meant nothing to him. He was being forced to dance with me. That was all I could think of that made sense.

"Where did you learn to dance?" he asked me.

This time, when I looked up at him, our eyes met. He was watching me. The green was darker in this lighting. Almost like a storm cloud over the sea. He was waiting on me to answer him. Nothing more. But my heart sped up, and when I opened my mouth to speak, I forgot my words.

What had he asked me?

"Who taught you to dance?" he asked me again.

"School," I said before I forgot the question. Maybe it was the champagne. It was affecting me. That was all this was.

He said nothing else, and the song finally ended. Blaise didn't let me go. Instead, his left hand slid from my back to my hip, where he firmly held me. I watched his throat muscles move as he swallowed hard before his gaze swung toward the table, where I knew Saxon and Trev were waiting on me to escape.

Another song started, and more couples walked onto the dance floor. Blaise's hand continued to hold on to my hip. Just below my waistline. It felt possessive. Something I shouldn't want at all, yet I was unable to move away from him.

Did those at our table notice this? Our standing here, his hand on me, as if I belonged to him?

I turned toward them, nervous of the reactions I would see. Although I was doing nothing wrong, it felt as if I were walking a thin line between sanity and danger.

Trev's eyes met mine, and he gave me a nod. I was sure that meant our exit was almost here. Trev stood up, and I glanced over at Saxon to see what his move was going to be.

He nodded his head toward the door, then mouthed the words, *I'll get you.*

There was no time for me to make a decision on what to do next. Blaise made it for me. He eased his grip on my hip, and I started to step back when the heat from his palm pressed firmly against my back once again.

"Come." The singular word was said as he began moving us off the dance floor. He guided me through the other couples dancing, but not toward our table.

I turned to look back at the others. Saxon was watching us as he spoke to his mother. She didn't seem to notice Blaise leading me out of the room. I didn't get to see if anyone else was watching before we were in a wide hallway I didn't recognize. We hadn't come into the ballroom this way.

"Where are we going?" I asked, my voice sounding strange to my ears.

Blaise said nothing as his pace increased until we were walking into another room. It was empty, and the only light in the room was the moonlight streaming in from the floor-to-ceiling windows.

I could hear my heart beating in my ears. We were alone.

Did I want to be alone with Blaise, or was I frightened? Should I be?

There was no time to figure out what I was feeling exactly. Blaise's hand left me, and he took several steps away from me before stopping. His back was to me, so I couldn't see his expression. I could see his shoulders rise and fall as he took a deep breath.

"Trev and Saxon will be looking for me," I said, needing to hear something other than my heartbeat. "We were planning on escaping."

"I know," Blaise replied, then finally turned around to look at me. "And I should have let you go with them."

I waited for more of an explanation. There had to be a reason we were alone in an unused room. He made a low sound in his chest, then muttered a curse.

"I can't even blame the dress," he said with clear frustration.

Then, his gaze scanned down my body, making me feel warm all over. Even my scalp tingled. This was bad. Very bad. I needed to snap out of this, and I was never going to drink alcohol again. Clearly, it made me stupid.

His intense stare locked on my face. I struggled to pull in a breath as I looked back at him.

"Why did you bring me in here?" I asked in a whisper, as if I wasn't sure I wanted a response. Perhaps I didn't want him to hear me.

Blaise's neck flexed, and his nostrils flared as he inhaled sharply. "I wasn't ready to let you go."

Of all the things I had thought he might say, that was not even in the same ballpark. I had no response to that. I simply stared at him. My face felt flushed, and I hoped he didn't hear my heart beating erratically, the way I did.

"This is wrong," he said with a fierceness in his tone, as if I were to blame.

"What is?" I asked, wondering if I truly wanted an answer to that.

Blaise closed the distance between us in three long strides, then stopped just inches from his chest touching mine. "You. Me. Us," he clipped out sharply.

I wondered if I hadn't drunk the champagne, would I have reacted differently. I imagined I would have. My temper and defenses seemed to be impaired. The Maddy I knew wouldn't be standing here, still looking up at him. She'd have never let him bring her in here.

Maddy on champagne, however, was not very bright.

"I wasn't aware there was an us," I replied. At least I was still honest.

His right hand cupped the side of my face, and he studied me. His gaze finally rested on my mouth. The look in his eyes made me feel things low in my belly and in the region a little further, which I'd never experienced before. I felt hot. As if my skin were on fire.

I should leave this room. Run from this room. But my legs wouldn't move.

"There isn't," was his hoarsely whispered response.

If the door to the room hadn't opened and the light from the hallway hadn't poured into the darkness, I was sure I would have said something I'd regret later.

A man cleared his throat, and Blaise didn't drop his hand from my cheek and step away. Instead, his eyes snapped up to glare at whoever stood behind me.

"It's Angel," the deep voice said.

With those words, Blaise's hand fell away from my face, and he stepped back.

"Who's with her?" Blaise demanded.

"Huck," the man replied.

Blaise didn't look back at me. There were no words for me. No explanation for what had happened in here. He simply headed for the open door. I turned to watch him go, thinking I had misunderstood. He couldn't just be leaving me. Without saying anything?

"Have Saxon get her," he said to the man who had interrupted us.

I recognized him from the pool party. One of the rodeo squad. I'd seen him have sex with the red head.

The man gave him a nod, then stepped back to let Blaise leave. I was frozen with confusion—or was it disappointment? The room had turned cold, and I shivered from the chill. There was no fire warming my skin any longer. That moment was gone.

"Follow me," the guy said and turned to leave.

I had to move or be left in here alone, unsure of where to go. I didn't want to walk back into the ballroom. I was sure my face would tell them everything. My legs fell into line, and I walked out of the room and into the brightly lit hallway, following behind the guy. He didn't look back at me or say anything. He didn't even check to see if I was indeed following him.

It wasn't until we reached the double doors leading to the outside that I recognized where we were. When we stepped into the night air, Trev was standing in front of a limousine. The guy who had led me here walked back inside without a word.

"The night is young! Where shall we take it?" he asked with a smile on his face.

Saxon appeared at my side. "Where do you want to go?" There was concern in his voice, unlike Trev's.

"Anywhere but here," I told him.

Saxon nodded. "Then, let's get in the limo," he replied.

Trev looked at me expectantly as I sat across from him in the limo. I knew he was waiting for me to tell him where I wanted to go, but I honestly didn't care.

"What do you want to see?" Trev asked me.

I shrugged. "I don't know."

"It's not like she's familiar with the area," Saxon told him. "She's barely seen anything other than your place and Moses Mile."

Trev nodded slowly, as if he was just realizing that. "You're right. Want to swim in the springs?"

I shook my head. "I can't swim, remember?"

He frowned. "We have got to fix that. If you're gonna live in Ocala, you've got to learn to swim and ride. We don't have much else going on in this area."

"I'm going to teach her how to ride," Saxon said, and I turned to look at him. He gave me a reassuring smile. "You're ready. You've got a bond with most of the horses. No point in continuing to put it off."

When I had arrived here, I hadn't been sure I'd ever be ready to get on a horse. However, I was getting comfortable around them. They intrigued me. I hadn't expected them to be so intelligent. My daily talks with Firefoot, Rig, and Jinx were something I looked forward to each morning. Empire had started watching me, and when I was sure that Blaise wasn't going to show up, I'd go over and talk to him some. He appeared to want me to give him attention, like the others.

"Okay," I finally said, although the uncertainty in my voice was clear.

Trev nudged my leg with his foot. "I'm still available if you feel safer with me," he said, then winked.

A small laugh escaped me. Trev was hard not to like. He was fun and charming. People were drawn to him and never felt uncomfortable around him. Nothing like his brother.

Yet Trev didn't make my skin heat up or my heart race. Apparently, my body reserved that for his elitist, intimidating, and detached older brother. I had no business feeling anything for a Hughes. I wasn't going to be here long enough for it to matter anyway.

"Which horse do you want me to start on?" I asked Saxon.

"Sunshine," he said, grinning.

I sighed in relief. Sunshine was a sixteen-year-old quarter horse. She was the only horse I'd led out of the stables and the only one whose stall I would go in when she was in there.

Trev rolled his eyes. "When you're ready to learn how to really ride, let me know. All you're gonna do on Sunshine is sit. I doubt she'll even trot for you."

"She does just fine, and she's perfect for beginners," Saxon told him.

Feeling a tug of excitement about my future lessons, I smiled and leaned back in the seat, relaxing for the first time since Blaise had held me on the dance floor.

"Whatever. That's not now. Where do you want to go?" Trev asked.

"Moses Mile," I replied honestly. It had been a long night. I was ready to be alone so I could think about it all.

Trev groaned. "Seriously?"

I nodded.

"Can we at least get drunk first? The bar in here is loaded," Trev said, leaning over and pulling out a bottle of whiskey.

I shrugged. "You two can drink all you want. I'll enjoy the ride."

Chapter
SEVENTEEN

MADELINE

Going to sleep last night, I'd been excited about the idea of learning how to ride today. However, my anxiety this morning made it difficult for me to eat breakfast. Melanie didn't notice as she drank her coffee and chatted about how impressive I had been last night. I hadn't felt very impressive, but if she was happy, then I was glad I hadn't embarrassed her.

After forcing a few bites of bacon and eggs down, I excused myself from the table and headed out the back door toward the stables. Saxon had told me to meet him at Sunshine's stall around eight. I still had about thirty minutes, so I made my rounds, visiting with Rig, Jinx, Firefoot, and Empire before turning to head down to the end stall where Sunshine was kept.

Just as I reached her stall, Saxon stepped inside the back entrance. I started to smile at him, but the look on his face made me pause. He looked tense and almost apologetic.

"Hey, bad time?" I asked him, thinking something must have come up and he needed to cancel today's lesson.

He took a deep breath, then shook his head, but didn't say anything. "No, uh, it's just that …" He paused, and his gaze looked past me.

"I'll be teaching you how to ride," a familiar, deep drawl said.

My eyes widened as I looked at Saxon, then turned to see Blaise walking toward us. His faded jeans fit him, as if they'd been made just for his long legs, and hung on his hips slightly. The black T-shirt he was wearing looked stretched across his broad shoulders. I swallowed nervously, not sure how this turn of events had happened. I hadn't agreed to this.

Blaise stopped a couple of feet from me and tipped his cowboy hat back with a finger. Those green eyes were locked on me. He was waiting for me to respond, although I knew by the look on his face that my reaction would mean nothing.

Why was he here? Last night, he couldn't get away from me fast enough.

Saxon cleared his throat. "Uh, yeah, Blaise came by earlier this morning to check in on Empire. I mentioned your riding lessons today, and he, uh, said he'd teach you."

Blaise raised his eyebrows just slightly as he watched me. It felt as if he were taunting me to refuse. What would happen if I did? This was Moses Mile. He had no power here. Although Saxon sure made it seem like he did. He hadn't even asked me if I wanted Blaise to teach me.

Lifting my chin, I glared back at Blaise. "Why?" I asked him simply. It was a fair question. One that needed answering. One he should have to answer.

"I'm the best," he said, and then a slight smirk touched the corner of his lips.

I fought against staring at those lips. Fantasizing about Blaise Hughes's mouth was never going to be a good idea.

I placed a hand on my hip and turned slightly toward Saxon but kept my eyes on Blaise. "Saxon can teach me just fine. I don't need the best. It's not like I plan on becoming a jockey."

"No," was Blaise's immediate response. The almost-teasing glint in his eyes vanished, and there was a warning there now.

"He's right," Saxon said quickly before I could respond. "Blaise is a great teacher. You'll learn quicker from him."

It was the tone in Saxon's voice that kept me from refusing to allow Blaise to take over my lessons. He was nervous and clearly didn't want me to argue with Blaise. *Why? Was he afraid that Blaise would take Empire away?* Blaise was his best friend's older brother. That was all.

"I've changed my mind," I told Blaise, deciding I'd handle this if Saxon couldn't. "I don't want to ride."

Blaise looked past me toward Saxon. "You can go," he told him.

I turned toward Saxon to tell him that I would start my stable chores, but Saxon nodded his head at Blaise, then walked away without one glance in my direction. Letting out a frustrated sigh, I glared at his back as he retreated. He was leaving me alone to handle this. I didn't want his help either. I'd get Trev to teach me. He'd stand up to his brother.

"You can't get on the back of a horse in that mood. He'll feel it," Blaise told me.

I didn't look at him. I moved my gaze to Sunshine. She was so gentle that I doubted she cared what my mood was. Not that I had agreed to let him teach me anything.

"Let's go," he ordered.

My eyes snapped to him then. "Go where?"

"To get you on a horse," he drawled slowly, as if I had difficulty understanding the English language.

I pointed at Sunshine. "This is the horse Saxon was going to use to teach me how to ride."

Blaise held my gaze. "And I'm not Saxon."

That was something I had not needed clarified. I was very aware of who he was.

Blaise started walking away from me, and I knew he expected me to follow him. I didn't want to do anything he told me to do. Well, a part of me didn't. The largest, most important part. There was a small, insignificant part that wasn't ready to stop this—whatever it was—with Blaise just yet. I needed to work on that part of myself. It was struggling to make good choices.

"Madeline, don't make me force you," Blaise said without looking back at me.

Gritting my teeth, I slowly followed him. Perhaps that small, insignificant part of me was slightly bigger than I'd realized. I should be stalking right back up to the house and locking myself away in my bedroom.

Blaise stopped in front of a stall. I knew that stall.

I shook my head. "I can't ride Jinx," I told him.

I loved Jinx. He was sweet and loved carrots. He was also a great listener. However, he was a thoroughbred. He wasn't an old mare.

"You can," Blaise replied.

I pointed back toward Sunshine. "That's who I agreed to ride."

Blaise sighed, as if I were being a stubborn child and he was growing weary. "That wouldn't be riding a horse. That would be lounging on one."

Placing my hands on my hips, I straightened my back and glared at him. "Saxon didn't think so."

Blaise patted the side of Jinx's neck. "Do I look like Sax to you, Madeline?" he asked me as he slowly shifted his gaze from Jinx to meet mine.

I inhaled sharply, then rolled my eyes. That was a stupid response.

"Do that one more time, and I'll put you over my lap and spank your ass," Blaise said. His voice was deeper and had a dangerous edge to it.

Two things about his response were a problem. The first one being that it was completely out of line and abusive. The second was, for some reason, my body hated me and tingled in areas it had no business reacting. Because of the second thing, I didn't say anything. I was afraid of my voice.

"Now," he said, "be a good girl and come here."

He was continuing to be degrading, and my traitorous body was continuing to react to it.

I took a step closer and kept my eyes on Jinx. I trusted Jinx. He and I had a bond. He was just big. Much bigger than Sunshine. However, right now, I needed to focus on something other than Blaise Hughes.

Jinx moved his head to meet my hand, and I smiled, relaxing some from the tension that Blaise's words had coiled inside of me. Maybe the best thing to do was get on with this lesson and focus on learning how to ride. Then, Blaise would go away, he'd stop making my body turn on me, and I'd get on with my life.

Blaise moved in close enough behind me that I could feel the warmth from his body. I stiffened in response, and my hand paused on Jinx's neck. Jinx sensed my change, and he danced slightly on his feet.

"Easy," Blaise said in a low voice. "He can feel your emotions. You need to stay calm."

I closed my eyes tightly. "I was fine until you got in my personal space," I replied through clenched teeth.

His hand touched my right side, and I pulled my hand away from Jinx, stepping back so my sudden rush of anxiety wouldn't startle him any more than I had already. Blaise's other hand grabbed my left side and held me firmly.

"This isn't calm, Madeline," he said so close to my ear that his breath heated my skin.

I shivered and immediately hated myself for it.

"Stop touching me." My words came out in a ragged breath.

Blaise's hands tightened their grip, and he pulled my body with one swift tug until my back was pressed against his front. His breathing was heavy as his chest rose and fell. We stood there for a moment, saying nothing. I wasn't sure if I could move. My legs didn't feel very steady.

"Your nipples are so fucking hard that I can see them through your shirt," he said as he moved a hand from my waist to my stomach. "You sure you want me to stop touching you?"

I was struggling to breathe. Talking wasn't something I could manage. Not yet. I had to get control of myself. But with his body rock hard against mine and his palm flat on my stomach with his thumb almost caressing the bottom of my right breast, it was hard to do that.

"That's better," he whispered. "Sweet and obedient."

His hands fell away, and I swayed slightly.

"Time to get you on a horse," Blaise informed me as he walked over and opened Jinx's stall.

I didn't move. My head was still spinning.

Blaise glanced back at me over his shoulder. "Lesson number one," he began. "Don't get distracted."

Chapter
EIGHTEEN

MADELINE

Blaise was an excellent teacher. I wanted to hate him for it. He was arrogant. He was cold. He was beautiful. I could hate him for those three things, if nothing else.

Only once did I notice Saxon while I was out in the lower round pen with Jinx and Blaise. Once I was on the back of Jinx, I found all my attention was focused on not falling off. My trust in Jinx was tested at first, but he seemed to understand my nervousness. He was attentive to my commands, and I relaxed quickly.

Blaise helped me dismount and had me lead Jinx to the stables. No more inappropriate things were said, and he hadn't touched me again. Relief that he would be leaving and I would have time alone to brush Jinx and start my chores had me smiling as I walked back to the stall.

I heard one of the jockeys call out Blaise's name, and I didn't look back to see if he stopped or not. I continued on, not needing any direction on how to do the next few steps. Hopefully, Blaise would get busy and leave without my having to speak to him. He had said something about teaching me to trot in my next lesson, but he hadn't said when that would be.

While I got Jinx settled in his stall, I praised him for being such a good boy. I liked riding. There was something about it that made me feel centered. Even while the rest of my life was unsure, I had felt as if all was right when I was up there on his back.

I wondered if my mother had felt that way. *Was that why she had loved to ride?*

Patting Jinx's side, I stepped around him and out of the stall to go get his brush. He deserved some pampering after all that. I was almost to the tack room when Blaise walked into the stables. His eyes swung from Jinx's stall to me. I waited to see what he had to say in hopes that he'd say it and leave.

I shifted my feet when he didn't speak, feeling nervous under his quiet stare. He started walking toward me, and I forced myself not to watch him. It was hard. Unfortunately for females, he was nice to look at.

"You did good," he said to me before stopping only inches from me.

That was entirely too close. I needed him to back up some. Give me my personal space.

"Thanks," I replied, barely glancing at him, then focusing my attention on the tack room door.

He stepped closer, and I inhaled sharply. My eyes snapped back to him. One more inch, and our bodies would be touching. The sensation between my legs started up again, and I tried to tell myself to look away from him.

Don't make eye contact.

It didn't work. I was locked in.

His eyes dropped from mine to focus on my mouth. He'd done that last night. Less than twenty-four hours, and here we were again. Too close. It was messing with my head. Confusing me. I should push him away and tell him that. I should.

But his left hand cupped my cheek, and he tilted my head back. I didn't breathe. The world fell away. It went silent. When he lowered his mouth to mine, my heart slammed against my chest wildly. His mouth was hot, demanding, and talented. Just like him.

His right hand gripped my hip tightly, and I swayed into him as my hands grabbed his upper arms. It all happened too quickly. Like a small taste of something forbidden yet intoxicating, and then it was snatched away. Reminding me it wasn't safe. It wasn't mine.

Blaise's hands and mouth were no longer touching me. His body no longer in my personal space. His eyes met mine for a second, and then he turned and walked away. Long strides meant to escape. As if he couldn't get away from me fast enough.

I fell back against the wall and tried to regulate my breathing. That hadn't been my first kiss. Not even close. But it was the first time a kiss had terrified me. It was the first time a kiss had owned me.

"Maddy?" Saxon's voice called out.

I blinked and took another deep breath before turning toward him.

"Yeah?" I replied, trying to sound normal.

"You okay?" he asked as he continued in my direction.

No. I wasn't sure I would ever be considered okay again.

"Yes," I lied to him.

He stopped in front of me and studied my face closely. There was a frown line between his brows as he did so. "You sure?"

I nodded, wishing he would let it go. I was sure my lips were swollen and my face was flushed. They felt that way.

"Blaise just sped out of here. Didn't seem like he was okay," Saxon said.

I shrugged and turned away from him to walk into the tack room.

I grabbed the things I needed for Jinx, praying my regular coloring would return and my heart rate would slow down. When I

119

got all I needed, I faced Saxon again, who stood where I'd left him. His concern had seemed to only get more intense.

"How was your lesson?" he asked me.

"Good," I replied, not needing to lie about that.

He sighed, then ran a hand through his messy hair. "Okay, well, uh, did he say he was going to continue teaching you?"

He had. But that had been before he kissed me, then vanished. I shrugged. "I think so."

Saxon nodded again. "Yeah, okay, well, I gotta get back to the vet. He's here to check on Iron War."

I held up the brush in my hand. "I'll be here," I said with a smile I didn't feel, then headed back to Jinx.

I was glad he couldn't ask me questions. Because I had no answers.

Two days later, and Blaise hadn't returned. Saxon didn't mention giving me lessons, and I didn't ask. It had given me time to get my head on straight. I'd been able to think through my reaction to Blaise and him kissing me. Sure, it still made no sense. He had made it clear he didn't approve of me. Why he wanted to be the one to teach me how to ride was still confusing. Garrett had mentioned it at the gala, but Blaise didn't appear to do anything his father told him. From what little I had seen and heard, their relationship wasn't the best.

I finished up for the afternoon at the stables and began walking up to the house when Saxon came running up from the main arena toward me.

"Hey!" he called out, and I stopped to wait on him.

There were a few times today I had thought he would offer to give me a lesson, but he hadn't. If Blaise didn't return tomorrow, then I was going to ask Saxon to teach me. I just wished he'd offer first.

He was grinning when he reached me. "I got an idea," he said.

"Okay," I replied, returning his smile.

"You need to learn how to swim," he said. "And it's been blazing hot today. I think it's a good time to learn. You've yet to get in our pool."

"As long as we stay in the shallow end," I replied.

He laughed. "We will today. But eventually, you'll have to move to the deeper water."

"Deal," I agreed.

He lifted his arm to wipe the sweat from his forehead. "I'll meet you out there in thirty minutes."

While I headed up to get changed, I decided I'd bring up the riding lessons while we were in the pool. I wanted to ride again. I'd enjoyed it, and if I had to wait on Blaise, I might never get that chance. I doubted he was coming back.

Chapter
NINETEEN

MADELINE

Within the thirty minutes since I had agreed to let Saxon teach me how to swim, we had managed to add Trev to our small gathering. He showed up, asking if we wanted to go to the springs tonight to a party one of their friends was having. Saxon told him he was teaching me how to swim and that the springs wouldn't be a good idea for me until I could swim.

Declan had sent Saxon several texts about the party, and he hadn't responded.

We had just gotten to the pool when she arrived at Saxon's, clearly angry. Trev looked over at me and wiggled his eyebrows as Saxon took her inside to talk to her.

"He needs to break that shit off," Trev said as he pulled his shirt over his head and tossed it on the closest lounge chair.

I agreed, but didn't say anything.

Trev ran and dived into the deep end of the pool. I watched as he swam up and then stuck his head out of the water. He shook his hair out of his eyes, then grinned up at me.

"You can't learn how to swim out there," he informed me.

I looked down at the towel wrapped around my body and sighed. He was right, but Saxon was supposed to be teaching me. Not Trev. I wasn't sure I trusted Trev enough for that.

"I won't let you drown, I swear," he said. "Just ease into the shallow end."

Glancing back at the house, I wasn't sure how much longer Saxon was going to be. There was a good chance Declan would be joining us tonight. Which meant he wouldn't be able to teach me how to swim.

I looked back at Trev. "Promise?" I asked him.

He swam to the shallow end, then walked toward the slanting entrance of the pool. "On my life," he assured me. "Get in here."

I took the towel and laid it on the table beside me, then slipped off my flip-flops before walking over to the water. I went in just deep enough that it hit my knees, then stopped. It was hot outside, and the cold water was a shock.

"How did you just dive into this?" I asked and shivered a little before moving slowly in until it hit my waist and I felt moderately covered up.

"Get in and get it over with—first rule. Easing in like that is harder," he says.

I started to argue that I doubted that when he moved his hands against the water, splashing my formerly dry upper body. I squealed as the icy water ran over me.

"Trev!" I yelled, moving to get out of the water.

He was laughing, and I glared back at him.

"I'm sorry! Don't get out. I was trying to get you used to the water. I won't do it again."

"Uh-huh," I replied, not moving up too far, just away from him.

"It felt good though, didn't it?" he asked, grinning as he walked closer to me.

I held out my hand to stop him. "Don't get any closer. I don't trust you," I said.

He stuck out his bottom lip, and I laughed.

"That's not nice," he said and moved like he was going to splash me again.

This time, I ducked and moved deep enough so that I could do my own splashing. My attempt wasn't as good as his, but I still got the side of his face just as he turned away. When he looked back at me, I knew I was in trouble. I'd started something.

"Game on, Maddy," he said.

I squealed, then stepped back, only to realize I couldn't touch.

Just as I went under, I saw Trev's eyes go wide before he shot toward me. My feet didn't even get a chance to touch the bottom before Trev's arms were around me and my head was above water again. I clung to Trev as I coughed up the water I'd swallowed. He moved me back to the shallow ground, but even after I could feel the bottom again, I didn't let go of him. I needed to hold on to something while I caught my breath and stopped coughing.

Just as I started to feel like an idiot and moved the wet hair out of my face, a deep, threatening voice said, "Get the fuck away from her!"

It startled me and caused Trev's body to tense up. My eyes snapped open as I blinked away the water falling from my lashes.

Blaise.

"Come here, Madeline," he commanded when my gaze met his.

I didn't move, but Trev did. His arms let me go, and he stepped back from me.

"You okay?" Trev asked me.

I nodded and looked back at him. He studied me for a moment, then turned his attention to his brother. The way his jaw clenched, I thought he might tell Blaise to leave or at least stand up to him. But he didn't say anything.

"Madeline, now," Blaise demanded again.

No longer coughing, I managed to glare at Blaise. "No," I shot back at him.

A laugh caught my attention, and I realized Declan and Saxon had also come outside. Saxon was shifting his gaze from Blaise to me while Declan had her hand over her mouth, looking surprised. I didn't want to have this … whatever it was in front of anyone. Especially someone like Declan.

I looked back at Blaise as he reached for his shirt and pulled it off, tossing it on the chair behind him. His gaze locked on mine. When he began unbuckling his jeans, I glanced at Trev, who shook his head as he walked into the deeper water before diving under.

I turned back to Blaise. "What are you doing?" I asked him.

"Coming to fucking get you," he replied and started to push his jeans down.

"Don't!" I yelled.

His green eyes darkened. "Are you going to come out?"

Afraid of what he was planning on doing if he came in the water, I gave in and nodded. When I began walking back up out of the water, Blaise pulled his jeans back up and fastened them, never once taking his eyes off me. His heated gaze slowly moved down my body, and I wished he hadn't done that. I didn't want to react to him. I wanted to feel nothing.

When I was completely out of the water, he walked over to grab the towel I had left on the table and then took four long strides to me. The towel was wrapped around my body tightly before his eyes met mine again.

"What are you doing?" I asked him.

"Covering your ass up," he replied, and then he walked away from me as I stood there, watching him. He didn't look back at me as he grabbed his shirt and pulled it back on.

"Why?" I was still trying to figure out what was going on.

This man was going to make me crazy.

He moved over to me and grabbed my arm, then began pulling me with him toward the house. Saxon said nothing as we passed him. He wouldn't even look at me; he just stared at the ground at his feet. Declan barely glanced at us before her wide eyes quickly looked in another direction.

I waited until we were inside and away from my friends and Declan before pulling my arm free of his hold. "What is wrong with you?" I asked him angrily. "That out there, what was it about?"

Blaise reached out and grabbed my chin in his hand. "Can you fucking swim?"

I wrapped my hand around his wrist and pulled his hand away from my face. "No!" I shouted.

The small distance between us was gone as he stepped so close to me that I had to tilt my head back to continue my heated glare at him.

"You went under," he said simply.

I waited for more, and he said nothing. We stood there like that for several seconds.

"Don't go in a motherfucking pool if you can't swim," he said in a low voice that sounded like a growl.

I leaned closer to him. "Saxon was going to teach me," I said through clenched teeth.

Blaise inhaled sharply. "No," he replied. Then, his hand wrapped around my upper arm again, and he began forcing me to walk through the house. When we reached the stairs, he stopped and looked down at me. "You need clothes," he said.

"Why? Are you going to force me to stay inside? What happens when you leave?" I taunted him.

"Either you lead the way to your room or I'll find it," he replied in a clipped tone.

Whatever this was, I decided to just let it play out. Maybe he'd leave if I did what he said. I wanted him to leave. A knot in my stomach, however, said another thing. The part of me that wanted him around was growing. I was obviously deranged and needed counseling.

I pulled my arm free from him again and held on to my towel tightly as I walked up the stairs. Every step I took, he followed me up.

When we reached my door, I waved a hand at it. "We are here. You can leave now," I informed him.

He took the knob and turned it, then opened the door. "Go," he said as he put a hand on my back and pushed me inside.

I stumbled inside and let go of the towel to steady myself. My temper spiking again, I swung my gaze back to him to demand he leave when the towel fell to the floor at my feet. Blaise's eyes moved from my cleavage to my stomach and stopped at the bikini bottoms. I didn't say anything.

The door closed behind him, and he was in front of me then. His cotton shirt felt soft against my chest. I closed my eyes and tried very hard to focus. This was Blaise. My body needed to snap out of it. I should be yelling at him to leave. Drawing attention to the fact that he was in my bedroom.

The tips of his fingers touched my stomach and brushed the bare skin. "This wasn't supposed to happen." His voice was low and raspy.

Those fingers moved lower and slid just inside the top of my bottoms.

"I can't stay away," he said, his head dropping forward. His breathing was heavy against my ear. "I should," he whispered as his hand moved until his fingers were between my legs.

I cried out as his middle finger ran against the sensitive, swollen flesh. My knees buckled, and Blaise grabbed my waist with both hands, then tossed me back onto the bed in one swift move.

My hands fisted the comforter as I lifted my body up, my breath now coming out in gasps. I opened my eyes to see Blaise was already climbing onto the bed, and his eyes were where his fingers had just been. His hands grabbed my knees and pushed my legs open to his view.

This shouldn't be happening. I knew it. He wasn't safe. Nothing about him was safe. But as he moved his hands up the inside of my thighs, all I wanted was for him to touch me again. I wanted his hands there. The desire was more powerful than anything else.

"AH!" I cried out as his fingertips brushed the thin strip of fabric he met when he reached my bottoms. "Please," I panted, lifting my hips.

Sanity was gone. It was just pleasure controlling me.

"This ..." he whispered as he slipped a finger under the fabric.

I moaned, and my body trembled at the contact.

"Soaking wet." His deep voice felt almost as good as his touch.

His finger slipped out of my bottoms.

"No!" I pleaded.

That beautiful mouth curled into a wicked grin as he pulled the bottoms down my legs with an aggressive tug that freed them from me quickly. My eyes were locked on his face. I was anxious for more. The finger he'd had inside me slipped between his lips, and he sucked on it, then grabbed my knees, pressing them back onto the bed. His head lowered between my open legs, and the moment his tongue licked my core, I cried out, fisting the covers in my hands and closing my eyes.

The tip of his tongue circled my clit before slipping inside me. Just when I didn't think I could take any more before exploding, he slid a finger inside of me as he continued to taste and suck. I wasn't sure what I screamed as the crest of my climax washed over me. It felt as if the wave was never going to let me go, and I shook, unsure if I could take much more when I slowly came back to earth.

I couldn't open my eyes. The reality of all that had just happened was sinking in. The bed moved underneath me, and I was afraid if I looked, I'd see Blaise leaving me. I wasn't sure I could watch that. Not when I was this vulnerable.

I pulled my legs up against my chest in an attempt to protect myself from the rejection I knew was about to come. Except this time, it had been more than a kiss. I'd been intimate with him.

"No," Blaise said as he grabbed my arm and pulled it away from my knees.

Opening my eyes, I looked up to see him standing over me.

"Get dressed," he said and inhaled sharply. "Quickly, or I'm going to fuck you right here."

My eyes flared at the words, and my sated body suddenly stirred awake again.

"Don't," he said, clenching his teeth tightly. "Get up and get on some goddamn clothes." He turned and stalked toward the window with his back to me.

I sat up and stared at his rigid back. He didn't look happy about what had happened. In fact, he looked furious.

"Just go," I said, wanting to lie back down, curl up, and cry.

"Not without you. Now, get dressed," he said with his back still to me.

I stood up and walked to the closet, as if obeying his commands were normal. I would stand my ground once I had my body covered. I quickly dressed in the closest sundress to me, and I slipped on panties, then walked back into my room.

He was still at the window, but he turned to look at me, and his eyes swept over my dress. Then, he glared at me. "Do you not have something that covers you up more than that?" he asked, clearly angry.

I had needed that. It was the face slap that I'd needed to get out of the haze he'd put me in. "Just leave! Why are you still here? Why did you ..." I stopped, unable to finish that question.

He shook his head slowly. "I won't be leaving without you. Not sure I can do that again," he replied. "I don't want to be here, but I can't fucking stop it. And, baby, now that I've had you on my mouth, it's about to get much worse. That sweet pussy just became mine."

Had he really just said that?

I stared at him with a mixture of fury, confusion, and desire.

What was happening? Why was he doing this to me? Where had my brain gone?

"I can't stay in here with you any longer. Wear the damn dress with no bra. You'd better hope no one looks because I'm not completely in control right now," he said, reaching for my arm and starting for the door.

Fear gave me the strength to jerk back from him. "I'm not leaving with you!" My voice cracked slightly, and I hoped he didn't notice.

He pushed me against the wall as his eyes held mine. The fury inside those green depths was mixed with need. It was as exciting as it was terrifying, and I realized that defined Blaise. He was equally both of those things.

"Madeline." He said my name and took a deep breath. "This is a real fucking thin line you're walking. You're gonna leave with me. You're gonna stop fighting me. There were other paths for you. Better fucking choices. But if another man ever touches you now, I'll have to kill him."

When his mouth covered mine, I forgot all my questions about what he meant by that and the concern that when he had threatened to kill someone, it had sounded like he actually meant it.

I was clinging to him, helpless to argue, unable to make good choices, and desperate to have more of him when he broke the kiss and grabbed my hand, then started for the door again.

I went.

I walked with him down the hallway, the stairs, and out the front door.

When he opened the door to his truck and lifted me up to put me inside, I didn't fight him. We were driving down the dark road as the scent of leather and mint surrounded me.

This wasn't safe. This wasn't going to end well.

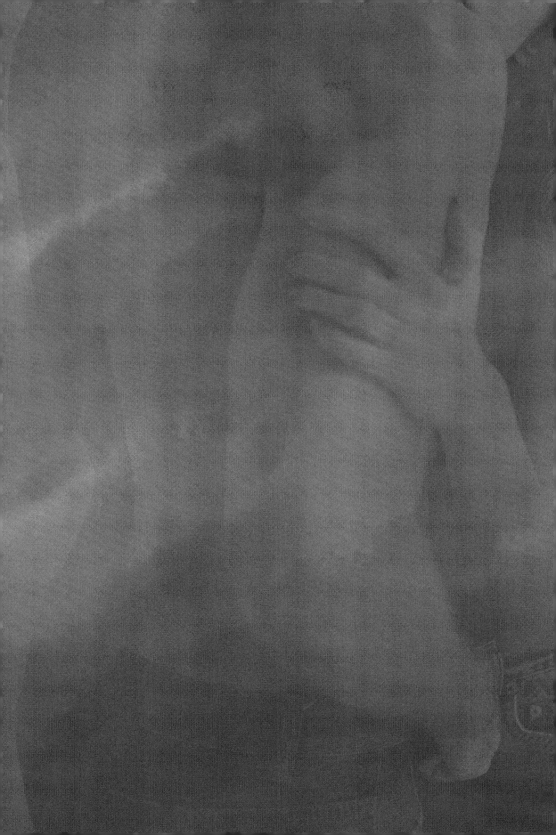

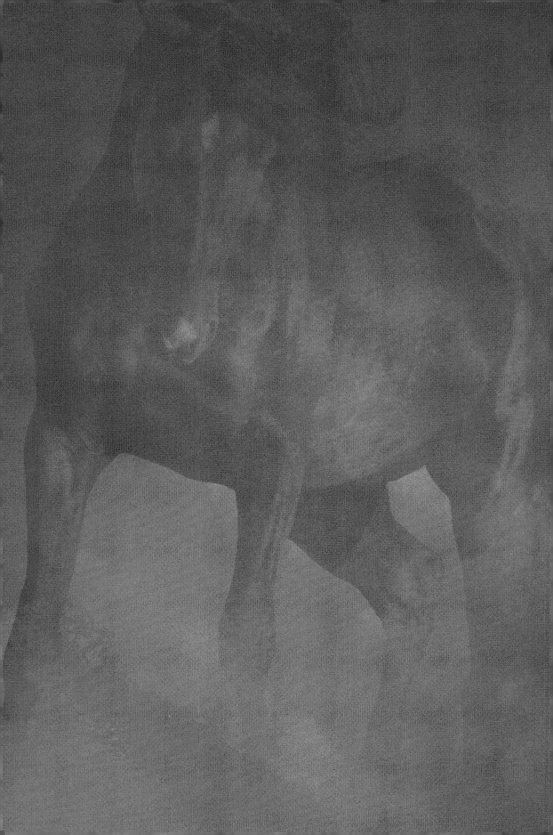

II

*It's not the demons you should fear,
it's the Devil who is charming.*

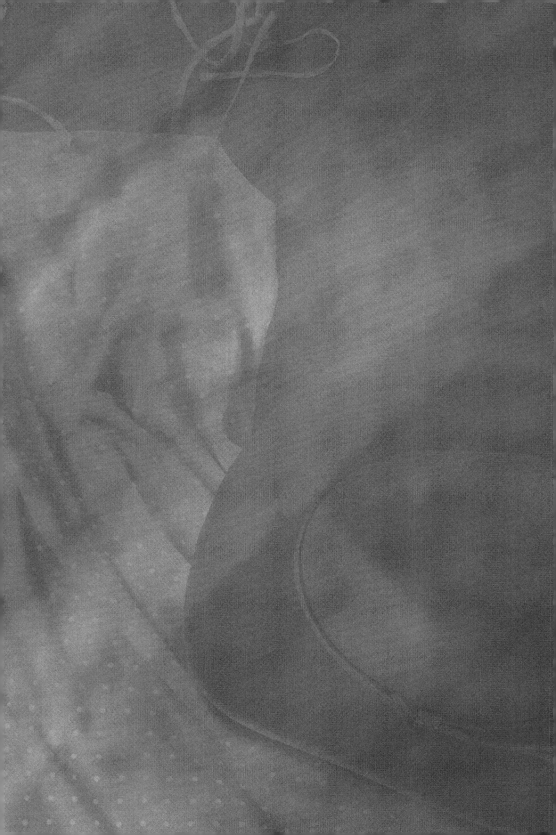

Chapter
TWENTY

MADELINE

Neither of us spoke on the drive. It was longer than just a short drive over to Hughes Farm. When he finally turned off the main road, we went down a long dirt one, and I glanced at Blaise several times, wanting to ask where we were going. I didn't. I wasn't sure I wanted to know or even if he'd answer me.

A tall iron gate appeared, and when we slowed to a stop, it swung open as motion lights came on and lit the now-paved road that led to a large brick house with massive columns. It wasn't as big as the Hugheses' mansion, but it was bigger than the Houstons' house.

Blaise drove past it, and one of five garage doors opened. He pulled in slowly, then cut the engine before looking at me. I thought he'd explain where we were or tell me something. He didn't. Instead, he opened his door and got out of the truck. I sat there and watched him walk around the front of the truck to the passenger side.

He opened my door and reached for my hand. I hesitated before giving it to him. His much larger one closed over mine and pulled me to him until he could pick me up and set me down. He didn't drop his hands right away. His nostrils flared as he stared down at me, and then he pressed his palm to my back and led me toward the door.

When he opened it, I stepped inside, and he followed so close that his chest brushed against my back. The room we walked into was dark, and Blaise didn't turn on a light as he walked me through it until we came to another door. He opened it, and thankfully, light flooded the darkness. I heard voices. We weren't here alone.

The room we had entered had large dark brown leather sofas, a fireplace, and exposed wooden beams in the ceiling. I was taking it all in when one of the rodeo squad stepped into the room, pausing when he saw us. His gaze went from Blaise to me, then back to Blaise.

"Things just got real fucking interesting," he said.

Another one came walking in the room with his arm around a barely dressed brunette. He looked at me, and then his eyebrows shot up. "Oh damn," he said and grinned. "All right then."

"That's Huck and Gage," Blaise said to me. "That's Gina," he added.

Gage was the one with the buzzed hair-cut. Huck was the largest and scarier looking one out of the group.

Gina barely gave me a glance before turning her smile to Blaise.

"We're going down," he told them.

"Okay," Huck drawled slowly when Blaise didn't say anything more.

"Should we be expecting Trev?" Gage asked.

Blaise shook his head. "No."

Huck let out a low whistle as Blaise led me through another door, then down a hallway before we came to a closed door. He pulled a key out from his pocket and unlocked it, then opened it. Stairs led down into darkness. Blaise reached for a switch, and lights came on.

"Go on," he said to me.

I took a few steps down, and then he followed me but first stopped to close the door and lock it. I watched him, and his gaze met mine when he turned back around. He simply nodded his head for me to continue.

I had come this far with him. I might as well go down into the underground with him. When the stairs turned, lights came on automatically, and the massive room surprised me. I wasn't sure what I'd expected, but this wasn't it.

The floor was made of stone but covered in several plush rugs. The center had a sectional sofa, fireplace, and television. A minibar sat to the right of it, and in the back left corner was a king-size bed with a black leather frame. There was an arched doorway that didn't have a door but led into a bathroom. From where I stood, I could see the opulence tucked inside.

"This is where you live," I said.

"Yeah," he replied.

"Why did you bring me here?" I asked him as I turned to look up at him.

He tucked a strand of hair behind my ear, then cupped my neck as his gaze traveled down to my breasts before coming back to meet my eyes. "To fuck you," he replied.

This was where I needed to tell him that wasn't going to happen and demand that he let me go back to the Houstons'. My arousal came to life and began to remind me how good he had made me feel. I wasn't sure I could walk away from him now.

"When you're done, do I walk back to Moses Mile, or are you going to give me a ride?" I asked him, feeling annoyed by my reactions to him.

He smirked before bending his head down to run the tip of his nose along my neck as he inhaled. "I told you earlier," he said as his hands cupped my butt and jerked my body up against him.

"No, you didn't." I shook my head and tried to stay focused.

This girl was not me. I did not forget myself for a man. I didn't lose my sanity over an orgasm. No man had ever given me an orgasm until tonight. Hank had always been worried about himself. All that aside, I was smarter than this.

He pulled my dress up with his fingers until he had it around my waist. "In your room," he said.

Then, he continued to peel the dress up my body until I had no choice but to raise my arms and let him take it off. The sundress fell to the floor at his feet, and his gaze heated my skin.

"What are you going to do to me?" I asked, fear mingling with need.

As much as I wanted him to touch me, I also knew I shouldn't be here. He was older, he was experienced, and I wasn't sure how dark he went.

"Fuck you, Madeline." His voice was husky. "Take off the panties," he demanded as he pulled his shirt off and threw it down.

My eyes went to his chest, and my fingers itched to touch him. He was made of solid muscle. I had to stay focused.

"Off," he repeated as I stood there, watching him.

I began to push them down until they slid the rest of the way, and I kicked them away once they reached my ankles. His eyes were on my breasts as my breathing grew faster from either panic or excitement—there was a fine line between the two right now.

I started to ask him again what would happen after he ... fucked me, but his jeans fell to the ground, and the boxer briefs he had on cupped his erection. Words didn't come. I'd never seen one like that. I had only ever slept with Hank, and he hadn't been that size. It had been a normal size.

He held up a foil package and ripped it open. I watched as he shoved his briefs down, and the full size of him was revealed. He rolled the condom down his length.

"Come here," Blaise said.

I shook my head, looking up at his face.

"Madeline." There was a warning in his voice.

When I didn't move, an evil smile curled his lips.

"You want me to make you beg for it?" he asked.

I was still unable to move, unsure if I needed to turn and run.

Blaise moved so quickly that I didn't have time to make a decision. He picked me up and carried me to the end of the sofa, then dropped me down. His hand wrapped around my left ankle, and he put it up on the back of the sofa. Then, he pressed his hands on my inner thighs, opening me until it was almost painful.

Maybe it might have been if his tongue hadn't slid over my clit, then down all the way to my bottom before coming back up to flick at every sensitive nerve he could find. It took him less than a minute to have me panting his name and begging. He pulled back, and I moaned, squirming. I was so close to coming that I felt frantic.

He moved over me, and the tip of his erection pushed inside me. It stretched me with a sharp pinch as he filled me with one thrust. The feeling wasn't what I had feared.

"Fuck," he groaned loudly as he began to move in me. "My tight little pussy."

I arched my back, wanting more. I wanted to feel more of the stretch, hear more of his moans and the dirty things he was saying to me.

"That's it, baby," he said as he held himself up over me. The muscles in his neck flexed as he looked down at me. "Take all that cock," he panted. "So damn wet."

Watching him grow closer to his climax stirred my own pleasure. The spiral was coming, and I grabbed at his biceps, lifting myself as the moment hit me. His shout and the jerk of his body inside me only sent me spiraling harder.

This time, when I came down, he was still there with me. His head was bowed down in the crook of my neck as his breathing returned to normal. I didn't move and wished dread hadn't started to set in already. It was done. He'd accomplished what he'd brought me here for. I didn't want to feel anything for him, but he'd somehow claimed a piece of me that I didn't think I could get back.

I held my breath as he lifted his head and then began to pull out of me. A gasp escaped me, and I realized I was sore. His eyes met mine, and he grinned before standing up. I watched him as he walked away, then closed my eyes as regret sank in, ruining all of it.

Forcing my body to sit up, I looked around for the dress he'd taken off me in hopes of covering myself back up before he returned. I winced slightly and looked down at the sofa to make sure I hadn't bled from the size of him. I didn't see anything and hurried over to grab my sundress.

"What are you doing?" Blaise asked me, standing at the opening to the bathroom, still naked.

I held up my sundress, hoping it covered my body. "Getting dressed," I replied.

He stared at me for a moment, then held out his hand. "Drop the damn dress and come here."

I looked at the dress in my hands and back at him. "We aren't done?" I asked.

"Don't think that day will come," he replied. "Either drop the dress and come to me or I'll come get you."

I dropped the dress and walked to him. I was obeying his commands, like everyone else seemed to do. How did he manage that? When I made it to him, he nodded his head toward the large iron bathtub that was being filled from some kind of waterfall.

"You need to soak. It'll help the soreness," he said, wrapping my hair around his hand. Then, he tugged me back against him with my hair. "I told you that pussy was mine. I don't say things I don't mean."

He let my hair go and ran a hand down my bare back. "Take your time. I'll leave you something to sleep in on the bed. I'll be back late. Get some rest."

I turned to look at him. "I'm staying here?" I asked. "What about the Houstons? Melanie will be worried," I told him.

"They know where you are. No one will worry," he replied, then walked away, leaving me there in his bathroom, naked.

I seriously doubted they knew I was naked in Blaise's bathroom.

Chapter
TWENTY-ONE

MADELINE

When my eyes opened, it was dark. I lay in bed and realized I wasn't in my bedroom at the Houstons'. Confused, I sat up and looked toward the only small glow coming from a doorway. I saw the iron bathtub from here, and I remembered.

I was at Blaise's. There were no windows, so I had no idea if it was morning or not. I looked beside me, and he might not be here now, but he had been. I'd fallen asleep easier than I'd thought after my bath last night. Slipping out of the covers, I stepped onto the rug and made my way to the bathroom.

The light came on automatically when I walked through the arched frame. I turned to the mirror to see myself. The shirt that Blaise had left for me to sleep in last night hit mid-thigh and hung off one of my shoulders. It smelled like him too. I walked over to the sink and picked up one of the white washcloths and turned on the warm water so I could wash my face.

There was a toothbrush still in its package and toothpaste lying beside it on the sink. This hadn't been here last night when I went to bed. All the things he'd said last night began to play through my head as I tried to figure out what we were doing. I had so many questions, including why Melanie didn't care that I was here with Blaise.

Knowing I had to get some answers, I went about getting ready the best I could before going to find my sundress. It was missing, and after looking for it for several minutes, I gave up and went back to the bathroom to get the black robe I'd seen hanging beside the shower. Slipping it on, I realized it wasn't meant for Blaise. It fit me. This was for a woman—or women. That fact left a sour feeling in my stomach.

How many had worn this before me?

I lowered my nose and smelled it. No perfume smell. It just smelled clean. Lifting my eyes, I stared at my reflection in the mirror and sighed. If I let myself get jealous just because we'd had sex one time, then I was in for a world of hurt. I shouldn't have come here. I was one of the many who had worn the robe now.

Not wanting to stand here alone and think about my mistakes anymore, I headed for the stairs. Blaise had to be somewhere, and I wasn't going to just stay in his cave until he came back to visit me. I needed to leave. Forgetting this had happened would be best.

I just hoped I could emotionally detach from Blaise after having sex with him. Having sex with Hank had caused an emotional attachment. When he'd cheated on me, it had been painful. Blaise and all that he encompassed was something I feared could crush me if I got attached.

The door was locked, and I unlocked it and opened it. The smell of bacon hit me immediately, and my stomach grumbled. I followed the smell of food and sound of voices until I was standing at the kitchen door. My gaze scanned the people around the table, then moved to the island in the center, where I found Blaise leaning against it with a cup in his hand while listening to Huck talk.

It was Gage who noticed me first. Although Gage was ex-military, something about him made me feel as if he were harmless.

There was a boyish look to his features, especially when he smiled. The others, not so much.

He flashed me a grin, then looked at Blaise before nodding his head in my direction.

Blaise put his cup down and turned to look at me. His gaze lingered on the robe for a moment, and then he motioned for me to come to him. I walked into the room slowly and wished I were dressed in actual clothes. That way, I could ask to leave. I didn't know these people. Waking up and coming out of Blaise's cave in a robe that his women wore made me feel as if they were all judging me. Comparing me to the other females who had slept over with him. I had to stop thinking about that. The more I thought about it, the more it bothered me.

Remain detached, I reminded myself.

"Fix her a plate," Blaise said without looking away from me.

I glanced around, confused as to who he was talking to, when I saw Gina over by the coffeepot, pouring a cup. She'd been with Gage last night. I wondered who she was to him. At the pool party, he'd not appeared to have a girlfriend. Yet she seemed comfortable here, and Blaise was ordering her around.

"Sleep good?" Blaise asked me.

I nodded and felt as if everyone in the room was looking at me. I kept my eyes on Blaise. Oddly enough, he was my only safe spot here. I never thought I'd think of him as anything remotely safe. Doing so now was stupid, but I had put myself in this position.

I kept a casual distance between us until Blaise reached out and grabbed the collar of the robe, pulling me closer to him.

When he had me against him, he bent his head and whispered near my ear, "Relax."

I wanted to laugh. As if I could relax. That was the absolute last thing I would be able to do this morning. Blaise tucked a strand of hair behind my ear and grinned down at me, as if I'd said that aloud.

Someone cleared their throat, and Blaise's eyes left mine to look toward the sound of it. I knew it was one of the rodeo squad at the table, but I didn't know which one.

"Should we be expecting Melanie to show up, pitching a damn fit?" Huck asked.

I recognized his drawl. His accent was so similar to a Texan's that I wondered if he'd always lived in Florida or if he had spent the first part of his life in Texas.

Blaise shook his head, and then his eyes came back to mine. There was a flutter in my stomach this morning when he looked at me. Sure, I'd felt something before, but today, it was more. I was so going to regret this.

"Do you want jelly on your biscuit?" Gina asked.

She shouldn't have to make me breakfast. I stepped back from Blaise to go take the plate she was holding and finish what she was doing.

"Whoa," he said, reaching for my arm this time to pull me back to him. "Where are you going?"

I waved my free arm toward the stove, where breakfast was laid out. "To make myself a plate."

He frowned. "I told Gina to."

That annoyed me. Was Gina the hired help? And if so, did she have to wait on all the women he brought over here? I wasn't like them. I didn't require someone serving me. I was starting to feel cheaper by the minute.

"I am perfectly capable of doing it," I told him, pulling my arm free, then turning to go take the plate Gina was holding.

She grinned at me like she wasn't sure if I was crazy or not.

"Thanks," I told her, then turned to the stove to see cheese grits, sausage links, scrambled eggs, bacon, white gravy, and biscuits. *Did they eat like this every morning?*

When Huck began talking about the bike he'd been discussing when I walked in, I was relieved that their attention was moved off me. I finished putting things on my plate, no longer sure I could eat. I should have just asked to go back to Moses Mile.

Taking the plate, I turned and found Blaise watching me. Pausing, I looked at him, waiting for him to say something. He smirked, then pushed off from the island he'd been leaning on to walk over to me.

"I'll be in later today," he said to Huck, who had just asked if he'd be by the shop. "I've got some things to handle first." He led me over to the table and pulled out a chair for me to take, then sat at the one next to it.

"Fuck it," Levi said, leaning back in his chair. "If no one else is asking, then I am." He looked at me, then at Blaise. "What is going on?"

Blaise lifted his eyes from me to meet Levi's. "She's mine," was the only response he gave.

I set the piece of bacon back down on the plate and turned my head to look up at him. *What did that mean exactly?* This conversation was about me. That I knew, but I was not Blaise's. Even if we were together, *she's mine* was a psycho, controlling way to describe it.

"I'm reading that signal loud and clear," Levi replied. "I think we all got that. But when did I miss how this happened?"

Blaise's eyes narrowed, and the room suddenly felt tense. I glanced around and saw that I wasn't the only one who felt it. No one spoke.

"When it becomes family business, then you'll know. Right now, this is my business," Blaise said in a low, commanding tone.

Levi didn't seem concerned. He shrugged, as if that was an answer. I, however, still didn't understand what was happening.

A small alarm bell went off, and Huck stood up quickly and walked out of the room. I took a bite of my bacon while waiting on someone to say something because the silence made it hard to eat.

"Now, it's family business," Huck announced as he walked back into the room. "Trev just drove through the gate."

Blaise muttered a curse, then stood up and picked up my plate. "Come on." It was an order, not a request.

I stood up, and before I could ask what we were doing, he started walking away with my food. Either I could stand in here with these people I barely knew or follow him. He hadn't left me much of a choice. I did as I had been told. I found I had been doing that more and more with Blaise, and it annoyed me.

We were at the door leading down to his cave when he stopped.

He held my plate out for me to take. "Go down there. Wait for me."

Was he serious? Because Trev was here? I'd told him my not coming home would worry the Houstons.

"Trev is my friend," I said, taking my plate from him.

He clenched his teeth and looked away from me. He couldn't get mad because I was stating a fact he had known.

"Just go down to my room and eat. I'll be there soon," he told me.

"Why? Can you explain that? Do you not want Trev to know I'm here? That we slept together? Because he knows I left with you last night. He was there."

Blaise closed his eyes and took a deep breath. When he opened them, he took my chin in his hand and lowered his face until our lips were almost touching. When he was close like this, I forgot that I was mad at him. I forgot that he frustrated me.

"Please, go downstairs. I'll explain later." His tone wasn't demanding. That was the reason I did what I had been told.

At least, I wanted to believe that was the reason, and not that his mint and leather smell had hit me, making me feel tingly. Reminding me of last night.

Chapter
TWENTY-TWO

MADELINE

I managed to eat most of my breakfast while I sat with my legs curled up under me on his sofa, watching an episode of *Friends*. By the time the guys moved into the big apartment and Monica made the small apartment pretty, Blaise walked into the room. I picked up the remote and turned off the television as I watched him walk toward me.

He sank down beside me so that my knee was touching his thigh. I waited for him to explain why I'd been sent away. I had several other questions, too, but I'd let him start with that one.

"The Houstons know where you are. You can call Melanie if you want. Trev wasn't here because of them. He was here because he's a spoiled brat. I dealt with him. He's gone."

Frowning, I sat there, waiting for more, but Blaise didn't say more. Instead, he ran his finger up my thigh as he stared down at my legs. Nope. I was not doing that. I scrambled off the sofa before he could grab me and stood up.

Once I had a safe distance between us, I put my hands on my hips and glared down at him the best I could. He was distracting. All of him.

Damn him for being so sexy.

"I'm going to need some more information," I told him.

He raised his eyebrows and crossed his arms over his chest as he stretched his legs out in front of him. There was a crooked grin tugging at the corner of his mouth.

"Okay," he replied.

"What am I doing here? How many girls have worn this robe? Please tell me it's been washed since the last one wore it. When are you taking me back to Moses Mile? What was that *she's mine* comment? Because that verged on creepy. And why are you suddenly being nice?" I had more questions, but we could start with those.

"I wanted you here. That robe is new. I don't bring girls down here. I want you with me, but if you want to go back to Moses Mile, I will take you. I told you last night, while I was licking your pussy, that you were mine. Nothing is creepy about that. You gave it to me, and I'm keeping it. And I'm done trying to make you hate me to save you. You made me weak. You made me jealous, and that's a weakness. I can't have weaknesses. Not in my world. So, I stopped fighting it and got a taste." He leaned forward then and rested his elbows on his knees while he looked up at me. "I've tasted hundreds, but you're a fucking drug I didn't know existed."

He stood up then, and I had to tilt my head back to keep looking at him as he towered over me.

"You can leave whenever you want, but you'll still be mine," he said as he pulled the belt on the robe free. "You'll still want me to make you feel good."

Every nerve in my body was now humming with anticipation. He shoved the robe off my shoulders, and it slid down my arms until it was on the floor around my feet. The hungry look in his eyes made me want to forget everything.

To stay here with him and do whatever he wanted me to do. That wasn't healthy, and I knew it. I struggled to care enough to stop it when his hands moved under the shirt I was wearing and cupped my butt as he pulled me against him.

"Tell me what you want, and I'll do it," he whispered against my neck. "So young and sweet. I tried to protect you from me. I fucking tried so hard."

He licked my collarbone, and I trembled.

"You're beautiful. I knew the boys wanted you. I told myself they could have you." A low chuckle vibrated in his chest. "Then, I saw Saxon dancing with you. His hands on you."

Blaise's hands slipped inside the back of my panties, and he slid them down my bottom until his index finger ran over the proof of my arousal. I jerked against him at the contact.

"I wanted to rip his arms from his body." His hoarse whisper was against my ear as he began to run the tip of his finger inside me, then back in a slow rhythm. "Your panties are already soaked. Even your pussy knows it's mine."

My knees were going weak, and I grabbed his shoulders to keep from falling. He pulled his hands free and sucked the finger that he'd been using inside me. I watched him with a mix of fascination and need.

"As much as I love the taste of your cum," he said, "I want to feel you come on my dick. Will you let me inside you bare?"

Bare. He meant no condom. I hadn't ever thought about that. He'd been with hundreds of women. Hadn't he just said that?

"I'm clean. I swear. I made sure," he said, then reached for the T-shirt I was wearing and pulled it up and over my head. "You're not on birth control." He said it like a statement, not a question, but I shook my head anyway.

His hands covered my breasts, and I could see the torn look in his eyes. As if he was battling his decision. Right now, I knew that I'd give in to anything he wanted. My brain seemed to shut off when he started touching me.

"Fuck," he muttered, then picked me up and started toward the direction of the bed.

I wrapped my legs around his waist. When we reached the bed, he set me down on it, then quickly began shedding his clothing. Unable not to look at him, I soaked in every detail.

Was it fair for a man to be this perfect? To not only have a face that made a girl act stupid, but to also have a body that did the same?

When he was naked in front of me, I tried not to look at his erection. I knew the reminder of how big it was would only make me nervous. He bent down, taking the sides of my panties and ripped them, then tossed them aside. I moved back on the bed, but he grabbed my legs and pulled me to the edge again.

"I fucked you hard last night. You're gonna be sore," he said as he went down on his knees. "Let me kiss it first."

I gasped as he pressed his mouth between my open thighs. His tongue shot out and flicked my swollen flesh several times.

"AH!" I cried out.

He was right. It was tender where he had stretched me, but it made the sensations stronger. My fingers threaded into his hair as I began to ride his mouth, lifting my hips.

He groaned, and the vibration went through me.

"Oh GOD!" I screamed, never wanting this to end.

He could control me with this power, and right now, all I knew was, I wanted more. A frenzy began to build in me, and I became frantic.

Blaise lifted his head, and I whimpered, ready to force his magical mouth back down. The look in his eyes was as wild as I felt. He tossed me farther back on the bed, then climbed on top of me, pushing my legs open just before he slid inside of me, bringing both pleasure and pain. I grabbed his biceps and cried out.

"Holy fuck," he said on a groan as he started to pull out, just before slamming into me again.

"Oh, please!" I begged, not sure if I was asking him to stop or keep going.

The pain from his size was more intense this morning, but my body was climbing toward its peak with each rock of his hips.

"Jesus, baby," he panted. "Too damn good." He shook his head. "Shouldn't have done this. I can't stop now." His breathing was heavy as he growled and began pumping into me harder.

It was there. I was there. The spiraling was coming to a head, and ecstasy rushed through me as I screamed and called out his name.

"Mine!" he roared as he jerked once, then pulled free of me.

I felt a warmth hit my inner thigh, then my stomach. I'd never seen a guy's cum, except in the end of a condom. But I knew what it was.

My high was slowly easing, and I opened my eyes to see him picking up his T-shirt. He began wiping me up, and I lay there and watched him. His eyes would linger on an area for a moment before he cleaned me. This felt different. I wasn't worried about what would happen next. I didn't regret this. How could I when I was already wondering when we would do it again?

When he lifted his eyes to meet mine, we didn't say anything. I didn't want to think about what we would do next. I couldn't move in with him, and I knew that. This was new, and we didn't know how long it would last. I had security at the Houstons'. I needed that until I could get my own place.

Before I left today though, I needed to know exactly what we were now. *Would he continue to date other people? Were we exclusive?* It all seemed like things I should know, but this relationship was nothing remotely close to normal. Blaise wasn't normal. His life … wasn't normal.

Chapter

TWENTY-THREE

MADELINE

The talk never came that day. After we showered together, Blaise brought me my sundress and then told me he had to go to Moses Mile to see Empire with a new jockey he'd hired. After that, he had to go do some other "horse business," and he'd leave me at Moses Mile, but he would pick me up at seven.

When we pulled up to Moses Mile, he kissed me, then told me to bring a bag with some clothes tonight. I started to argue that I couldn't sleep over there again, but he walked off toward the stables. I could follow him and push the talking-about-our-relationship thing, but I didn't. Truth was, I wanted to be with him tonight. Watching him walk away from me made my chest ache a little, and that wasn't a great sign.

Blaise Hughes was addictive.

I walked around to the side door that led into the kitchen. I wanted a bottle of water before I went up to my room. Also, I wanted to avoid Melanie if she was still here. She knew I had stayed with Blaise, and facing her wasn't something I was looking forward to. It was an awkwardness I knew I'd have to deal with eventually, but I was going to put it off.

Opening the door slowly, I listened for voices and didn't hear anything. Relieved, I stepped inside and quietly shut the door behind me. As I headed over to the fridge to get a water, I heard Saxon's voice. He sounded angry, but the only word I made out was my name. I tiptoed over to the hallway and heard Melanie, but she was talking softer. They sounded like they were in the library. I eased closer until I heard Melanie clearly.

"Yes, that's what we will do." Her voice was calm.

"She's nineteen. She has no idea who he is or what this is. Can't you protect her?" Saxon was upset. Not just angry.

I bit my lip as I waited.

"I don't know what you expect us to do. It's not like we are talking about some random guy. It's Blaise," Melanie said. "I had hoped Trev would be the one who won her over, but with her being as charming and beautiful as her mother was, I should have been more prepared for this."

"Would her mother have wanted this?" Saxon shot back at her.

"That's hard to say, and it truly isn't of importance here. You've grown up in this world. You know how things are done and how they are handled.."

Frowning, I tried to figure out what she had meant by that exactly. *How things were handled? In the horse racing world? What did that have to do with me?*

"Dammit!" Saxon shouted. "Can you talk to Garrett? Can Dad? Someone needs to fucking do something. She has no one protecting her."

Was Saxon this scared of Blaise? I wasn't being beaten and held against my will. Maybe I needed to explain things to him. Saxon had this idea of Blaise that was far scarier than reality.

"She is more protected now than anyone in the family. There is no better protection. You're letting your feelings for her get involved, and, son, if those feelings are deep, you had better check

153

them now." She sounded like she was warning him. Her voice had lowered, and she'd snapped out the last part.

"That's it then? We just stand back and let Blaise have her?" Saxon sounded defeated.

"He's the boss," she replied.

"Not yet!" Saxon argued.

"He might as well be. Loyalties are already shifting. You've seen it too."

The boss? Loyalties? What in the heck were they talking about? I needed to google horse racing, apparently.

Melanie's heels clicked on the hardwood as she began to walk. I hurried back to the kitchen and slipped out the side door before either of them saw me.

My gaze went to the stables as the conversation I'd just heard replayed in my head. Those other questions I had for Blaise had just tripled. Tonight, I needed some answers.

Did he know that the Houstons were scared of him? Or that Saxon thought he was taking me against my will? He'd said he'd let Melanie know I was with him. *Wouldn't he know if they were concerned?*

I heard footsteps inside coming closer, and I took a deep breath, put a smile on my face, and opened the door, as if I were just getting here. Saxon was inches from the door when I walked in, and he was scowling when his eyes met mine. It fell away, and he seemed to instantly calm down.

"Hey," I said, hoping I sounded surprised to see him.

"Uh, hey, Maddy," he replied. "You're back."

I laughed. "Yeah, I am."

"Oh, there you are, Madeline," Melanie's voice called out from the other side of the kitchen.

The awkwardness I had worried about was gone. Instead, I was now struggling to pretend I hadn't heard anything they said. As if I wasn't confused and baffled. I was never a great liar.

"Yes, I am sorry I didn't take my phone. I forget I have it at times," I told her. That sounded like something I would have said before.

She shrugged and continued smiling at me. "I understand. It's fine. Blaise let me know the moment you left with him. Are you staying for a while, or do you have plans? I can make sure Mrs. Jolene brings you lunch to the house."

Melanie was an excellent actress, which didn't make me feel better.

"Oh, yeah, I'm going to stay here for a bit, if that's okay. I can go eat lunch out at the barn kitchen though."

Melanie shook her head and waved a hand, as if that was silly. "No need. She will be coming up here anyway. Saxon, honey, let Mrs. Jolene know to bring lunch up to Madeline," she told him with a smile that was a little too tight.

I might not have caught it before, but I was looking now. She was giving him a silent warning.

What did she think he was going to say to me? I decided to push this a little.

"I'll go with Sax down to the stables. I need to do my chores too," I told her.

She frowned. "No, those have been handled. You are free to relax, enjoy the pool, read a book."

"Oh. Well, I'll go visit the horses then. They'll wonder where I am if I don't show up with their treats," I said.

"Is Blaise here?" Saxon asked before Melanie could come up with a reason I shouldn't do that.

"Yes," I replied.

Saxon looked at his mother. "She'll be safe then," he said before opening the door and walking out.

I turned my attention back to Melanie to see her expression. She shrugged and shook her head, smiling, as if to say she didn't understand Saxon's response. I debated on confronting her with what I had heard, but she hadn't sounded like the one I would get my answers from. Going down to the stables, I doubted I'd get much information either. I decided to get my phone and google horse racing and the Hughes specifically.

Chapter
TWENTY-FOUR

MADELINE

Nothing. Google knew nothing. At least nothing more than the number of champions the Hughes Farm had in their ranks. It also had pictures of Blaise with more women than I cared to see. Rarely did he take the same female to a race or event. That should make me feel better, but the fact that he went through females so quickly didn't. Also, my age stood out. He had women on his arm. They were his age. They weren't teenagers. I only had two months before I wasn't a teenager anymore, but twenty wasn't a big deal.

Tossing my phone back on the bed, I glared at it in frustration. That had given me no answers and only made all these unanswered questions worse. It was easy to forget everything when I was with Blaise. He consumed me. Admitting that wasn't helpful either.

He was coming to get me tonight. I was supposed to take a bag of clothes with me. Although I was confused and unsure of what was going on, I still wanted to go. I wanted to be with him. I was overthinking this. That was what I got for eavesdropping.

I had put on new panties the moment I got in my room, but I'd not changed out of my sundress. Going into my closet, I found a pair of hot-pink shorts and a lacy white halter top that Melanie had bought me when we went shopping that one time after I went to Trev's. I stopped and looked at my choices, realizing I was trying to dress older. Normally, I'd come in here and pick out the most comfortable items I could find. The pictures of the women Blaise had dated were getting to me.

I waged an internal battle, and in the end, I put on the dang halter top. Yes, I was dressing for Blaise. I had to accept it. I liked him more than a lot. Pushing that thought aside, I put some things in a bag and placed it on the bed, then decided to go eat lunch. I was about to walk out the door when my cell phone alerted me of a text. Stopping, I went back to get it. I rarely got a text or call. Melanie and Trev were the only two who had texted to contact me. Saxon just came and found me.

Blaise's name was on the screen, and I frowned. I'd not put his number in my phone. I didn't know his number. We hadn't exactly been on good terms until last night. I opened the text.

Keep your phone on you at all times.

That was it. That was his message.

Why? And when did we exchange numbers?

I sent that and stood there, waiting for a response. It came almost immediately. As if he had known what I was going to ask.

Because I want to be able to get in touch with you.
Melanie gave me your number.

That didn't explain why his name was in my phone.

But your name is in my phone.

I waited again, and his response came quickly.

Melanie probably added it.

If I hadn't heard the conversation earlier, I would have found that odd. But he was right. She probably had. After all, she had given me the phone and told me my passcode to it. She could use my phone anytime she wanted. I had nothing to hide, and she paid for it.

I slipped the phone into the pocket of my shorts before leaving the room.

When I entered the kitchen, I hadn't expected Saxon to be sitting at the bar, eating a sandwich. He looked at me when I walked in and pulled out the stool next to him. There was a plate beside him with an identical lunch. I was glad he had come inside to talk to me. I trusted him, and I felt like he would answer some of my questions.

"Thanks," I said, taking the seat beside him. "I love Mrs. Jolene's Reubens," I said, looking down at my plate.

He nodded while chewing the bite he had taken. I took a drink of my water and waited before taking my own bite. When he swallowed, he turned to look at me. I was hoping he'd start the conversation.

"I think I missed something," he started. "Last night, what was that?"

Okay, good. We were going to talk. Melanie hadn't scared him off from discussing Blaise with me.

"Well, it confused me too. At first. Blaise hadn't been nice to me since I'd arrived. Then, at the gala, things got weird." I paused. Not sure how much I should tell Saxon.

This was new to me, too, and I didn't want to share details about Blaise and me with him. That seemed dishonest.

"There was something there. Then, the horse riding lesson. He showed up. You were there." I shrugged. I didn't think Saxon wanted to hear how Blaise had affected me from day one. That even when he was a jerk, I noticed him. "Until he came here and we ... talked ... I'd misunderstood things."

"I don't think that's changed," Saxon muttered under his breath, but I still understood him.

"What?" I asked, wanting him to clarify.

He shook his head and stared down at his plate of food. I waited. He was thinking about his words. I could tell he wanted to say more.

"Blaise is twenty-five. You're nineteen. He's done some shit. He's dated daughters of some powerful people. Don't you think his coming over here and taking you to his house like—" He stopped then, and I was glad.

This wasn't the conversation I had wanted.

Saxon was verbalizing my insecurities, making them feel legit rather than something I'd made up in my head. Knowing he thought I didn't compare to his previous girlfriends wasn't easy to hear.

"I don't know why he came over here and why he is …" *What, dating me?*

We never had that talk. Instead, we'd had sex again. He had called my vagina his, but that was about it. I was pretty sure that had been a heat-of-the-moment thing.

"What are y'all?" Saxon asked me.

I was the one studying my plate of food now. I could feel Saxon looking at me. He was waiting for an answer I didn't have.

I managed to shrug. "I think we are dating."

"Exclusively?" he asked.

I turned to meet Saxon's gaze. "I'm not sure. It happened fast. We kinda let the moment and all we were feeling happen."

Saxon scowled and turned his eyes to look out the window. "The moment, huh?"

I didn't reply.

"Did he say when he'd see you again?" Saxon asked through clenched teeth. He was angry, and although I knew that, I was surprised he was letting me see it.

"He's picking me up tonight," I replied.

His gaze swung back to mine. "To stay with him overnight again?"

I started to nod, but the sound of heavy footsteps caused me to pause, and we both turned to see Huck walking into the kitchen. It was odd to see him inside the Houstons' house.

Was Blaise back already?

"Those sound like questions you might want to let go of, Sax," Huck said and gave him a tight smile that didn't meet his eyes.

Saxon looked stiff as he stood up from the stool. "Yeah." He took his plate from the bar. "Didn't know you were here. Looking for Dad?"

Huck shook his head as he studied Saxon. "Nope. I know where he is. I was just out, checking on things. Thought I'd step inside. See if Mrs. Jolene had any of her sweet tea made."

Huck had just been walking around Moses Mile? Since when did the rodeo squad show up here?

Saxon didn't look confused. He simply nodded and put his plate in the sink.

"Might want to go on out yourself. See how things are going. Think your dad might be looking for you," Huck told him.

Saxon took a deep breath and gripped the edge of the sink before nodding. "Okay," he finally replied, then gave me one last glance before leaving out the back door.

I stared at the door, trying to make sense of the scene I'd just witnessed, then remembered Huck was still here. I looked back at him.

He gave me a nod, then walked over to the fridge. "Sax is a good kid," Huck said as he looked around. "But he's a guy. Sometimes, a pretty face can make us stupid."

I said nothing. I was waiting for him to get to his point.

He reached into the fridge and pulled out a gallon of tea. "Takes us males a while to grow up. Understand what's more important," Huck told me as he placed the tea on the bar. He smiled at me then, like he was having a chat with an old friend.

"Is there a point to this?" I asked him finally.

161

He nodded. "Yeah." He pulled a glass down from the cabinet. He had been here enough times to know exactly where the glasses were. Maybe he had come to check on Empire or something, and I'd never seen him. "Sax might say something stupid that could end real bad. Don't want to see that happen. If he's your friend, then you don't either. You got questions, ask Blaise. You get asked questions, tell them to ask Blaise."

He poured tea into the glass and took a long drink. When it was clear he wasn't going to say any more, I stood up.

"I'm not even sure what Blaise and I are. We haven't talked about it. I don't think that after one night in his bed, I'm now supposed to go through him for all communication. Sax is my friend. We talk. I trust him."

Huck put the glass back down and sighed loudly. "In the kitchen this morning," he began, "he called you his."

He had. We'd kinda talked about that. We had sex again after that, and he made me think nothing in the world mattered but the two of us. But that had been in the moment. Out here, away from his private cave, things weren't so clear. This was new. We were new. There were no actual ties, except the sex and obvious attraction.

"You might not understand it yet. But Sax does," Huck said, then drank the rest of his tea in one long gulp before placing the glass in the sink and heading for the back door.

I wanted to stop him and tell him to explain to me what that meant. Something was wrong here. I could tell myself I was overthinking it all. I wanted to, but there was a secret I didn't know. A secret where Blaise was dangerous or obeyed or whatever.

I wasn't sure, but the thought occurred to me, *What if the secret is why my mother left? Who were these people?*

Chapter
TWENTY-FIVE

MADELINE

The book I'd gotten from the Houstons' library didn't distract me much, but it was the best thing I could think of to occupy my thoughts until Blaise arrived. It was almost five when my bedroom door opened and Blaise stepped inside. I stared at him as he walked over to the bed and picked up my packed bag.

"Let's go." It wasn't a request; it was a command.

I didn't move. I sat there with my book and studied him.

His eyes locked with mine. He was angry. This was the Blaise that I was used to. The one who had taken me to his cave blindsided me. He'd confused me and made me forget things. Like the fact that Blaise was normally an asshole.

"Now, Madeline."

I wasn't scared of him. Everyone else could be if they wanted to be, but I wasn't. He was pissed. Probably because Huck had told him I'd had lunch with Saxon and the questions Saxon had asked me. I didn't care. We hadn't done anything wrong. Saxon was my friend. I lived in his house.

"I don't obey orders," I replied putting my book down and crossing my arms over my chest defiantly.

Blaise's nostrils flared as he inhaled, and I knew I was pushing him. I still didn't care. He didn't have to walk into my room and treat me like his property. I'd had sex with him, not signed over my life to him.

"Please," he said through his teeth.

I raised my eyebrows and said nothing.

Blaise muttered a curse and tossed the bag down on the floor, then stalked over to me. I didn't move an inch. I wasn't going to show fear. He wouldn't control me. Whatever god complex he had wasn't going to be encouraged by me.

"If you don't move your sweet ass right fucking now, I'm going to carry you out," he threatened.

"Really? You think tossing me over your shoulder and walking out with me is the way to handle it? Instead of … I don't know … being *nice*?" I said. "It's not so hard. You were real nice in your bed this morning."

Blaise took another step, towering over me. "If that's an invitation to fuck you right here, then I'll take it, but it's gonna be hard, and it's gonna hurt."

I swallowed, wishing that his sex threats didn't turn me on. I had a point to make. I did not need to be controlled by sex.

"That's not what I meant, and you know it," I replied.

He smirked then, and although it was arrogant, it still softened the anger in his brow. "Let's go," he said in a somewhat-softer tone this time.

"You came in here angry. Why?" I wasn't going to leave with him until he clarified some things.

"Your lunch with Saxon," he replied.

"We had sex, and now, I can't have lunch with my friend?" I asked as I stood up.

Blaise shoved his left hand into my hair and grabbed it, then jerked my head back. "You have questions? Talk to me." He lowered his head and ran the tip of his nose up my neck.

164

I was not going to get distracted. I was not.

"Saxon asked me questions first," I said.

"He won't again," Blaise replied, then eased his hold on my hair.

"Why is he scared of you?" I asked him, not taking my eyes off his face. I was looking for anything in his expression that would confirm what I was asking.

"I'm older, bigger." He moved his hand from my hair to trace my jawline with his fingers.

"It's more than that, Blaise," I pushed.

He shrugged. "The racing business is what defines his family, just like mine. Moses Mile needs the Hughes Farm. We are powerful. It will be mine one day." He said this as if it made complete sense.

"And Trev's," I added.

He shook his head slowly while he continued to run his fingertip along my bare skin. "No. Just mine. There can only be one boss," he replied. "Trev was never the one. He's too soft."

Boss. That was what Melanie had called him. She'd been referring to Hughes Farm. That made sense. If Garrett was handing it over to Blaise, then the Houstons didn't want to make an enemy. Especially over a girl they had just brought into their home.

I sighed, feeling like an idiot. My head had gone in so many directions today, and I blamed my stupid eavesdropping for it all. I should have minded my own business.

"Okay," I said. "We can go."

Blaise didn't move as he ran his fingers over the cleavage the halter top showed. "I like this top," he said, lifting his eyes to meet mine.

I felt a blush warm my neck and face. I'd worn it, hoping he would. "Thanks."

His hand slid down my stomach and then between my legs. "Not a fan of the shorts. They're in my way."

I smiled then and stepped around him. "Sometimes, you have to work for it. You can't just take what you want, when you want it."

I went to pick up the bag he'd dropped.

"Keep talking to me like that, and I'm going to spank your bare ass when I get you home," he warned.

The idea of being hit should make me cringe. It should. But thinking about Blaise doing it only made me squirm.

"We need to leave," Blaise said as he headed for the door, taking my bag from me on the way.

I walked out as he held it open.

"It's only five," I said, noticing the grandfather clock in the hallway. "You're early."

"You were having lunch with Saxon," he replied.

I frowned. "That's why you're early?"

He nodded his head once.

I followed him down the stairs and to the front door. Pausing, I looked back. "I should tell someone I'm leaving."

"They know," he said.

Of course they did. Apparently, Blaise had Melanie on speed dial. I didn't want to witness a confrontation between Saxon and Blaise anyway, so I left the house without telling anyone bye.

When we got to his truck, he opened the passenger door, then tossed my bag inside. I started to get in, but then he picked me up and put me inside. While I watched him walk around to get in on the driver's side, thinking about how sexy he made a pair of jeans, I saw someone standing off by the far round pen. It was Saxon. He was watching us. I wished he weren't so worried. But I didn't know how to ease that concern for him.

Blaise climbed inside, and we pulled away. I didn't look back at Saxon.

Chapter
TWENTY-SIX

MADELINE

There was a crowd here. The moment we pulled up, I noticed extra vehicles outside the house. Three big, expensive trucks, some kind of sports car, and a few SUVs.

"Fight night," Blaise said simply as we pulled into the garage.

"MMA?" I asked, thinking that season was over.

My dad and brother had watched it when they could get it on TV. Most of the time, they'd had to go to a bar that was showing it.

"Boxing," he replied.

"I didn't know you were into boxing," I told him, but then I didn't know that much about his likes and dislikes.

"I'm not. The guys are," he explained as we got out of the truck.

I followed him inside as he carried my bag in his hand. This would be his crowd. Not just the rodeo squad, but also his group of people. They were going to be older than me, and I wished I'd put on some makeup so I felt like I at least looked older. Saxon's words about our age difference came back to haunt me.

The television was loud, and people were sitting everywhere. Some standing. The kitchen had voices coming from it too. I felt somewhat better about things. I could blend in easier with so much going on.

That thought was instantly wiped out when a large man with red hair and a beard saw Blaise walk into the room. He waved his beer in the air.

"Boss!" he called out loudly, and every eye in the room was now looking in our direction.

"You didn't bet!" another man shouted, who was covered in tattoos and had a piercing in his face. "It's an easy win," he added, throwing his hands in the air.

A tall, curvy bleached-blonde, wearing a short pink dress, walked up to Blaise with a glass of whiskey in her hand. He took it from her, then reached back to take my hand as he made his way through the room. Everyone moved out of his way, like the parting sea.

"We got jambalaya in the kitchen. The good shit that Tanya makes," someone told him.

Blaise kept moving until we were in the empty hallway. He was taking me to the cave. We weren't staying up here with his friends. When he opened his door with the key, I didn't move to follow him down. He turned and looked up at me.

"You don't want to stay up here?" I asked him. I felt like something he was trying to hide.

"We're coming back," he said. "I was going to change and let you put your things away."

"My things away?" I asked, not sure I understood that exactly.

The corner of his mouth curled up. "Yeah, this bag. Your things. Put them in the closet."

Oh. I was putting my things in his closet. Okay. I had not expected that. I stepped down and closed the door behind me. He continued on, and I followed him. The cave looked exactly like we'd left it earlier today.

Blaise took my bag and dropped it on the bed, then turned around to look at me.

"Come here," he said sitting his drink down.

I walked to stand in front of him.

His gaze dropped to my shorts and he unzipped them before looking back at me as he slid his hand inside my panties and cupped me.

"Still sore?" he asked while gently massaging my slit with his fingers.

"A little," I said, then gasped as he drove his index finger inside me. Okay, more than a little.

"Mmm," he replied as he sat down on the edge of the bed.

He rested his forehead on my breasts as he continued to play with me. I whimpered and braced myself by holding on to his shoulders.

"If I lick it, I'm gonna need to fuck it," he said, then bit down on my right nipple through my top.

If he kept touching me, I was going to strip naked and beg for it.

His hand eased out of my shorts, and he held his finger to his nose and inhaled. I watched his eyes flare as he did it again before sucking it into his mouth. He zipped my shorts back up.

"I want your panties wet," he told me, then stood up. "I'll go change, and we can head back up. You can unpack later. If I stay down here with you much longer, I'm going to fuck your brains out."

"Okay," I replied, but it came out in a whisper.

I didn't move from that spot until he walked back out, wearing a pair of navy athletic shorts and a T-shirt. His feet were bare. Other than naked, I'd only seen him in his jeans and boots. He had tanned feet, which I found odd for a guy who always had on boots.

"Let's go," he said and waved for me to go on before following me.

It wasn't until we were walking up the stairs and he ran a finger under the bottom of my shorts that I understood why he had wanted me to go first.

I jumped and looked back at him.

"Shorts barely cover your ass. You need more fabric," he said.

I rolled my eyes and opened the door. Once we were back on the main floor, he took my hand and walked me into the large living room. A guy who looked closer to my age jumped up from the sofa, and Blaise took his spot, pulling me down to sit on his lap. He let go of my hand and rested it between my legs.

"Still got time to bet," the tattooed guy told him.

Blaise grinned and shook his head.

"He only bets on the track," Huck called out from the doorway.

"He always fucking wins. I need him to bet on other shit so I can follow his lead," the tattooed guy replied.

The red-haired man leaned forward from further down the sofa. A brunette was on his lap, and she had on nothing but a bra. I hadn't seen that earlier. Her boobs were enormous, and I wasn't sure that bra was going to be able to hold them.

"He bets on his horse," Red said and chuckled. "Won't bet on anything but his own."

The blonde from earlier walked in and put another drink in Blaise's hand, then ran her hand over his shoulder before walking over to sit in Gage's lap. Gage looked from the screen to her and slid his hand up her dress, shoving her legs open so that she was straddling him.

I jerked my eyes off them and decided I might need to just watch the television. There were other females here, but not as many as there were guys. I was afraid to scan the crowd to see what the others were doing. I'd already witnessed the rodeo squad at the Hugheses' pool. I knew they didn't need to get a room to enjoy sex.

"You hungry, Blaise?" a female asked, but I didn't turn to look at her.

"Not right now," he replied, then squeezed my leg. "Are you hungry?" he asked me.

I shook my head.

The girl walked off, and Blaise talked to a guy sitting to his right about the first prequalifying race of the season and who all he was sending. I didn't know anyone here, except Huck, Gage, and Levi. I hadn't seen Gina yet, but I didn't really know her either. I realized Blaise wasn't introducing me to people. While that made it easier for me, it also made me think that he didn't see a point in it.

Blaise's thumb made circular motions on my inner thigh as we sat there. I watched the television mostly and listened to bits and pieces of information. No one engaged me in conversation, but I didn't hear the other females talking much either. I made the mistake of looking over to where the blonde and Gage were and saw her still sitting in his lap, facing him now with her dress pulled down and her boobs bared while she rocked back and forth on him.

I glanced around to see if anyone was watching them and saw the tattooed guy had his hand in his jeans, rubbing himself while looking at the blonde's bouncing boobs. I swallowed hard, not sure how bad this was going to get in here as the night wore on. Shifting in Blaise's lap, I thought about going to get a drink of something to calm my nerves.

"You good?" he asked me.

I looked down at his whiskey, then took it from him and drank. It burned, and I tried hard not to cough. When I handed it back to him, he was watching me with an amused grin. I covered my mouth to cough, and he chuckled.

"Easy, baby," he told me.

I started to ask if there was something less toxic I could drink when things seemed to quiet down, and I turned to see what had happened. Blaise tensed under me just as my gaze landed on the reason why.

Angel was here. Her eyes were on Blaise and me as she stood there with her timid, haunted look. She was wringing her hands nervously and looked ready to bolt, like a deer scared by a sound. Blaise moved me off his lap and stood up. He didn't say anything or ask me to follow him. He made his way through the room until he was in front

171

of her. I watched as he took her hands and talked to her, then led her out of the room.

She was one of those questions I hadn't asked him about. We'd not had time for that, seeing as all our alone time was sexual.

"Here. Drink this and sit down."

I looked over to see Gina standing beside me. She had a clear drink with ice in her hand, and because I knew people were watching me, I took it. I felt like the elephant in the room. No one wanted to talk about what had just happened to me.

"Sit," Gina demanded.

I sat down in the spot that Blaise had left. It was still warm from his body, and why that made me feel like crying, I didn't know. I should be mad. Or embarrassed. Or asking questions. Instead, I wanted to cry.

"I swear to God, if you fucking cry, I will slap you. Drink the vodka," Gina hissed close to my ear and sat down on the armrest beside me.

I took a drink and realized it wasn't as hard to swallow as the whiskey had been. I drank the rest quickly. Anything to make this easier. I would leave, but how? This place was like a fort, all locked up. No one was getting in unless they knew it.

"Let that sink in, and I'll get you another," Gina said to me.

I nodded because what else was I going to do?

"Mattia," the guy sitting beside me said. "You want some chips?" He held out a bag he had been eating from.

I looked down at the bag, then back up at him. He had black hair and an olive complexion.

"Thanks," I said, afraid to turn them down.

I didn't want to insult anyone. I was alone here, and right now, I was ready to cling to Gina, who I knew nothing about.

Reaching into the bag, I took several out and began to eat one.

"You bet?" he asked me.

I shook my head. I had no money to bet, and if I did, I wouldn't gamble with it.

"Like boxing?" he asked me.

I shook my head again, and then an unexpected laugh bubbled out of me. Mattia grinned, and that made me laugh again.

"I'm Maddy," I told Mattia, realizing he'd introduced himself and I hadn't done the same.

"I know," he replied.

"You do?" I asked, wondering if I'd been introduced to him and not remembered.

"Everyone knows who you are," Gina informed me.

I turned to look at her. "How?"

"Gina." Huck's sharp command stopped whatever she was going to say.

She pressed her lips together, but said nothing.

I turned to look at Huck, who was standing behind the sofa with his arms crossed and his eyes on the television. He didn't look at me or Gina.

"It's time!" someone called out, and everyone's eyes went to the television. It got quiet again.

Gina stood up, and I looked up at her. She nodded her head toward the kitchen, then turned to walk in that direction. I stood up and followed. I didn't want to sit in here with strangers.

When I walked into the kitchen, I found Gina and one other woman I didn't know. She looked to be in her mid-twenties and had long, dark hair that hung straight around her shoulders. She was drinking a beer and looking at her phone.

Gina took a tortilla chip from a bowl and dipped it in salsa. She looked over at me. "Get whatever you want," she said before taking a bite.

The other girl looked up then and studied me for a moment. I smiled at her.

"Hi. I'm Maddy," I said.

"I know," she replied, then looked back down at her phone.

"Jesus, everyone knows who you are. Stop introducing yourself," Gina said. "That's Rose. She's pissy tonight. Ignore her."

I looked behind me to make sure Huck hadn't shown up in here to stop me from asking a simple question. When I didn't see him or anyone else, I turned back to Gina.

"How?" I asked her, knowing she'd understand.

She took another chip and waved it around in a circle. "You're his," she replied, as if that explained everything.

There was that possessive-belonging thing again. I didn't belong to Blaise. Currently, I wasn't sure I would ever come back to this place or have anything to do with Blaise. He'd been gone for half an hour now.

I wished I hadn't left my phone in the damn cave. I could call Trev since I didn't want Saxon getting in trouble with his parents. He could pick me up at the gate. I felt insignificant and abandoned.

I glanced at the phone in Rose's hand, then looked at Gina.

"Do you have a phone?" I asked her.

Gina raised her eyebrows at me and smirked. "Yeah, and I'm not handing it over to you so you can call the Houston kid to come get you."

I smiled, impressed she was so close to my idea. "I wasn't going to call him. I was going to call Trev," I replied.

She laughed then and shook her head. "I wish you would. That would be epic. But it's not happening on my phone. I know better," she said, then took another chip while laughing some more. "God, Rose, could you see it? Trev showing his ass up here to take her away?"

I looked over at Rose, and she was smirking now as she looked down at her phone. Maybe she'd let me use hers. I started to open my mouth, and she lifted her gaze to meet mine and shook her head.

"Who is she?" I asked Gina.

Gina frowned and picked up her glass. "You talking about Angel?" she asked me in a whisper.

"Of course she is," Rose replied while tapping away on her phone.

I nodded, finding myself relieved that he didn't call her angel as an endearment. It was her actual name.

"I don't think I can talk about that," she said, still whispering.

"Not if you want to live," Rose replied.

Gina glanced at the other woman and nodded in agreement, then went back to eating chips.

Secrets. There were still things I wasn't being told. The racing thing, the boss thing, the power thing—he'd explained those, but what about the weirdness with his friends? What about Angel? Why did everyone act like I was his possession?

"Can I have another drink?" I asked.

"That I can do for you," Gina replied and pulled out a glass. Then, she put in ice cubes and poured vodka and soda water into the glass. When she handed it to me, she smiled. "Drink up!"

Cheering came from the other room.

I drank it down quickly and looked at the food, but I wasn't hungry. I'd lost my appetite along with my date.

"I'm guessing you wouldn't give me a ride?" I asked Gina.

She scrunched her nose and shook her head. "Sorry. I like you. But I can't do that."

Rose chuckled again from her seat.

"Madeline."

Blaise's voice startled me, and I spun around to see him standing just inside the kitchen entrance. He seemed tense, but I didn't care. He motioned with his fingers for me to go to him.

I shook my head. "I'm good, thanks," I replied and turned my back on him.

This time, Rose looked up from her phone. She looked at me like I was insane. Gina's eyes went wide, and she put another chip in her mouth.

"Madeline." His warning tone annoyed me.

I didn't care how he said my name. I wasn't going to go running to him.

I thought about telling him that just then when his hand clamped around my upper arm. I tried to pull it free, but he didn't let go. Instead, he forced me to walk past Gina and Rose. We were headed to his cave, and I wiggled, trying to get free.

"Stop it. You're hurting me," I said as he used his free hand to unlock and jerk open the door.

He released my arm and pressed my back to the open door. "Calm the fuck down," he ordered.

I felt the urge to cry again. This was frustrating. Everything about this was confusing. He was confusing. He was giving me whiplash with his mood swings.

"This was too much, too soon," he said then, his tone and eyes softer now. "I pushed for too much, and I needed to give you time."

Was this how he was going to end it and send me home? My chest started to ache, and the idea of this being over, my time with Blaise ending suddenly, felt much bigger than all the other stuff. Tears stung my eyes. That wasn't what I wanted.

"Fuck," he whispered, then picked me up and began carrying me down the stairs like a child.

I buried my face in his chest, wishing the tears would go away. I didn't want to cry over this. Having sex with him had made me this way. I wasn't mature enough to have a sexual relationship and not get attached. My emotions were involved now. I was being *that* girl.

Blaise sat down while still holding me in his lap. I wanted to hit him for making me act like this. I had lived through bad things. Much worse than this. A guy should not have this kind of power over me. Yet I stayed there in his lap and let him hold me.

"I'm sorry I was gone so long," he said.

I understood that Angel had issues. I got that. I had witnessed it. This wasn't jealousy. It was more of the feeling that I was being held at arm's length. Not allowed inside the world of Blaise. He wasn't telling me things. His world was one I was hanging on the outside of, looking in.

I stayed silent, searching for the right words. To try to explain exactly what was bothering me. Also, the warmth of his body comforted me. I had never been held as a child, or if I had by my mother, I had no memories of her. My father hadn't held me or hugged me. I hadn't known what it felt like until now. This wasn't sex or something sexual. It was simple comfort.

His lips pressed against my head. "I didn't mean to hurt you. I was trying to get us away from an audience. I should have been easier with you."

My arm wasn't going to be bruised. He hadn't hurt me that bad. I might have used that as an excuse to get him to let me go. Feeling guilty, I turned to look up at him. The concerned line between his brows eased some when my eyes met his.

"I had to deal with Angel," he said gently. "She had known about you, but she hadn't seen us together yet. I knew if I didn't take her upstairs and talk to her, then she'd find the first fucking knife she could and start cutting herself."

I sat up, and his arms stayed around me. I hadn't planned on getting up, but his explanation of Angel wasn't enough. He needed to expand on her cutting because of seeing us together.

"Why would she be upset by us?" I asked, wondering if I wanted this answer. *Was I ready for the truth I kept demanding?*

He sighed, as if he had hoped I wouldn't ask more. That didn't help my growing dread.

"Angel hasn't always been like this. We were kids together. Grew up in this world together. She was my first girlfriend. My first kiss. We were young, and at that time, we thought we'd always be us." He paused and studied me for a moment.

"She was with her parents when they were killed. She was shot last. She should have died, too, but the gunman didn't check to see if she was dead. The gunshot to her head didn't go into a critical part of the brain. It went in with a high enough velocity that it didn't wobble or move, but it went clean through. Her parents weren't as lucky." He let out a heavy sigh.

"She was thirteen years old. It took a year of therapy before she could walk, talk, feed herself, do common tasks again. She was able to remember things. All the events of that night. But her brain didn't mature. She remained the same intellectually.

"My dad brought her home. She lived with us. He had special nurses move in for her. When Gina's mom—one of my dad's ex-wives—left, Gina stayed. She was there with Angel through all of this, and she became a sister to her."

I sat there, silently digesting this. My heart hurting for all she had suffered. Feeling like a complete bitch for acting the way I had when Blaise left me there. Gina had been so nice to me when she knew I was upset about Angel.

"Angel lives here. On the third floor. Gina does too. She refuses to leave Angel, and honestly, I don't know what I'd do if she did. My dad tried to get me to let Angel and her nurses stay at the farm, and for the first few years, I did. That's when the cutting started."

I closed my eyes and exhaled. *How horrible.*

"I'm sorry," I said, knowing that wasn't enough. Not for what all she'd been through and all he'd done to help her.

"You didn't know. I didn't tell you. Don't apologize," he said.

"Gina was so nice to me tonight," I whispered mostly to myself.

"Gina knew this was going to be hard for everyone. She also knew you didn't know the story," he replied, taking my hand and threading his fingers through it.

"I've not been up front with you about a lot. I don't share things with women. I keep my life closed off. It was always sex for me, but I didn't give them anything else. I never brought them here. This was my sanctuary. I didn't plan on keeping someone long enough to tell them about Angel or show them my life."

He stopped, and I lifted my gaze from our hands to meet his eyes.

"But you brought me here," I said.

He nodded. "Yeah, I fucking did. I couldn't get you in my bed fast enough. From the moment I gave in to this pull you have on me, fucking you was all I could think about." He smirked. "But I fucked you here. In my sanctuary. I had known before I did it that you were mine."

I bit my bottom lip to keep from smiling. It felt wrong after all he had shared with me. "I was referring to it as your cave in my head," I admitted.

He cupped the side of my face and ran his thumb over my lips. "As long as you're in it, you can call it whatever you want."

Tonight, he'd told me a lot. The heaviness of it still sat on my chest. I had more questions, but the raw truth I'd just heard was enough for now. I wasn't sure the other answers mattered so much. Yes, he had power and money. His group of friends treated him like he was their king. It was strange, but none of that changed how he made me feel.

Safe, wanted, needed, cared for, and like I had a place where I belonged.

"Why me?" I asked him, swearing to myself that was the last question for now.

"I knew long before you did that you'd be mine. I fought it. I hated it. I didn't want it," he said, and then he rested his forehead against mine. "Until I saw someone else touching you. Looking at you like he wanted you to be his. That undid me. Flipped a switch that wasn't ever going back."

I started to point out that we hadn't known each other that long, but I let it go. What he had said was sweet, and if he wanted to make it pretty with flowery words, I'd listen. I liked fairy tales anyway. Fiction was always better than reality.

Chapter
TWENTY-SEVEN

MADELINE

Blaise woke me up with a kiss the next morning and told me he had some business to go handle, then said it was early for me and to go back to sleep. I immediately fell back asleep, and when I did finally get up, I checked my phone to see what time it was.

Just after seven. It felt like I'd been sleeping a long time, but maybe I had just slept deeply. I took a shower and got dressed before going upstairs. I wondered who had stayed last night and if there was going to be a crowd in the kitchen for breakfast. I doubted it, considering Angel and Gina lived here. *Did the rodeo squad live here too?*

More questions I had no answers to.

After last night, I wasn't ready to ask anything more just yet. I'd let my emotions be controlled by my insecurities. That wasn't me—or at least, it never had been. I didn't like that side of myself. I hoped it never reared its ugly head again.

Gina was at the kitchen table with a bright red mug that said *Queen Bitch* on it in white letters. She looked up from her phone she'd been studying when I walked in the room.

"Morning," she said and held up her cup. "Coffee is made, but that's about it. Guys aren't back yet, so I haven't made breakfast."

I went over to the coffeepot and filled a mug up. "They all had to go?" I asked, thinking it was odd that they had business this early that required all of them.

Gina was looking down at her phone again and didn't look up this time as she nodded her head.

Right. She didn't like the questions. No matter how close I felt to Blaise in the cave, when I returned to the real world up here, things still seemed odd.

"There is good creamer in the fridge. I like the caramel-flavored one, but there is also vanilla and chocolate mocha. That powdered shit is Levi's," she said.

I put the powdered creamer down, thankful I wasn't going to have to use it, and went to get the vanilla from the fridge. The bowls of fresh fruit surprised me, as did the number of eggs inside. There had to be at least eight dozen eggs.

"If you want any of the fruit, help yourself. I buy it so Angel and I have something healthy to eat. The guys rarely touch it," Gina informed me.

I reached in and took some strawberries before closing the door. I popped one in my mouth as I walked over to sit at the table. Seeing as we were alone, I thought this would be a good time to apologize for my behavior last night.

"I didn't know about Angel. I'm sorry ab—"

She held up her hand to stop me. "You didn't know. I don't hold it against you. I'd have acted worse in your position. You held it together way longer than I'd expected. I should have stayed upstairs with Angel. It was my intention, but she was determined to come downstairs and see what the noise was. Then, she saw you, and, well …" Gina shrugged. "I let Blaise deal with her, and I stayed with you."

I took a drink of my coffee, not sure what to say to that. I didn't want to ask her more questions, especially about Angel. Besides, I didn't have to know everything about Blaise and his life right away. That was what getting to know people consisted of. Finding out as we went along. Blaise just had a lot of things in his life that were strange. That was all.

"How long do you think they'll be?" I asked, then added, "I wasn't sure if I should call Melanie to come get me."

"Fuck no. Please, for all that is holy, do not call one of the Houstons or Trev to come get you. The shit that would hit the fan." She shook her head. "Trust me, he doesn't need that distraction right now."

Okay, so he was going to keep me here? I did live at the Houstons'. I started to ask why that was an issue, but decided against it. I drank more coffee instead.

After a few moments of silence, I felt Gina's eyes on me, and I glanced over at her.

"You're not asking questions. That concerns me. You like to ask questions," she said.

I smiled and took a bite of my strawberry.

"I'm serious. Don't leave here until Blaise returns and takes you himself," she warned me.

I nodded.

Wanting to change the subject from her worrying I was going to jump ship, I decided to talk about the racetrack. Since I knew now that she had grown up with racehorses too.

"So, do you have a horse?" I asked her. "That you race?" I added.

She shook her head. "Never got into it. I can ride one, but they were not something I cared for that much."

A door opened, and that stopped me from inquiring about the track and if she went to races. Her head snapped up, and she looked toward the door.

"They're home. Better get breakfast going," she said, standing up and slipping her phone into her pocket.

I stood up too. "I can help. You tell me what you need, and I'll do it."

She raised her eyebrows at me. "You know how to cook?"

I laughed then. I'd been cooking meals since I had been tall enough to stand in a chair and reach the stove. "Anything you need, I can do it," I assured her.

She nodded. "Okay then. You start the eggs. Scramble up about two dozen."

Holy crap! No wonder they had so many eggs. Who all were we feeding?

I didn't ask though. I went to get the eggs out of the fridge.

"Skillets are under there," she told me, pointing to a cabinet to the left of the sink.

"I'm hungry, G!" Levi said as he entered the kitchen and tossed his cowboy hat on the table. "You've not started yet?"

Gina shot him an annoyed glare over her shoulder. "Didn't know how long y'all would be. Did you want a cold breakfast?"

Huck walked in and slapped Levi on the back of the head. "Stop bitching," he grumbled, and then his eyes met mine. "You cooking?" he asked, sounding surprised.

"Helping," I replied.

Blaise walked into the room, and seeing him in the daylight with his hat, pearl snap shirt, and faded jeans made my stomach feel funny and my heart beat faster. Yep, I was in this entirely too deep. I cared more for him than I should, but there was no reversing it now. Seeing him made me happy.

His gaze locked on me as he continued around the others until he was close enough to slip a hand around my waist and pull me in for a kiss. The scent of leather and mint washed over me, and I sank into him. His body was hard and warm. It felt like being wrapped up in sunshine.

When he stopped kissing me, he hovered over my mouth with his for a moment.

"Good morning," he whispered.

"Good morning," I replied softly.

"Fuck, when did you get so damn mushy?" Gage asked.

Blaise turned his head to look at Gage, but didn't let me go. "Got a problem?" he asked.

"He's just jealous," Huck replied with a laugh. "He's not got a hot piece of ass walking around the kitchen, making him breakfast."

Gage nodded. "Sounds about right."

Blaise turned his gaze back to me and pressed one more quick kiss to my lips. "You want to cook?" he asked me.

"Yes," I replied.

"Okay," he agreed, then let me go and walked over to get a cup of coffee.

It took me a second to remember what I'd been doing. His presence easily distracted me. When I was good again, I went to the stove and started working on the eggs. Gina was making biscuits on the counter beside me, and the guys were talking about their morning. Or at least, that was what I assumed they were talking about. I didn't understand most of what they said, and I was almost positive that was on purpose.

Gina didn't seem to be paying any attention, so I tried to block them out, too, as I finished the eggs and started on the grits while she moved on to the bacon. Other than asking her where things were and how she liked things cooked, we didn't say much. I almost asked if Angel would be coming down to eat, but I didn't. Talking about her seemed like a sensitive subject, and I didn't want to make everyone uncomfortable.

The guys came and served themselves once we were done while I helped Gina clean up the mess we'd made. We sat at the table with them and ate as they talked. Blaise's hand stayed on my upper thigh through the meal. It seemed to keep inching closer and closer to the crotch of my panties. I'd worn a sundress for him, and he was taking advantage of it.

When his fingers brushed the satin fabric and found it was already damp, he stood up and reached for my hand. He didn't excuse us or say we'd be back. Blaise just began walking to the door to his cave. With every step he took closer to it, my body grew with anticipation.

He jammed the key into the lock, then jerked it open before leading me down the stairs. We made it to the bottom before he grabbed me and pushed me against the nearest wall. His hands yanked my dress up to my waist, and he slid his hand into the front of my panties. My body arched toward him as I moaned with pleasure.

"God, you're dripping wet," he said, shoving his finger into me with more force than usual. "I had no fucking clue what any of them were saying," he said, pressing a kiss to my collarbone. "All I could think about was getting buried inside this sweet, tight pussy."

I made another sound as he continued playing with me. His mouth trailed kisses along my chest, and then he covered my nipple with his mouth and sucked on it through the fabric. My knees buckled. He moved then, pulling my dress off. He stepped back, and his eyes looked hungry as they moved over my body. I was only in a pair of panties now. They were the nicest ones I had. Melanie had bought them for me, and at the time, I'd thought I would never wear them. The thin strip up the back did little to cover my butt. Seeing Blaise's reaction to them made me glad that I had worn them.

He jerked his shirt open, the snaps letting go easily, and shrugged it off. I wanted to reach out and touch his chest. My eyes, however, moved down as his jeans and briefs fell away, leaving him completely naked.

They should make statues of this man.

Unable to help myself, I reached out and ran my fingers down his abs, then lower until his thick length was in my hand. The vein in it pulsed against my palm, and I ran my thumb over the top. Blaise didn't move an inch, so I continued my exploration. This wasn't the first penis I'd touched, but it was by far the largest. It was also the only one I'd wanted to touch. The other times had been when Hank stuck my hand down his pants and ordered me to rub it.

This was a different experience.

I moved my hand down his length and back up again. Blaise hissed, and my gaze shot back up to his. His jaw was clenched tightly, and I felt him tremble. I knew men enjoyed being touched. This couldn't be hurting him.

"You've got five more seconds," he said through his teeth.

I looked back down at my hand and made a decision. Before he could stop me, I went down on my knees and slid the tip into my mouth.

"Fuck, baby," he whispered.

I lifted my eyes to watch him. He leaned forward, bracing himself with both his hands on the wall behind me. His eyes were locked on my mouth, and I continued to take in more until it reached my throat. His mouth fell open as he breathed heavily. The power I felt excited me.

I began to move my mouth back and forth in a pumping motion, letting my tongue lick the tip before sliding it back inside. I could hear his breathing and feel his body shaking.

"Holy shiiiit," he groaned and began to pant. "Fuuuuck, baby, suck it."

He started to move his hips in rhythm with my mouth. His moaning was getting louder, and each sound sent a shock of pleasure to my core. The wetness soaked through my panties, and I could feel it on my thighs.

"That mouth on my dick," he groaned. "Hottest damn thing I've ever seen."

His right hand left the wall, and he grabbed the back of my head. "Yes, that's it. Suck it." His hand trembled. "I'm gonna come." His voice shook. "Do you want it?" he asked me.

Our eyes met, and I nodded once, taking him deeper into my mouth.

"Christ!" he yelled. "GAHHHHH!" His hips jerked, and his release coated my throat.

I swallowed and continued until I felt him go weak, his knees slightly buckling.

When I moved away and started to stand, his eyes watched me. I licked my lips and smiled. That had been fun. Having Blaise's pleasure completely in my control was something I was going to want to do again.

The corner of his mouth lifted. "You liked that."

I nodded.

"I'm trying not to dwell on the fact that you suck dick like a fucking porn star. I don't want to know how you learned to do that." His gaze darkened.

"What would you say if I told you that yours was the first one I sucked and I'd learned it from watching porn?" I replied, surprising myself that I'd admitted it.

I had been curious when I started dating, and my dad was not someone I wanted to ask about sex. So, I had gone on the internet and found that porn was very informative.

Blaise shook his head slowly. "Fucking hell. When I think I can't get more addicted to you, you do and say shit to prove me wrong."

He reached for me and pulled me against his chest. His hand cupped my face as he stared down at me and caressed my bottom lip with his thumb.

"This is mine. All of it. I'll die before I let you leave me," he said in a hoarse whisper.

The possessiveness of that comment should have terrified me. Warning flags should have gone off. Instead, I wanted more of him. I wanted to sink into this world of his and get so wrapped up in this man that I could never leave. I didn't want to leave. I could think of nothing that he could do to make me leave him.

Was this love? Or was it obsession? Or were they the same?

If I had known what was to come, would I have still felt this way?

Chapter
TWENTY-EIGHT

MADELINE

It was almost a week before Blaise took me back to Moses Mile. In that week, I had come to realize I wouldn't be staying at Moses Mile. Moving in with Blaise seemed too quick, but what we were doing wasn't a normal relationship. We weren't dating. We had skipped that step completely. We'd gone from enemies to lovers so quickly; there was nothing in between. The Houstons didn't seem to mind my staying with Blaise.

Melanie had called to see how I was and asked if she needed to bring me anything. The way she had talked, it was easy for me to think this was acceptable behavior. Even if deep down, I knew it wasn't. However, I'd never been in love. I had never had stability. My life had been something where I woke up every day with the mindset to fight through it and survive.

Being with Blaise, I never felt that way. Security and safety for someone who had lived a life like mine were powerful things. I didn't want to let it go. The bubble we were living in couldn't remain though. He had a life outside his house, and I needed to get one too. However, when I had mentioned getting a job, he'd shut me down immediately.

I was waiting to broach that subject again. Preferably when he couldn't throw me back and make me forget everything with his very talented tongue. Today was a good thing for us. I was going to stay at Moses Mile for three days while Blaise went to New York on ranch business. There was a horse there that Hughes Farm wanted, and he was going to make the deal. He had only agreed to let me stay with the Houstons if I would pack up everything I had there and move it to his house when he returned.

Melanie had been thrilled I was coming to stay when we spoke on the phone. She didn't mention Saxon, and I'd not spoken to him since the day in his kitchen when Huck showed up. I missed him and Trev. They had become my friends, and it seemed unfair that I couldn't keep in contact with them. I'd mentioned it to Gina, and she'd informed me that, for now, it was for the best. Trev and Blaise had a very complicated relationship. I had already known that.

If I had to choose, however, it would be Blaise. I wasn't willing to lose him.

I looked down at his hand as he held mine. He had seemed tense all morning. Even when he had taken me into the shower and given me not one, but two orgasms, he'd seemed to need it. As if he were marking me and making sure I was there. I didn't know any other way to describe it.

Moses Mile was up ahead, and I smiled over at him. He didn't want to leave me, and I liked knowing that he wanted me close. My insecurities had all but faded away completely. Angel had come downstairs with Gina twice this week while I was there, and she'd done well around me. Granted, these were times that Blaise was not there. Gina had said it was better if she got used to me being there first. If anything, Angel was my only insecurity now. I feared she might always be.

When Blaise parked his truck, he squeezed my hand. "I'm not going to get out," he said. "I've got some things to do before I head to the airport."

Talking about him leaving me here for a few days and actually doing it were completely different. I felt a slight panic that once he left, things would never be as they had been. Something would change. I'd lose him.

Blaise reached up and grabbed my chin with this thumb and forefinger. "Whatever the fuck is going on in that head of yours, don't," he ordered.

If only it were that easy.

"Thirty minutes ago, I was telling you how obsessed I was with you while I had you riding my dick. How did that switch inside your head flip so quickly?"

I smiled. "I just already miss you," I replied.

He leaned forward and kissed me. "Three days, baby."

I had to stop being so clingy. Mentally scolding myself for it, I nodded. "I know." I couldn't say more though. I reached for my bag and opened the door.

When I stepped out, it felt like much longer than a week since I'd been here last.

"Bye," I said, turning back to look at him.

He winked at me. "Keep your phone on you at all times," he reminded me for the thousandth time.

"Yes, sir," I replied teasingly.

An arrogant grin crossed his handsome face. "I like that. Next time we fuck, I want you to call me sir."

I laughed then and shook my head before closing the door. I wanted to stand there and watch him drive away, but seeing him go would only make me sadder. Taking my bag, I headed for the front door. Wondering if I should ring the bell or walk inside. My things were still here. It wasn't like I'd officially moved out yet. When I reached the top step, I paused and glanced back, unable to stop myself.

He'd backed up to turn around, but he hadn't left. His window was rolled down, and he was watching me.

"I'll leave when you're inside," he called out.

My chest felt warm, and that feeling of safety was there. I blew him a kiss, then turned and walked inside the house. It didn't feel like home, but then again, it never had. This was simply a house I had lived in.

I heard Melanie's heels before I saw her.

She beamed brightly at me as she entered the foyer. "Oh! You're here. Wonderful. I'm going to the club, and I thought you might want to go with me. We can have lunch and maybe do some shopping."

I wanted to say no because neither of those things appealed to me. However, the look of excitement on Melanie's face made me feel guilty. Saxon had said she had always wanted a daughter and I'd fill that void. In reality, I had barely gotten to know her, and now, I wouldn't be staying here. She had been the one to come and get me. If it wasn't for her, I'd never have come to Moses Mile. I'd never have met Blaise.

"That sounds nice," I lied. "Do I need to change?" I asked her, hoping I'd get a brief reprieve before having to rush out the door.

She took in my outfit that she'd bought for me. "Hmm, go change into the baby-blue linen skirt with the sleeveless white blouse that has the scalloped hem around the waist. Maybe pull your hair up into a twist." She lifted her eyes back to mine and smiled, pleased with her decision.

I nodded. "Okay," I agreed.

"Take your time. I need to make a few calls," she told me as I turned and headed for the staircase.

When I reached my bedroom, I opened the door, and the crisp, clean smell wafted over me. It reminded me of Melanie. Somehow, everything in this house had that same smell. I wondered if it was the laundry detergent. Dropping my bag by the door, I moved to close it when I saw Saxon standing in the hallway, watching me.

"Hey," I said, surprised to see him inside at this time of day.

"Hey," he replied. His hands were in his front jeans pockets, and he looked as if he wanted to say more, but didn't.

I hated the awkward silence between us. "How've you been? Trev have any wild pool parties lately?" I asked, wanting to lighten the mood.

A crooked grin touched his face, and he flashed one of his dimples. "A couple," he replied. "How's Fort Blaise?" he asked me.

I frowned but realized he was referring to the fact that Blaise did live down a long dirt road and had an iron privacy fence around his house. I smiled at the thought of them calling it Fort Blaise.

"Good," I replied, not wanting to talk about Blaise with him. It felt like I was doing something wrong now. "I'm going to the club with Melanie," I told him.

"Ah, yes. She's got you for a few days. She'll want to make the most of it," he said. "I'll let you get ready. But tonight, if you're back in time, a group of us are going to the movies. You're welcome to join. Better than sitting here, alone."

The movies. I hadn't been to the movies since my last date with Hank. The more things I did, the quicker time would pass. Staying in this room alone would make three days feel like an eternity.

"I'd like that," I told him.

He gave me a full grin then. "Cool. You can ride with me," he said. "Trev has a date and needs to go pick her up first. Declan is bringing some friends, so we will meet them there."

I nodded. "Okay. I'll see you tonight then," I replied before closing the door and going to change into the outfit Melanie wanted me in.

Chapter
TWENTY-NINE

MADELINE

When Melanie introduced me to friends of hers at the club, she didn't mention Blaise, but several times, one of them would say something like, "You're the beauty who has won Blaise Hughes's attention." Or, "Garrett has mentioned you. He is so pleased you're dating Blaise."

Melanie always controlled the conversations, so I never had to say much. This wasn't a world I saw Blaise in. Not after seeing the people he had over to his house. His group of friends didn't look as if they'd walked out of a country club. Even at the gala, Blaise had had an air about him that was edgy, wild, untamed. Nothing like the people his father surrounded himself with. I did enjoy getting to see this side of his life though.

Garrett wasn't someone we ever discussed. It was interesting to me that his father cared who Blaise dated. He had known my mother. Melanie had known my mother. Yet I still knew very little. I'd tried bringing it up more than once with Melanie, and she always changed the subject or skirted over it. Never giving me the details I wanted to know.

While we were shopping, Melanie insisted on buying me two different dresses, which I tried to decline, and a pair of heels she swore I would need if I was going to be accompanying Blaise to events. Again, something I hadn't thought about. He never talked about this world, but then again, we were new. This was all new.

It was after five when we arrived back at Moses Mile. Saxon had texted me that we were leaving at six to go get dinner before the movie. I wanted to change into something else, but I wasn't sure if I had time. Melanie went directly to the kitchen to speak with Mrs. Jolene while I hurried to the bedroom with my new clothes. I found a pair of navy-and-white checked shorts and a top to match, then slipped on a pair of sandals before taking my hair down.

I almost walked out of the bedroom without my phone, but remembering Blaise's insistence that I take it, I slipped it into my pocket and headed for the door. Saxon was coming down the hall from his room, and I waited on him to catch up to me.

"Enjoy your day?" he asked with a smirk, knowing it wasn't my thing.

I shrugged. "Who doesn't love mimosas, rich-people gossip, and spending five hundred dollars on a pair of heels?"

He laughed then. "Sounds like my mom."

"I just hate her spending the money on me," I admitted.

He didn't look at me when he said, "I wouldn't worry about that."

We walked out to the garage entrance, and once inside, Saxon grabbed a key fob from a box hanging on the wall and pressed it. A black sports car's lights flashed, and he grinned at me. "Dad is letting me take the Porsche."

The inside was red leather, and it was tiny. Good thing no one else was riding with us. I didn't think they'd fit. Saxon turned on some music from the Spotify app that appeared on the screen, then pulled out of the garage and headed for the main road.

"Trev was glad to hear you were coming. He's been worried about you," he said, cutting his eyes to me. "You know how he feels about Blaise."

I nodded. "Yeah, they aren't real close, but there is more to Blaise." I knew I sounded defensive, but I felt like they didn't really know him.

"You mean, he's not always a controlling asshole?" Saxon asked me, but the humor in his tone made it clear he was teasing me.

I rolled my eyes at him and laughed. "No, he's not. Surprised me too, trust me," I replied.

"I've seen him with Angel," Saxon said. "I know he's not."

I was surprised he'd mentioned Angel. "You know Angel?" I asked him.

He nodded. "Yeah, of course. She moved in at the Hughes Farm when I was seven. I knew her before the accident too. She and Blaise were always together." He paused then and cleared his throat. "Anyway, yeah …"

When he didn't say more, I was disappointed. Blaise had told me about everything. I just wanted to hear more from someone else's point of view.

"How is she doing with, you know, you being there?" Saxon asked me.

"Uh, better," I replied.

Saxon grinned. "Been rough, huh?"

I shrugged. It wasn't that it had been rough exactly. It had just been difficult when she was around. It was clear that my presence upset her. It didn't matter how nice I tried to be to her.

"Anyway, enough about that. How do you feel about Mexican food?" he asked me.

"I like it," I replied.

"Good. That's what we're eating. Everyone is meeting for dinner. It's a taco truck really, but hands down, they make the best tacos on earth."

I laughed. "Earth? Really?"

He shrugged. "Well, the Southeast at least," he replied. "There *might* be better in the Southwest," he added.

My phone vibrated in my pocket, and I pulled it out. I'd sent Blaise a text earlier, telling him about my plans with Melanie. He hadn't replied, so I never explained my evening plans.

Where are you?

I typed back.

In the car with Saxon. We are meeting Declan and a group of friends to have dinner, then see a movie.

I didn't think this would be an issue, but then it was Blaise. He could possibly not like the idea of me being with Saxon. I'd purposely left out Trev's name.

While I waited for his response, my phone rang, startling me.

"Hey," I said, already nervous that he was calling instead of texting his response.

"Give the phone to Saxon," he ordered.

"Why?" I asked, not liking his tone of voice.

"Madeline." He clipped out my name.

"Fine!" I snapped at him, then handed the phone to Saxon.

His face made it clear he knew who it was and why. He took the phone.

"Blaise," he said simply.

I couldn't hear what was being said, and I watched Saxon's face.

"Yes. Of course. I understand."

He sat there, listening to something more, and then he handed the phone back to me. I wanted to end the call, but I knew I'd regret that. As mad as I was at him for this reaction, I still missed him.

"Yes?" was my short reply.

"The next time you want to leave Moses Mile, I need to know beforehand. I'm not there, Madeline. I can't make sure you're okay unless I know in advance." He sounded irritated.

"Blaise, I am going to get tacos and watch a movie with friends. I am not headed to the inner city to hunt down drug dealers and ask them if they want to play ball," I pointed out.

He didn't say anything at first, and then he chuckled. "What the fuck kind of example is that?"

I shrugged, although he couldn't see me. "I don't know. I'm mad."

He sighed. "Just ... trust me. Please."

I did trust him. I just didn't understand what that had to do with my eating tacos and watching a stupid movie.

"That isn't the problem," I told him.

He was quiet for a moment. "It is. You've got to trust me. Keep your phone on you all night. Don't go anywhere alone."

"I won't," I told him.

The concern in his voice tugged at me. Had anyone ever cared about my safety this much? No. My dad and brother hadn't. Sure, they loved me. In their way. They just hadn't been worried if I was out late. No one had warned me to be safe. I was new to this.

"I'm sorry I didn't tell you. I was waiting on you to reply to my first text. I didn't want to keep texting and bother you."

"Text me, call me, whenever," he said.

"Okay," I replied.

"Enjoy your movie," he told me.

"I will."

Then, he ended the call.

I tucked the phone back into my pocket.

"Ready for the world's—or the Southeast's—best tacos?" Saxon asked me as he parked in a gravel parking lot.

"Yes," I replied. "Let's do this."

We got out of the car, and he didn't mention the text or phone call. I wanted to ask him what Blaise had said to him, but it wasn't the time. An SUV full of girls pulled up, and Declan was driving. I mentally prepared myself for Declan's less than cheery personality while we waited for her to get out.

She was smiling when she walked around the Mercedes SUV. She went straight to Saxon and wrapped her arms around one of his. She placed a kiss on his lips, then looked at me and smiled. "Hey, Maddy. Glad you could join us."

That was not the response I'd expected. There was no snarky comment, and she didn't look pissed about me being here at all.

I smiled, confused. "Thanks."

Chanel walked by and smiled at me and gave me a little wave.

I glanced at Saxon, and he didn't appear to find this strange at all.

The other girls all greeted me as we walked toward the taco truck. I recognized a few from Trev's. None of them had spoken to me then. Now, one would think we were all friends. I was in the twilight zone.

Chapter

THIRTY

MADELINE

The tacos were delicious. Everyone talked and was friendly. Trev talked to me and not once mentioned Blaise. He acted like we'd just seen each other yesterday. No questions about how I'd been. Nothing.

By the time we arrived at the theater, I finally began to relax. I'd been expecting something to be said that I would have to defend or for Declan to make a rude comment. This was too easy. I decided to embrace it and enjoy the rest of my night. Trev sat on one side of me, and a girl named Vivy sat on the other side of me. I couldn't decide if she and Chanel were dating or not.

Trev had his date on his other side, but he talked to me some. Mostly, we focused on the movie. I'd eaten a few bites of Trev's massive bucket of popcorn, and I was thirsty. I decided to go to the restroom and get a bottle of water.

I stood up and slid past Trev and his date to the aisle. Once I was out of the darkness and could see, I looked for the restroom sign.

"What are you doing?" Saxon asked me.

I spun around to see him behind me.

"Uh, going to the bathroom and getting water," I replied.

"Wait. Let me get Declan to go with you into the restroom," he said.

"Are you serious right now?" I asked him incredulously.

"Very," he replied.

I shook my head. "I can go to the restroom by myself," I told him and started that way.

He fell into step beside me. I looked at him and saw he was scanning the area.

"What are you doing?" I asked him.

"Going with you," he said, his face tense.

"No," I replied. "I am not letting you go to the bathroom with me. This is ridiculous," I told him. "Did Blaise tell you to do this? Not let me go alone?"

He nodded.

I sighed and threw my hands up in the air. "Fine. I'll go in and check the bathroom and let you know it is all clear. You stay out here."

"Fine," he replied, crossing his arms over his chest.

I went inside, and it was empty. Walking back over to the door, I stuck my head out and informed him I was alone. He could relax.

"I'll be out here," he replied.

I used the restroom, annoyed that Blaise had Saxon following me around. We were going to talk about this. He could worry about me being safe, but this was verging on insane. I walked out of the stall and went to the sink. Still thinking about Blaise and his demands.

When I looked up in the mirror, however, all those thoughts fell away. My gaze locked on the eyes staring out of the holes of a ski mask. I started to scream when the person moved fast. My scream was muffled by the cloth crammed in my mouth, pulling it back and tying it behind my head.

My heart started slamming against my chest, and I knew I had to do something. Kick, fight, anything. I spun around and kicked, swinging my arms. I was sure it was a man once I saw the body attached to the mask. Aiming for his crotch, my foot was caught in his hand, and I fell back, hitting my head on the sink.

Sharp pain vibrated through my skull as darkness began closing in, taking me under. I tried to fight against it as the wave covered me.

The throbbing in my head kept me from opening my eyes. I tried to figure out where I was and why my head was hurting. There was darkness when I slowly pried them open. Panic gripped me. I tried to move but realized my hands were tied together, and so were my feet. The rough, cold floor beneath my cheek felt like concrete. I blinked, and realized there was a blindfold over my eyes.

Was I dreaming? I fought hard to remember something. *Where had I been last?* The pain radiating from my skull made it difficult. I slowly inhaled from my nose. I could breathe. I needed to focus.

Tacos. I'd eaten tacos with Saxon … and Trev, Declan … and then we went to a movie. Trev had been beside me. I groaned as my head felt like it was trying to split in two. Long, deep breaths again through my nose.

I felt the vibration of the footsteps before I heard them.

I wasn't alone.

The restroom. I'd been in the restroom, alone, but then I saw someone in a black mask in the mirror. Saxon had been outside the door.

This wasn't a dream.

My head pounded again, reminding me how very real my pain was. I smelled blood then. *Was it mine?*

A deep voice began speaking, but it wasn't English. I had barely passed Spanish in school, but I knew that wasn't Spanish. I tried to concentrate on the words, but the excruciating pain in my head was making it impossible. Not that I would recognize the language anyway.

Another male voice spoke in the same language. There were two of them. I had only heard one walking, so the other must have already been here.

Had they been watching me try to move? I stayed frozen, barely breathing.

I felt the heaviness of the booted foot on my shoulder before he pressed down, rolling me over. The movement almost sent me back into the blank space. The pain was incredible and made it hard for me to stay conscious. He began talking again, and I did all I could to think about breathing. Just breathing.

Was Saxon here too? Had they taken him? Was he alive? God, I hoped he wasn't hurt because he had been trying to keep me safe. He'd been doing what Blaise had asked.

I swallowed.

The metallic taste of blood was in my mouth. I could still smell it. The voices stopped, and then one whispered. I heard them moving.

The darkness was pulling at me. I couldn't let it take me. I was afraid if I did, I might never wake up again. *But did I want to? What were they doing with me? Was I going to be one of those missing girls that no one ever saw again and was sold in some sex trade? They wouldn't keep Saxon. They didn't take boys, did they?*

Tears stung my eyes, and I squeezed them tightly. Maybe I should let the void take me. Death would be better.

Blaise. I'd never see him again. I'd just found him, and that was all I would get of happiness. He was worried about my safety. I thought it was ridiculous. He had been right to worry. How strange that seemed.

My chest began to ache with the loss.

A gunshot rang out, and feet began to move. I closed my eyes tightly and waited to die. *Would I feel it? Had I been shot?*

The men were talking fast. They sounded surprised. Maybe even scared.

Another gunshot, and something fell. There was running, but it stopped, and a new voice began to speak. It was a man, and he was speaking English.

"You gonna run now?" The voice sounded familiar. "NO? Can't talk with my Glock in your fucking mouth?" the voice taunted.

The pain in my head was getting worse, but I tried to focus on the voice. I knew that voice. *Why did I know it? Why did they have a gun?*

The gun went off then, and I heard the thud of a body hit the floor.

"Oops," the voice said in a cold tone.

Then, the steps drew near me and stopped.

"Fuck," he swore.

More feet were running, and I remained as still as I could. I prepared for more gunshots or my last breath. However one prepared for that, I didn't know, but I feared I might find out.

"Motherfucker!" a voice called out.

And this time, I knew exactly whose voice that was.

"She's bleeding. It's her fucking head. Get her untied. I'm going to make sure these two send out the message loud and clear," the first voice said, and now, I was able to place it too.

Relief washed over me. They weren't here to kill me. I was going to be okay.

"Is she conscious?"

"I don't know."

Hands began to untie my ankles, and once they were free, they moved to my wrists. Then, the gag in my mouth was pulled away. I cried out and gasped.

"Easy, Maddy," Gage said. "Your head doesn't look good. We are going to leave the blindfold on for now. I'm afraid to mess with it. Might be helping to stop the bleeding. Do you understand me?"

"Yes." I choked out the word, then winced.

"Do you know who I am?" he asked me.

"Gage," I whispered.

"Ready?" Huck asked then.

"Yeah. I'll lift her and wrap this around her head, too, and then you carry her out," Gage told him.

They began to move me, and I whimpered. It hurt more than any pain I'd ever experienced.

"He's gonna kill 'em all," Huck said in a low voice.

"Yeah," was all Gage said.

I didn't know who *he* was and who he was killing. I just knew I was going to fade into the darkness again. I wasn't going to die. I wouldn't lose Blaise. I'd see him again. The comfort in that was enough.

I began to slowly fall away, but before I did, I heard Gage say, "You hung the fuckers upside down on a cross?"

Followed by a laugh, and then there was nothing.

Chapter
THIRTY-ONE

BLAISE

She's alive. I'd repeated that over and over the past twenty-four hours to keep from losing my goddamn mind.

The machine beside my bed beeped as it took her blood pressure. Since I'd walked into this house, I'd not left her side. She was so fucking pale. The bruising on her body was turning a dark purple. Every time the nurse pulled the covers back, I felt a cold rage burn through my veins.

I heard the footsteps coming down the stairs. Glancing at the clock, I knew it was the nurse. My eyes went back to Madeline. Even with the bandage around her head, dark circles under her eyes, and the lack of color in her skin, she was the most beautiful woman I'd ever seen.

I had hated her for being beautiful. The first time I'd had to go find her, start checking in to make sure her so-called father was keeping her safe, she'd been thirteen. I'd been her age now.

She was even beautiful then. She wasn't like any female I'd ever known. She was selfless, kind, tough, caring. The older she got, the harder it was for me. I fought it. God, I fucking fought it. This wasn't the life I wanted her to get. She deserved to be given the perfect family. The family she never had.

Then, in one second, my plans for her changed. It was to save her, and I swore I would keep my distance. Saxon was a good choice. I'd fucking chosen him for her. He was in the family but far enough removed that she could enjoy life without this darkness.

It might have happened just like I had told my father it would— if I'd been able to let her go.

Garrett had seen me the night of the gala, unable to stop looking at her, and he'd laughed in my face. All my plans, all I had wanted for her, I couldn't give it to her because I couldn't let someone else have her.

The nurse checked her stats, then looked at me. "I'll stay with her. Go eat."

Lynn had been working for the family for the past ten years. She was the only one we brought into the house. Other than Carmichael, the doctor that the family had used for over twenty years. He would be here in an hour. He'd been coming to check on things every eight hours.

"No," was all I said to her.

She didn't argue. She just nodded.

"Any change?" I asked her.

She smiled down at Madeline. "She'll be awake soon."

Was I ready for that? Facing her after she had almost been killed because of me?

I dropped my head into my hands. I was going to be haunted by this for the rest of my life. Knowing she had gone missing and I was a thousand miles away.

A small moan came from Madeline, and I snapped my head up to look at her. I watched her breathing. Another small moan, and her lashes fluttered.

She whispered something. Her eyes still closed. I moved, leaning closer to her, and covered her hand with one of mine.

"Bl-a-ise," she said softly, and my heart slammed against my ribs.

"I'm right here, baby," I said, pressing a kiss to her hand.

She blinked again and slowly opened her eyes. Those blue eyes met mine, and everything in my world felt like it was centered again.

"You're okay," I told her. "I've got you now."

She looked over at the machine beside her and at her hand, which still had the IV attached.

"Not the hospital." Her voice was just above a whisper now.

I shook my head. "The hospital came to us," I told her. Something she would understand soon.

My keeping this from her until I thought she was ready had almost gotten her killed. I should have trusted she'd not leave me. I should have told her the fucking truth before. She would know soon.

"He shot them," she said as she looked at me. "I didn't see it. But I heard it."

I nodded. The guys hadn't known how much she'd heard. It didn't matter now. The family was not going to be a secret I kept from her any longer.

"And I will answer every question you have for me. I swear it. But first, I need you to heal. Rest. Let me take care of you."

She said nothing for a moment and stared at me, only blinking slowly. "I thought I was going to die," she said.

If someone had taken a fucking knife and sliced open my chest, it would have hurt less than hearing her say that.

I swallowed hard and took a deep breath. "I won't let that happen."

She looked down at my hand holding hers. "That wasn't the first time they'd killed someone."

She had heard it all.

"No, it wasn't."

When she finally lifted her eyes back to mine, she gave me a weak smile. "And you're the boss."

Chapter
THIRTY-TWO

MADELINE

Blaise looked like he hadn't slept in days. He was looking at me like he would do anything I asked. There was pain and relief in his eyes. It wasn't clear, everything that had happened, but pieces were coming to me as I looked at him.

"I'm going to let the nurse know you're awake and get the doctor here," he said.

"Sax?" I asked, remembering he had been there. Outside the restroom.

"He's fine physically. Mentally though, he's beating himself up. There was another door to the restroom. It went into an employee entrance. He didn't know you had been taken or hurt until he waited eight minutes, then went in after you. You were gone, but he saw the blood. He called me immediately."

I sighed in relief. He was okay. I hadn't been the cause of him getting hurt.

He let my hand go and pulled out his phone. I listened to him tell someone I was awake and that Carmichael needed to get back.

Once he was done, he put his phone away and reached for my hand again.

"My head doesn't hurt like it did," I told him. There was still a throbbing, but it was nothing compared to what it had been.

"You're on pain meds," he replied with a small grin that didn't meet his eyes.

"They're good ones," I told him, and this time, he laughed. I liked hearing him laugh.

"It wasn't a coincidence was it?" I asked him, realizing that his fear had been for a reason.

He hadn't simply wanted me to be careful. He'd known something.

"What?" he asked me.

"When I was lying there, tied up, in pain, I thought it was odd." I paused and swallowed. My mouth was dry.

Blaise moved and held a straw up to my mouth. "Small sips," he told me.

I wanted to suck it all down, but I did as he'd said. When I was finished, he took the cup and set it back beside the bed.

"You thought it was odd that I'd been worried for your safety and someone had taken you," he finished for me, understanding what I had been saying. "No. That wasn't a coincidence. I kept things from you. Things I didn't think I could tell you yet. And my fear was that I'd lose you if you knew before …" He paused and took a deep breath. "Before I could get you to fall in love with me. I thought you'd leave. I doubt I will ever forgive myself for that. If you'd known then, this wouldn't have happened."

I was listening to him, but the words *fall in love with me* were the ones that kept replaying in my head. We hadn't talked about love. There hadn't been enough time for that, had there?

"You want me to love you?" I asked him.

"If you love me, then you won't leave me," he said.

I didn't think that was a good reason to want someone's love, but I didn't know how to say that. There wasn't time to either because the doctor and nurse both entered the room.

"There's our patient," the doctor said with a friendly smile. He had white hair and a short white beard. "How do you feel?" he asked me.

"Good," I replied.

"Where does it hurt?" he asked and began to check my head.

While he examined me, Blaise stood on the other side of the bed with his arms crossed over his chest, watching. I kept looking over at him and getting distracted. I knew he was going to tell me things I wasn't going to like. I knew now that the power I'd thought the Hugheses had wasn't exactly the power people were referring to. Blaise was dangerous. But he was mine.

When faced with death, you realized what was most important to you. He was all I had thought about. The only thing on this earth that I didn't want to leave. That must be love. After all, he was my home now. After losing my dad and brother, I'd thought I'd never have one again. That wasn't the case.

"Blaise, do you mind stepping out of the room?" the doctor asked.

My eyes flew from the doctor to Blaise. Why did he have to leave? I didn't know these people. I wasn't ready to be left alone with them.

"No," he replied.

"She's having a hard time answering my questions with you in here. She is, uh, distracted," the doctor told him.

Blaise's eyes didn't leave mine. "I'm not leaving her."

The doctor sighed, and I turned to look at him.

"I'll pay attention," I assured him.

He began asking me questions, and I answered them the best I could, only glancing over every few moments to make sure Blaise was still there. He never left.

When the doctor finished and the nurse took the IV out of my arm and detached all the equipment, I was tired. I felt my eyes closing and fought it. Blaise spoke to the doctor, and I began to drift off. His voice made me feel safe, and I knew he would stay while I slept.

"Door stays locked. No one comes down here," Blaise said in a low voice.

I blinked, slowly opening my eyes to see the lights were off, except for the television and the bathroom. Blaise stood with a towel around his waist and his back to me as he talked on the phone.

"Nothing yet. I'll make that plan when she's better." His bare shoulders lifted and fell in a sigh. "I'll deal with Garrett."

He ended the call and tossed the phone on the chair in front of him. Then, he turned around, and his eyes met mine. A slow grin stretched across his face as he walked toward me.

"You're awake," he said.

I could see the water droplets on his chest from his still-damp hair. He'd taken a shower. I thought about our last shower together.

"You need to eat," he told me, coming to sit on the side of the bed. "Let me help you up so you can use the bathroom, and then we will get you some food."

Both of those things sounded good. I started to sit up and winced.

"Easy, baby," he said, reaching for me. "The strongest pain meds have worn off. We need you to take some of the new ones once you eat something."

I let him help me up, and when I was finally standing, I looked down to see a soft, pale blue silk nightgown that came about mid-thigh on my body. I lifted my eyes back to meet his.

"I sent for some things," he told me.

"From where?" I asked, knowing this had not come from the things Melanie had bought me.

"Paris originally, but it was from a boutique that I own. The manager sent over things in your size that I asked for," he said.

"You own a boutique? With women's lingerie?" I asked.

He smirked. "I own several things. I'll give you a list later. Right now, I need you to stop swaying in place. My stress can't handle it. Let's stay focused."

I let him walk me into the bathroom, but refused to let him watch me use the toilet. That was when I noticed I wasn't wearing any panties. When I was finished, I stood up to walk out, and he was there again, holding on to me.

"Do I have panties here?" I asked.

"Many," he replied.

"Could I put a pair on?" I asked.

He grinned. "Yeah, I'll get that when you aren't walking around. I'm not letting you go."

When I was sitting on the edge of the bed, he told me to stay and went into his closet. Then, he came out with a pair of panties that looked like they matched this gown perfectly. He bent down in front of me, and I let him put them on since he seemed determined that I couldn't.

I stood, and he slid them all the way up. His hands ran down over my butt before moving away.

"These are new?" I said to him.

"Yes, they are," he agreed.

"Blaise?"

"Hmm?" he replied, moving me back to the bed.

"How many new items from Paris do I have?"

He shrugged. "A few."

"As in three?"

"Or more," he replied. "Now, stop grilling me on your lingerie and move back against the headboard. I'm going to have food brought to the top of the stairs."

I obeyed.

Chapter
THIRTY-THREE

MADELINE

It took a week of Blaise waiting on me, nurse visits, and rest before I felt normal again. My head was tender, but Tylenol killed most of that. Luckily, my stitches were low enough on the back of my head that the hair that had been shaved was underneath and not visible. My bruises were starting to fade on my body.

Blaise had gone upstairs an hour ago to handle some work. I had been upstairs once a day for the past four days. I had needed sunshine. Gina had been chatty and good company when Blaise left me with her the times he needed to leave the house.

Yesterday, I'd seen Gage and Huck for the first time since they'd saved me. My memories were all back from that night, and I knew now that they had clearly killed without remorse. They had found me. They had been trained at what they did, and this had nothing to do with horse racing.

I thanked them for saving me. They both looked uncomfortable, but then Gage made a joke about being glad Sax and Trev hadn't also been killed. Huck had hit him and given him a warning look.

The bathtub was filled with lavender salts and bubbles when I sank down into it. I had been waiting patiently for Blaise to be ready to talk. I knew he didn't think I could handle it yet with my injury, but I was fine now. He pampered me and made sure I had everything I could possibly want. I needed to know what had happened that night.

Why me? Why had his closest friends found me? How had they known where to look for me? Why were they trained killers? You know, normal stuff.

I laughed at my train of thought.

"Glad I didn't miss this," Blaise said as he walked into the bathroom.

"Want to get in with me?" I asked, hoping he said yes.

He had been careful with me. So careful that there had been no intimacy at all. I missed it.

He looked at my breasts, then back at me. His jaw clenched, and I knew he missed it too.

He shook his head. "Bad idea," he said finally.

I sat up straighter so that the bubbles didn't cover my naked breasts at all. "I think it's a really good idea," I replied.

He inhaled sharply through his nose. "How is your body? Sore?"

I shook my head. "Not sore. But a little achy. Especially between my legs."

His eyes narrowed, and he walked toward me. "How about your head?"

I stood up then and let the water and suds run down my body. "It's good," I said, reaching out to tug on his shirt. "Take that off. Please."

He picked me up under my arms and took me out of the tub. Grabbing a towel, he began to dry me while I stood on the rug. When he got to the top of my thighs, he slipped his finger inside of me, and I shivered from the touch. He continued drying me, placing a kiss on each bruise he came to until I was dry.

He scooped me up into his arms and went to the bed and sat me on the edge. He pushed open my thighs with his hands and went down on his knees. When his tongue licked the inside of my thigh, I began to pant. He worked his way up until his tongue ran across my clit and then all the way back, flicking along the sensitive areas as he went.

I watched him, my hands in his hair. He lifted his eyes to look up at me as his finger went inside me. I bit down on my bottom lip and rocked my hips against his hand.

"Ah, yes," I panted, wanting more.

Blaise stood up and discarded his shirt, then removed his jeans and briefs quickly. I started to scoot back on the bed, and he grabbed my leg and shook his head. Then, he flipped me over so that my bottom was sticking up on the edge of the bed. His hand began to caress each cheek. A soft slap to the right side made me jump, and then he ran his hand over it before pressing a kiss to the spot.

I arched, wanting more, and he slapped the other side. My clit began to throb with arousal. I shook it back and forth, looking back at him over my shoulder.

His eyes went from my butt to my face. "You like me spanking you?" he asked.

"Yes, sir," I begged, drawing out the last word.

His eyes flared, and he gave me a harder slap. I cried out and wiggled some more. He gave the other side a firm hit. The pulse between my legs was surprising me.

"Please, sir," I begged, and he growled before slapping my right cheek, then left cheek.

I was close to an orgasm, and I snatched fistfuls of the sheets, begging him for more.

His hands grabbed my hips then, and I felt his erection slide behind me until it was pushing inside me. When he was completely in me, it was deeper than he'd ever been. I felt slightly crazed, needing to feel that release.

"FUUUUCK!" he roared as he slapped at my right cheek. He began to pull back, then slammed back into me. "GAH! I needed this pussy," he shouted.

My clit was swollen, and I knew if I reached between my legs and touched it, I'd shatter into the pleasure I was climbing to. But I wanted more. I didn't want it to end.

I looked back over my shoulder at Blaise. His arms were flexed, veins and muscles standing out on them. His heated gaze was on my butt, but it lifted to meet mine.

"Spank me, sir," I panted.

The muscles in his neck flexed, and he slapped my right side hard. "My ass," he growled. "When you're better, I'm gonna take that ass. Fuck it like I fuck this pussy," he told me.

The heat in his gaze excited me. I felt it as the wave of my orgasm broke free, and I cried out his name, pushing back on him. He started to pull away, and I was still there. Riding it. I wasn't done yet.

"Fuck me! Harder!" I begged. "Harder! Fuck me!"

His grip on my hips tightened, and he began to growl as he pumped into me harder. "Fuck!" he panted out. "God, baby!"

I was trembling from the pleasure when another orgasm broke free, and I screamed his name. Clawing at the sheets.

His pumping got faster, and I pushed back on him, meeting each thrust.

"FUUUUCK! I'm gonna come!" he roared.

I knew he needed to pull out, but I was out of control, rocking back on him.

"AAAAAHHHHHH!" he shouted out as his body jerked against mine, his cock hitting inside of me as he released with each thrust.

I shook as I felt the warmth inside me.

When he pulled out of me, I collapsed on the bed, gasping for air.

He lay down beside me and pulled me against his chest. His hand slid down my stomach and between my thighs. I jumped when he touched me. It was still too sensitive. He ran his finger inside of me, then pulled it out and began to run it along my thighs.

I didn't think I could get aroused again so soon after that, but it was happening.

"You need to go get this out of you," he said in a husky whisper near my ear. "But I fucking want to feel it on your skin, coming out of your pussy. Knowing that I've filled you."

He ran his fingers around my clit, and I gasped. It felt too good. My eyes closed, and I enjoyed the heat seeping out of me as he began to rub it around.

"My pussy," he said hoarsely. "Soaking wet with my cum leaking out."

His words, mixed with the way he was touching me, had me rocking against his hand.

"This is dangerous," he said. "So fucking dangerous. We need to get you on birth control."

Yet, as he said it, he didn't stop touching me. My thighs were wet with it, and I began to moan as the build got stronger.

"Baby, I can't stop this if you don't make me," he warned. "Stop rocking."

I tried, but I couldn't. "Feels so good," I whispered.

"Fuck," he growled and pushed me on my back before sliding inside of me again. "You make me fucking insane."

I whimpered, lifting my hips, knowing this was bad, but unable to care about anything more.

"Holy fucking hell," he swore and held open my legs to look down at where he moved in and out of me. "Shit," he breathed.

I held on to the covers until I was once again crying out his name and lifting my hips to meet each thrust.

When he came, he pulled out this time and shot his release on my stomach and breasts. He stayed there, looking down at me. His eyes taking in my body. "Mine," he said.

And I knew that I was. Completely.

Chapter
THIRTY-FOUR

MADELINE

It was three days later when we came up for breakfast to find Gage, Huck, Levi, and Garrett sitting at the table, eating, and I knew it was time I got my answers. Garrett had never been here. Seeing his father, who he seemed to hate, here was shocking.

"Madeline," Garrett said in greeting. "You look healthy. I'm glad you are healing well."

"Thank you," I replied, then glanced up at Blaise.

He pressed a kiss to my head and nodded toward the table. "Let's go ahead and talk. Gina will bring us a plate."

I looked over at Gina, who was by the stove. I didn't want her serving me. She winked at me and nodded her head toward the table.

Walking over to sit down, I waited for Blaise to pull out my chair simply because I wasn't sure where to sit. Once he did and took the seat next to me, I felt relief. I was going to know it all now. No more questions.

Garrett leaned back in the chair and crossed his arms over his chest. "As you've figured out, there is a lot you don't know."

I nodded.

"Your grandfather was a man named Eli Marks. He was one of the best men I have ever known. He was my father's best friend and closest confidant. When my father was killed, I was ten years old, and it was Eli who took over raising me and preparing me for the role I would one day hold. Eli held that role in my place until I turned twenty-one.

"Eli's daughter, Etta, was like a little sister to me. She was nine years younger than me and was only with him on the weekends. She lived with her mother most of the time. However, when she was sixteen, her mother was killed in a car accident. Etta came to live with Eli, and that was the first time she truly saw the family and its workings."

He paused, cleared his throat, took a drink of coffee, and I waited, holding my breath. He was telling me about not only my mother, but also my grandfather. I'd never had a name for anyone, except my immediate family.

"The family can be referred to as many things. Some call it the mob, others the Mafia. We just call it the family because that is what it is. Not all are blood, but once they are family, that is the only thing that matters. Blood can't always be trusted. The family can.

"Now, Etta knew because her mother, Yvonne, had told her just enough so she understood things. Yvonne hadn't wanted to be a part of the family, and she gave Eli a choice. It was her or the family. He chose the family. Your mother's birth wasn't something he knew about at first, but once he did, she was protected. He demanded a relationship with her.

"Etta loved Eli, and she enjoyed being with the horses. The track was her favorite place to be. She accepted this life and lived it to the fullest. Until she met a boy at one of the races, who she fell in love with. She kept it hidden for a while, but eventually, Eli found out about him. Being who we are, he checked things out, and the boy, Liam, was the son of a group that we do not associate with. Their form of organization and ours are not the same. They have no standards. No guidelines." He stopped then and took another drink of coffee.

Blaise's hand found mine under the table and squeezed it gently. I needed that. I knew more was coming, and I wasn't sure I was ready for it. I hadn't known this was going to be my family history. The one I never thought I'd truly know.

"When Eli told Etta what he'd found out and that Liam had singled her out on purpose because of who she was, she was devastated. She was also pregnant. With you. I had taken over as the boss at this point. Eli thought she wanted to abort it, but he struggled with that option. Etta didn't want an abortion, but she never talked to me or Eli about her decision.

"One day, she was just gone. Of course, I sent out the best, and we found her. Etta, however, knew us. She knew how we worked. She got better at running. Until, one day, we couldn't find her. It took years.

"Eli died, not knowing where she was, where you were. If either of you was alive. I'd sworn to him I'd find you both. He had a heart attack and never recovered fully. He never made it home from the hospital. With his last breath, he had made me promise that when I found you, I would keep Etta's wishes. Let you live your life but protect you."

My dad wasn't my father. That news kept reeling through my head. Over and over. Cole wasn't my brother. No. I didn't believe that. They had been my family. All I'd known.

"How do you know I'm that baby? I had an older brother, Cole," I said, thinking that made more sense.

"It was Blaise who found you. Living in Texas with a man you believed was your father and a brother. We sent someone into the apartment you lived in to take hair from your brush and test your DNA. It was a match. You are also an exact replica of Etta. I have pictures, when you want to see them," he said, looking at me pointedly.

"Blaise was nineteen when he got the lead that sent him to you. Eli was like a grandfather to him. He adored the man and was determined to find Etta and you. What Blaise found instead was that Etta had been gone for sixteen years, which was why finding her had been so difficult.

"Luke Reese had lost his first wife and was raising his son alone. We know that he met Etta at a bar, where she was waitressing. They married, she became the mother of his son, and he became your father. The death of your mother, however, placed him with two kids to take care of. He was a weak man and eventually turned to a few addictions, as you know. You were the one who kept them fed, cleaned the house, made sure they made it home at night. What Blaise found infuriated him, and he was ready to charge in and take you out of that life. But I steered him away from that. You appeared to love Luke and Cole. I agreed that Blaise could keep an eye on things and check in to make sure you were safe. He did for six years. The time you were living in a shelter and the man appeared giving your dad a job wasn't luck. It was on Blaise's order. When food arrived at your apartment with no explanation, that again was Blaise making sure you were fed." He paused and looked at Blaise. "So, it wasn't until you were left alone that we sent Melanie, your mother's closest friend, to come get you."

Garrett stood up then. "The rest of the story is Blaise's to tell." He turned and picked up his cowboy hat and put it back on his head. "Thanks for breakfast, Gina. Delicious, as always, my dear."

"You're welcome," she replied.

"I'll leave you to the rest," Garrett said, then turned and walked out of the house.

I sat back in my seat. I realized food had been set in front of me at some point, but I wasn't hungry. I didn't want to eat. I had to digest this. I needed the rest of the story. I turned to look at Blaise.

"You watched me for six years?" I asked him.

He nodded. "Yes, I did."

I was confused. He had looked for me, found me, and watched over me, so why had he treated me the way he did when I came here?

I shook my head. "I am not understanding things. When I came here, you hated me," I said.

"No. I hated what I felt for you. I didn't want to. You had lived a shit life. Saxon was perfect for you. He'd give you all the things you never had, and he wasn't the future boss. He was just part of the family."

Wait. What?

"You wanted me for Saxon? You didn't even know if I'd like him. If I could love him. You can't decide that for someone."

Blaise sighed. "Trust me, I know."

"What changed your mind?"

A small smile touched his lips. "You."

He squeezed my hand again. "You're not even bringing up the fact that you've been told that the family is organized crime. We are the mob. I will be the boss in the next few years. This will never change."

I nodded. "Yeah, but I had started to piece some of that together anyway." I looked over at Huck and Gage. "I heard more than you all realize," I said. "Huck hung them on a cross after shooting them. That's not normal."

Gage chuckled and tried to cover it with a cough.

"The men who took you, they did it because of me. You became something I had never had before. A weakness. You're a target. My claiming you made you that. It's why I'd tried so damn hard to stay away from you."

"They were another mob?" I asked.

He snarled, "No. They were fucking lowlife dealers. We have enemies. That happens in this life."

I felt like there was more to that than some drug dealers, but right now, I had too much to process. "How did they find me? How did you?" I asked him.

"Your phone. Melanie gave it to you, but I'd bought the phone. I'd put the tracking device in it. They took the phone, of course, and turned it off. They wanted something from me, so they wouldn't destroy the phone. They kept it to contact me directly. But the device wasn't in the phone. It was in the case."

It was all starting to fall together. His insisting I take the phone. His number being in it that time he had texted me.

"How does horse racing fit into this world?" I asked.

"It's how the family was started. It's also a big part of who we are. Gambling, politics, controlling drugs inside and outside of the track."

I knew something was being left out, but I didn't push.

"That's everything?" I asked him.

"Yes," he replied.

I didn't say anything, and I heard the chairs move as the others stood to leave. The kitchen cleared out, and when it was just the two of us, I looked at Blaise.

"I wouldn't have run from you if you'd told me," I told him. "But I understand."

He studied me. "Can you ever love me? Knowing all this?"

I laughed at his question. "You are worried about me falling in love with you? What about you? You're not only beautiful, sexy, and wealthy. You will also have power. You already do. Women are drawn to that. They'll throw themselves at you. I see them do it now. I should be the one worried about you falling in love with me."

An arrogant smile curled his lips. "You think I'm beautiful and sexy?"

I rolled my eyes.

Blaise cupped my face with his left hand. "Baby, I've been in love with you for fucking years. I fell in love with you before you ever laid eyes on me. Truth is, I was in love with you when you were jailbait."

My mouth fell open. "What? You didn't know me. You couldn't have loved me."

He leaned in and pressed a kiss to my lips. "You were that damn special. So strong and loyal. I almost killed that fucker Hank when he cheated on you. I hated him for having you, but to have you and not realize how damn lucky he was? The shit didn't deserve to breathe the same air as you."

"I need a moment," I told him. "Maybe give me time to process all this before you tell me any more."

He kissed my lips again. "Take all the time you need."

"There is one thing you should know," I told him.

He frowned. "Okay."

"You're my home. And I realized that when I thought I was going to die. You were the only thing I didn't want to lose. Nothing else mattered but you."

He kissed me again, then whispered, "I love you too."

Chapter
THIRTY-FIVE

MADELINE

The next month, things all began to make sense. I didn't feel like I was being kept out of something or being lied to. I convinced Blaise to let me get a job. It was working for him, of course, and I was enjoying it. I didn't clean stalls at Hughes Farm, but I did start helping with bookkeeping and running the stable offices. Blaise moved Empire back to the farm too.

Trev came around some, but he treated me differently. He no longer flirted or tried to get me alone. We talked, and he made jokes about me and Blaise. It was nice to feel like I fit in. Garrett brought my mom's pictures to me and told me to keep them. It was Eli's albums, and he said my grandfather would have wanted me to have them.

Angel came downstairs more often now, and she watched me quietly more than anything. I thought we were getting closer to a breakthrough—or maybe it was wishful thinking. I wasn't giving up on that though.

Blaise had left early this morning to handle some family business, and I showered and dressed before heading upstairs. When I reached the top step, there was a large envelope sticking out from under the door. I opened the door, then picked it up. My name was written on the outside. Thinking Blaise had left it for me, I smiled and went to the kitchen. It was empty.

I walked over to the island and leaned against it while I opened the envelope. There was a thick stack of papers inside, stapled together, and photos further down. I pulled them out and set them on the counter. The first thing I saw was a picture of my dad and Cole. That hurt. I'd struggled with the fact that he wasn't my father and Cole wasn't my brother. I had decided that just because they weren't my biological family, they'd still been mine. Our life hadn't been easy, but there had been good times. Especially when I was younger. Before Dad got further into the world of alcohol and Cole wasn't using.

Picking them up, I flipped through the photos, seeing they were all of my dad and Cole. Some together, some alone, some with people who looked shady. There was one of my dad with a needle in his arm, and I froze. My stomach twisted, and I put it down.

What was this? Blaise wouldn't have left this for me.

I grabbed the papers and began to read. They were copies of text messages at first. From my dad to some number I didn't know. Then between Cole and Dad. My world started to spin as I began glancing through the papers. Then, there was the one that would shatter the only happiness I had ever truly found.

The papers and photos fell from my hands, and the image of my father and brother with gunshot wounds to the heads, lying on the ground, stared up at me.

I shook my head.

The words below it read, *It's done, boss.*

I covered my mouth, but the scream came anyway. Moving away from it, my entire body began to shake.

I was in a nightmare. A horrible nightmare. I had to wake up. That wasn't how my dad and Cole had died. They were in a car accident. My dad was drunk, and he ran a Stop sign. I had been told all of this by the sheriff.

I heard my name, but I was staring at the floor as another scream came from me.

Gina called my name again, and I looked up at her, feeling frantic. She had to know what this was. She could explain it to me. I wasn't seeing this. This was not real.

"Maddy, breathe. I called Blaise," she said calmly.

Blaise. She had called Blaise.

I pointed at the papers and photos on the ground. "That's—" I cried. "That is my dad. My br-br-brother. That's them. They were in a car accident. They were," I said, shaking my head. "But that's them. There are gunshot wounds in their heads."

"Shit," she whispered and bent down to pick up everything.

"Someone followed them. They had their text messages. They had pictures of my dad shooting up. He didn't do drugs. Not like that."

Gina glanced up at me, and I saw pity in her eyes.

Why was she looking at me like that?

"That was them," I said more for myself than anything. Because that was my dad and brother. They were dead by gunshots to the heads.

I stepped forward and grabbed the papers from her hands.

"Maddy, no."

She reached for them, and I screamed. She jerked her hand back, startled. Her eyes wide.

I searched through the papers until I found the text again. I slowly read it. Not once, but three times. My body was numb. The place where my heart should be felt empty. Hollow.

When I heard Blaise's voice say my name, the pain from it sliced me to shreds. That voice that I loved so much. That I had trusted. He had betrayed me before I ever saw his face. I lifted my eyes to meet his, and I saw the horror I felt reflected in those beautiful green eyes I loved.

"Madeline." He said my name, and the agony in his voice was more than I could take.

I swallowed the bile in my throat. "I'm calling a cab. I'm leaving. Don't follow me. Don't come after me." My words were void of emotion, yet every horrible emotion one person could feel was coursing through me.

"Please, baby. You've got to listen to me," he said, taking a step toward me.

I backed up, shaking my head, feeling like I would splinter into a million pieces if he touched me.

"Madeline, don't do this. Please, you need to let me explain."

"SECRETS! YOU SAID I KNEW EVERYTHING!" I screamed at him, throwing all the papers I had clasped in my hands at him. "I didn't know that you had my father and brother killed. That was something you didn't tell me."

Blaise's nostrils flared, and he ran his hands through his hair like a man who was close to falling apart. I was already there. I had fallen apart, lost in my own reality.

"Jesus, how did she get these?" he roared, looking at Gina.

"How doesn't matter. What matters is that you let me fall in love with you. You had taken my family from me and lied to me. I've been living this life, being happy, fucking you, wanting you, and you killed the only family I had left in this world. NO! NO!" I backed away. "I am leaving, and you, *boss*"—I spit the last word at him—"will let me go."

I walked away then. Without my phone, without a purse, without anything but the clothes on my back. I opened the front door and walked out into the August heat. Down the stairs. Down the long drive. When I reached the iron gate, I pressed the keypad to open it. I watched it swing open slowly, then stepped through and onto the dirt road. I had to leave. Get away from this place. From these lies. I had accepted and embraced.

I didn't get far when a familiar truck pulled up beside me and stopped.

I looked up at Saxon, then kept walking.

I heard his truck door open, but I didn't look back. I knew why he was here. Blaise had called him, and Saxon always did what he was told. A good little soldier. Like they all were. One of those soldiers had killed my father and brother. My stomach rolled, and I paused, sure I was going to throw up.

"Maddy, I didn't know. I still don't know much. Blaise called me, and he was not okay. He asked me to pick you up and take you wherever you wanted to go."

I bent over and heaved. Staring at the dirt and wishing I'd died on that concrete floor. That would have been easier. When the heaving ended, I spit, then stood back up and turned to look at Saxon.

"You didn't know Blaise had my dad and brother murdered?" I asked him.

Saxon's face told me more than words could. He hadn't known. His horror reflected my own. But then Saxon was good. He would never do anything like that.

"Oh God, Maddy," he whispered, looking like he might cry.

I couldn't walk forever, and I had no way to get a cab, hotel, anything.

"I don't want to go to Moses Mile. I want out of this town," I told him.

He nodded. "Anywhere you want to go."

I walked back to his truck and climbed in.

He started the engine, and we turned around and drove. Neither of us said anything. We sat in silence. It was over an hour later when he pulled into a service station.

He looked at me when he stopped. "You need something?"

I shook my head.

"I'm sorry," he said.

Those two words seemed to crack something open inside of me. A loud sob broke free, and I wrapped my arms around my waist.

How could a heart hurt like this and not kill you? I felt like I had just lost my soul.

Saxon moved over to me and put his arm around me. I didn't lean into him. He couldn't comfort me. All I had ever loved in this life, I had lost.

"It's going to be okay," he said.

No. It would never be okay.

I took a deep breath, trying to stop my breakdown. Get control of myself. This wasn't going to help me. There was nothing that could make this go away.

"Even now," I whispered, "knowing this … knowing what he did … I feel like I left my soul back there. I'll never be the same."

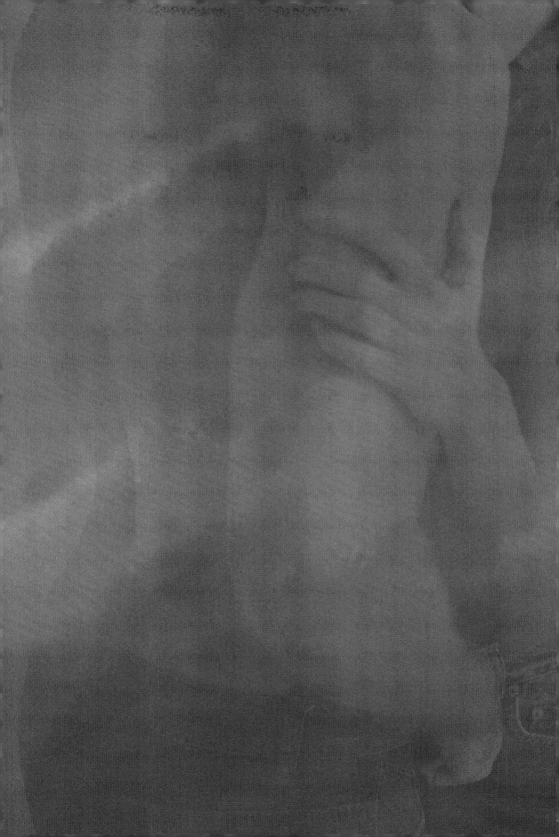

Their story isn't over...

FIREBALL

SNEAK PEEK

My eyes flew open and I laid there in the dark looking around. The moonlight was enough for me to see the bedroom clearly. Footsteps. I sat up in bed and tossed the covers off before grabbing my phone. Was I imagining it? Had the footsteps been what had woken me up? They were soft but I heard them again. I pressed Saxon's number then ended the call. He was hours away from me. Possibly even back in Florida. I needed to call 9-1-1.

Tip-toeing to the bedroom door, I stepped out to peek over the balcony overlooking the living room and kitchen. I pressed 9-1-1 and held my finger over the send button waiting to see if there was actually someone in this cabin or if my imagination was out of control. I didn't want this to be like the rental car drop off yesterday. I moved closer to the railing and held my breath for fear of being heard.

"Put the phone down," a deep voice said behind me.

Startled, I screamed and dropped the phone then spun around to find Huck standing a few feet away at the top of the stairs. Huck was here. He wasn't here to kill me. I was almost positive he wasn't. Maybe he was. Maybe my knowing about Blaise killing my dad and brother had put me on their kill list. Assuming they had one of those. Why hadn't I thought about that?

"For fucks sake, Maddy. Stop backing up. If you fall over that damn railing then Blaise will put a bullet in me," he drawled then held up an unlit cigarette. "Mind if I smoke this?"

I stared at him but said nothing. Why was he here? If Blaise didn't want me to fall over the railing, then he didn't want me dead. Yet Huck was here, in this cabin, miles away from Ocala, in the middle of the night. I was confused.

Huck shrugged when I didn't answer and lit the cigarette between his lips and took a long pull from it. "Go back to bed," he said with a grunt.

"What are you doing?" I asked him instead.

He raised his eyebrows as if that was a stupid question. "Did you honestly think you were up here in the fucking mountains alone, without protection?"

Yes. I did think that.

"Fuck," he drawled and took another pull from the cigarette. "You're a naïve one. Go back to bed. I'm just headed to my room."

Frowning. "Your room?" I asked confused.

He pointed his cigarette toward the room to his left. "Yeah."

I shook my head then. There was no way I was letting him sleep in this cabin with me. "No, you can't sleep here."

He chuckled. "Maddy, honey, I've been sleeping here since you arrived. Apparently, you're a light sleeper when you think you're alone."

"You've been here the whole time? Does Saxon know?" I asked.

Huck smirked at me. "Yeah, he knows. We take care of our own. You may be pissed about how things were handled but that doesn't change shit."

My fear had turned to anger. He acted as if my family's death wasn't a big deal and I was overreacting. "I'm not pissed! My dad and brother were killed! I am...I'm destroyed." I was also in this alone. Saxon had lied to me. If he was my friend he would have told me Huck was here. He was loyal alright, just not to me.

ACKNOWLEDGMENTS

-Those who I couldn't have done this without-

Britt always is the first I mention because he makes it possible for me to close myself away and write for endless hours a day. Without him I wouldn't get any sleep and I doubt I could finish a book.

Emerson for dealing with the fact I must write some days and she can't have my full attention. I'll admit there were several times she did not understand and I may have told my six-year-old "You're not making it in my acknowledgments this time!" to which she did not care.

My older children who live in other states were great about me not being able to answer their calls most of the time and they had to wait until I could get back to them. They still love me and understand this part of mom's world.

Annabelle gets a shout out because she read this in its unedited form for me in one day. I needed feedback and she put down the Jennifer L. Armentrout book she was loving to help her momma out. Love you big! Even if Armentrout is your fav.

My editor Jovana Shirley at Unforeseen Editing for not only doing this last minute because I suck at deadlines but also for helping me make this story the best it could be.

My formatter Melissa Stevens at The Illustrated Author. Her work always blows me away. It's hands down the best formatting I've ever had in my books.

Beta Readers who came through on a minute's notice, Jerilyn Martinez and Vicci Kaighan I love y'all!

Enchanting Romance Designs for my special edition book cover. This cover could not be more perfect.

Abbi's Army for being my support and cheering me on. I love y'all!

My readers for allowing me to write books. Without you this wouldn't be possible.

SMOKE SERIES

Smokeshow
Fireball
Smoke Bomb
Straight Fire
Firecracker
Whiskey Smoke
Smokin' Hot
Burn
Scorch
Ashes

GEORGIA SMOKE SERIES

Slay
Slay King
Sizzling
Storm
Demons

ABOUT ABBI

Abbi Glines is a #1 New York Times, USA Today, Wall Street Journal, and International bestselling author of the Rosemary Beach, Sea Breeze, Smoke Series, Vincent Boys, Boys South of the Mason Dixon, and The Field Party Series. She is also author to the Sweet Trilogy and the Black Souls Trilogy. She believes in ghosts and has a habit of asking people if their house is haunted before she goes in it. Her house was built in 1820 and she finally has her own haunted house but they're friendly spirits. She drinks afternoon tea because she wants to be British but alas she was born in Alabama although she now lives in New England (which makes her feel a little closer to the British). When asked how many books she has written she has to stop and count on her fingers and even then she still forgets a few. When she's not locked away writing, she is entertaining her first grade daughter, she is reading (if everyone in her house including the ghosts will leave her alone long enough), shopping online (major Amazon Prime addiction), and planning her next Disney World vacation (and now that her oldest daughter Annabelle works at Disney she has an excuse to frequent it often).

You can connect with Abbi online in several different ways. She uses social media to procrastinate.

https://www.facebook.com/abbiglinesauthor
https://twitter.com/abbiglines
https://www.instagram.com/abbiglines/
Snapchat: @abbiglines